CAUGHT IN THE ACT
New York Actors Face to Face

CAUGHT IN THE ACT
New York Actors Face to Face

Photographs by Susan Shacter

Interviews by Don Shewey

NAL BOOKS

NEW AMERICAN LIBRARY

NEW YORK AND SCARBOROUGH, ONTARIO

For information address New American Library

Published simultaneously in Canada by
The New American Library of Canada Limited

ACKNOWLEDGMENTS
The photographs of Kevin Bacon, Griffin Dunne, and Ken Marshall
appear courtesy of *Interview* magazine.
The interview with John Lone originally appeared in a different form in
The New York Times.
The interview with Wallace Shawn originally appeared in a different form
in *Esquire.*
The interview with John Malkovich originally appeared in a different form
in *American Film.*

NAL BOOKS TRADEMARK REG. U.S. PAT. OFF. AND FOREIGN COUNTRIES
REGISTERED TRADEMARK—MARCA REGISTRADA
HECHO EN WESTFORD, MASS., U.S.A.

SIGNET, SIGNET CLASSIC, MENTOR, ONYX, PLUME,
MERIDIAN and NAL BOOKS are published *in the
United States* by New American Library, 1633 Broadway,
New York, New York 10019, *in Canada* by
The New American Library of Canada Limited,
81 Mack Avenue, Scarborough, Ontario M1L 1M8

Library of Congress Cataloging-in-Publication Data

Shewey, Don.
  Caught in the act.

  1. Actors—United States—Interviews. 2. Actors—United States—
Biography. 3. Theater—New York (N.Y.) I. Shacter, Susan. II. Title.
PN2285.S484   1986   792′.028′0922   [B]   86-12834
ISBN 0-453-00523-3

Designed by Julian Hamer

First Printing, November, 1986

1 2 3 4 5 6 7 8 9

PRINTED IN THE UNITED STATES OF AMERICA

Contents

Introduction

Why do actors hold such fascination for us? Offstage as much as on, they seem to constitute a separate, even elevated species, a class of their own. I'm startled and thrilled as a starstruck fan to spy Peter Evans on the subway, Lindsay Crouse in the audience for a Pinter play, Harvey Keitel walking his dog on Charles Street. These people aren't what you'd call celebrities; they're just talented actors whose work I've admired intensely, but I get as much of a charge seeing them "in real life" as I would seeing Barbra Streisand or Dustin Hoffman.

It's not as if the process is a mystery to me, this job that looks so easy and yet never ends. I was trained as an actor, but couldn't get beyond the self-consciousness of living in public, could not take that step good actors must take from "impersonating" someone to "being" someone onstage.

One reason we're so fascinated with actors is that we're taught as children not to stare, not to judge people by how they look, not to scrutinize strangers. Actors, however, make their living by being looked at, and we have license to look at them as long and hard as we like, whether on the stage or on the screen, and that carries over to the street. Since many performers are especially good-looking, we can ogle them without seeming rude. And when an actor plays a role we respond to, we feel we know that person. When we've seen him in several roles, that actor becomes (disconcertingly) several people we know.

I've been watching actors in New York for more than ten years. Whether in basements or lofts in lower Manhattan or the plushest theaters on Broadway, there's nothing like seeing a good actor perform live. It's magic without props. That actor is breathing the same air we are and came in the same door we did; his watch has the same date on it that ours does, yet he's changing the temperature of the room and calling forth waves of emotion and thought with just the force of his own belief in his role. Bored with the crushing routine of work, often uncertain of our own role in a script that changes faster than we can learn it, we lean forward, mesmerized by this creature who finds the passion and humor of existence and acts it out with such clarity.

But acting is hard work. They call it "playing," and it's not supposed to show, but you can always tell a hardworking actor, whether onstage or on-screen. And in recent years a lot more good New York actors have been seen in major movies. In the late 1960s and early 1970s, a new generation of antiestablishment film directors came of age, directors whose urban-oriented, street-smart films demanded a gritty "realness" and an ethnic vitality not often found in Hollywood's gorgeously manufactured land of make-believe. Films shot on location in Manhattan provided access to the thousands of fine New York actors whose training in the theater gave them essential advantage over California actors who ply their trade under a less rigorous discipline on television. With their emphasis on creating an individualized, even idiosyncratic look, films like *Manhattan*, *An Unmarried Woman*, and *Raging Bull* use actors very differently than big-budget, star-studded Hollywood movies do. Directors like Woody Allen, Paul Mazursky, and Sidney Lumet prefer to find specific, not necessarily familiar faces to represent the particular world of a film; they want individual performances rather than the interaction of "types."

The integration of these two worlds, New York theater and contemporary movies, has created a new breed of actors whose careers are defined by an ability to go back and forth from plays to films. This versatility has both financial and aesthetic advantages to the artists themselves, but we are the beneficiaries of their sweat and craft. Hollywood in the studio era marketed glamour and worshiped stars, and yes, they had faces then. But we have something better: we have actors.

In conducting the interviews for this book, I wanted to know the biggest and the smallest questions about acting as a job, as an art form, as a way of life. Actors seem to me to be the repository of a certain amount of acquired wisdom they often are not asked to share in celebrity interviews. Although I had a number of general questions I asked everyone, I tried to let each conversation be defined by whatever was happening in the actor's life at the time. Such details are the key to universality; one actor's specific thoughts and feelings about being out of work, raising a family, or learning his lines are very likely shared by many other actors at different times in their careers. The final form of these interviews is impressionistic. Distilled from sometimes lengthy transcripts, they are not meant to be comprehensive biographical sketches. (An appendix listing the major credits of each actor is provided to refresh the reader's memory.) What emerges, I hope, is a composite portrait of the working actor culled from the individual experiences of 54 men.

Susan and I selected these men from a long list of people we admire and think of as New York actors—admittedly an elusive term. But if they trained in New York, made their names in New York, continue to work onstage in New York, and/or appear in films ostentatiously set in New York, we decided they were New York actors. We chose only men for practical purposes. In a book of this size, only a limited number of people could be featured, and including both men and women would have allowed us to choose only the best-known actors and actresses. By focusing on men, we were able to represent New York actors of all ages, acting styles, levels of recognition, and range of experience. We would like to see a companion volume do the same for women.

By no means does this book exhaust the list of New York actors. Many other wonderful actors could just as easily have been chosen: F. Murray Abraham, Danny Aiello, Seth Allen, Woody Allen, Tom Aldredge, Phillip Anglim, Mark-Linn Baker, Graham Beckel, Matthew Broderick, Len Cariou, John Cassavetes, Joseph Chaikin, Hume Cronyn, Robert De Niro, David Dukes, Charles (Roc) Dutton, Robert Duvall, Larry Fishburne, Peter Friedman, Peter Gallagher, Victor Garber, Ben Gazzara, Keith Gordon, Bob Gunton, John Heard, Hal Holbrook, Jonathan Hogan, James Earl Jones, Jeffrey Jones, Richard Jordan, Harvey Keitel, David Patrick Kelly, Frank Langella, Joseph Maher, George Martin, Chris McCann, Greg Mehrten, Barry Miller, Donald Moffat, Michael Moriarty, Paul Newman, Kevin O'Connor, Al Pacino, John Pankow, Austin Pendleton, Anthony Perkins, Lonny Price, Randy Quaid, Remak Ramsay, Bill Raymond, Jason Robards, Eric Roberts, Tony Roberts, Mickey Rourke, John Rubinstein, Bill Sadler, Jay O. Sanders, George C. Scott, Ron Silver, Josef Sommer, Vincent Spano, Daniel Stern, David Straithairn, Keith Szarabajka, Rip Torn, Ron Vawter, Eli Wallach, Jeff Weiss, Max Wright, and Chip Zien. And there's more where they came from.

I set out to do this book hoping to dispel—or at least to understand—the awe I feel about actors. It didn't work. Meeting these men and hearing them speak with—at times—exhilarating eloquence only increased the respect, wonder, and joy I experience watching them work.

—*Don Shewey*

I guess I've always been a voyeur. I love to watch people. I'd do it without a camera if I could, but it's not polite. Taking pictures gives you permission to examine people microscopically; in a way, so do movies and plays. The first Broadway show I ever saw was the musical *Carnival*, starring a very young Jerry Orbach. When I went to my first movie at the age of four, I got so excited I nearly fell out of the balcony. My sister, seventeen years my senior, acted in college. She didn't pursue it after she graduated, but I inherited her love of live theater. On weekends, she would take me to see children's plays at the Cricket Theater. I don't know which was more attractive to me then, the show or the free jellybeans they'd give out afterward, but before I knew it I was hooked.

I've always had a great deal of respect for actors and their work, and all the men in this book are people whom I've watched and admired over the years. I wanted them to look as they really did. I encouraged them not to dress up for the photo, but to wear clothes that were comfortable. We worked in daylight studios, friends' apartments, and in the streets of New York. Sam Waterston and I met in a parking garage near Westbeth, and I took Brad Davis to an area of the city known as "the trucks" where a couple engaged in an interesting sexual activity while we worked not four feet away. Basically, we went anywhere the light was right. I didn't set out to alter the image by which these men are usually perceived, but somehow that is what happened. Several of the actors I photographed weren't able to recognize their closest friends in my pictures.

Almost all my subjects told me that the thing they hated most about their profession was doing still photographs—they never knew where to look, what to do, or who to be. This is what they said, but when I started shooting, they knew, to a man, exactly what to do.

—Susan Shacter

We were going to have Montgomery Clift in the picture [*Sunset Boulevard*] but his agent said that it was impossible for an actor to become a star playing a gigolo. I was surprised at this; you know New York actors, they'll play anything.

—Billy Wilder

An actor is someone who in early childhood consents to exhibit himself for the rest of his life to an anonymous public. Without that basic consent, which has nothing to do with talent, which goes deeper than talent, no one can become an actor.

—Milan Kundera

Once launched upon the fury of his task, an actor requires infinitely more power to keep from committing a crime than a murderer needs courage to complete his act.

—Antonin Artaud

CHRISTOPHER
REEVE

Christopher Reeve

Years before he was immortalized as the Man of Steel, Christopher Reeve appeared on Broadway with Katharine Hepburn in A Matter of Gravity, *held down a continuing role on* Love of Life, *and lounged nearby while William Hurt skinny-dipped onstage at the Circle Rep in* My Life. *Every summer he can, he joins the star-filled acting company at the Williamstown Theater Festival in the Berkshires, even crooning tunes in the festival's cabaret tent after hours. He prides himself on the versatility his Juilliard training gave him. And lest anyone confuse him for a brainless hunk, he speaks about his craft with earnest articulation.*

Still, his image remains formed by his iconic presence in Superman, *Superman II, and* Superman III. *When he was filming* The Bostonians, *he was frequently embarrassed to be stopped outside the studio by mobs of teenage girls while his costars, legendary actresses such as Vanessa Redgrave and Jessica Tandy (the original Blanche DuBois) walked by completely unrecognized. Even on the set, Tandy tended to go unnoticed as she sat quietly in a corner in the makeup and costume of a much older, feebler woman. One afternoon, during the shooting of an outdoor scene, a silence fell over the set as the sound crew strained to hear if any aircraft threatened to intrude upon the scene. "Is it a plane?" asked someone, and a tiny voice from Tandy's corner called out, "No, it's Superman!"*

When we met, Chris wasn't feeling especially super. He had ground down a disk in his back and was in a lot of pain, especially since he was performing eight times a week as Count Almaviva in Andrei Serban's strenuous production of The Marriage of Figaro *at Circle in the Square. So he sprawled out flat on one huge sofa in his airy Upper West Side duplex apartment while we talked.*

Did you always want to be an actor?

Since the age of twelve. Growing up in Princeton, New Jersey, I was exposed to theater at an early age, and it became part of my life. I was invited to play small parts at the McCarter Theater, that grew to bigger parts, and pretty soon I realized I was committed to this. I felt it was something I could do that nobody else was doing—the way kids look for some kind of experience that sets them apart from the group. By the time I was fifteen I had worked as an apprentice at Williamstown, and at sixteen I got my first real professional job. I got the grand total of $440 for an eleven-week summer season in Boston at the Loeb Drama Center. I thought: This is it. When I was a senior in high school, my mother and I had a little negotiation—I wanted to go to professional school, Carnegie Tech, Northwestern, Yale, one of those. She said, "Please don't do that, please go to college. You need time just to read some books and think and have friends."

So I went to Cornell and read English and music theory and skied for four years and went off on acting jobs in the summer. I picked Cornell because of its inaccessibility to New York and temptations to work. I had an agent by this time, a very important New York agent named Stark Hesseltine, who was starting to send me up for things. I was meeting David Merrick and Joe Papp; Lynn Stalmaster, who eventually cast me in *Superman*, was constantly calling me in on big movies, things like *The Great Gatsby* and *The Godfather*. But by this time I had the idea of balance in mind. Many of the actors I knew seemed very limited as people. They were so career-oriented and so obsessed with getting ahead, they really didn't have much else going for them. I began to see the point of being able to discuss other subjects, to be interested in history and politics and government and music and Russian and French. So the decision to go to college was a good one. After I got out, I quickly picked up the professional pace again. I went to Juilliard for one year, but I dropped out at the end and said, "I've held back for ages, and I'm now going to call myself a full-time actor and go for it."

I was living on a budget of $40 a week, and I wouldn't spend more than $20–25, so I decided to get some money right away for security. I took a job on a soap opera, *Love of Life*, for two years. Suddenly I was making $750, $1000 a week. Whoa! That was incredible. While I did it, I also appeared all over town in plays—at Theater for the New City, Manhattan Theater Club. Then Stark got me an audition for a Katharine Hepburn play called *A Matter of Gravity*. This was a big ego boost, because she decided she wanted to see [*he does his Hepburn imitation*] "all the new actors in New York." Out of all this "modern" talent, she decided that I should be her grandson. Of course, everybody thought that was my big break. Now I'd made it. My friends were looking at me as if I was a big star. In fact, I was supporting Katharine Hepburn in a Katharine Hepburn play. When the play closed, suddenly I felt a terrible letdown. I quit the television show in June. Two years on a soap opera is plenty. If you stay on a soap opera too long, you get used to—oh, I don't know, making heavy drama out of pouring coffee.

Then somebody suggested, "You should be in California. You really have it to be in the movies." So I hopped on a red-eye and went. California was a shock to me. I couldn't believe the things that people took seriously out there.

What do you mean?

I remember being up for a series called *The Man from Atlantis*, about this guy from Atlantis who's part fish. They said, "God, you mean you don't want to go up for that stuff?" I said, "No, I don't. You have to understand. I'm a deadly combination of a preppy and a snob, and I just don't get this stuff. Leave me alone."

I had gotten my pilot's license a couple of years before. I took all my savings from that soap opera, and instead of getting a decent place to live, I spent $4000 on a second-hand little airplane called a Cherokee 140, which is like a Volkswagen engine with wings on it. This for me was freedom. So when I was supposed to be going to callbacks for *The Man from Atlantis*, I'd be up gliding in the Tahachapi Mountains at 12,000 feet. I could not make myself take it seriously. I'd been nurtured on a classical theater that had value, and I just couldn't see cashing in. To play those parts, all you had to do was show up and look nice. That's not enough to justify getting out of bed. I was looking for a greater challenge. I look at those six months in 1976 when I was in California as the nadir of my professional life, when I was completely without enthusiasm and just couldn't get motivated at all.

Finally I said to myself, "I really belong back in the theater." So I put the sleeping bag and food in the back of this little Cherokee, took two weeks, and flew across the country. As soon as I was back in New York, I felt the energy, the electricity, the excitement, and I found my mentor, Stark Hesseltine, saying, "Well, we wondered how long it'd take you to come crawling back here." I had two auditions immediately. One was for a play at Circle Rep called *My Life* —Bill Hurt was playing the lead, Jeff Daniels was also in it—and the other was to play Harker and stand by for Frank Langella in *Dracula*. I went to both auditions in one day, got both jobs, and immediately went to work in this play *My Life* and thought: Ah, I've landed again! I'm happy, busy, busy, busy.

I say all this as a prelude to what's coming next, because suddenly, having been reestablished in the theater, I got another one of these temptations—to go and screen-test for *Superman*. I remember sitting in the dressing room with Bill and Jeff, saying, "You'll never believe what happened today. The phone rang. They are going to make a movie out of *Superman*." They said, "Which? Shaw's *Superman*? Or the one with the cape that goes 'up, up, and away'?" We all had a good laugh. Movie? That sounds ridiculous, it would be stupid. Then I began to think: Well, at least I can read the script. Bit by bit I was getting hooked. I read the script, and I immediately saw a way to play this guy as a gentleman and a scholar in the old-fashioned sense, as opposed to just a muscle-builder.

Then I heard they've got Marlon Brando, Gene Hackman, Susannah York, and so on, and they're going to shoot in London, and I could probably bag a quarter of a million dollars—good-bye! I went to London and screen-tested for the part. The idea of going to London for the weekend struck me as unheard-of, outrageous. But a part of me just had to try something terribly unlikely. The screen test was the first week of January '77, and we started shooting March 28. I left the play January 15 and went to London and trained for two months.

Were you a bodybuilder before?

You wouldn't catch me dead in a gym. No way. I was 6′4″ and I weighed 190. By July of that year, I weighed 215, and it was all newly acquired muscle. The oddity is that I really saw *Superman* as a performance opportunity. It was an interesting challenge to turn people's expectations around. They're expecting it to be a cartoon, a joke, camp, something laughable—and with a little luck we can make it romantic and stylish. I think we were able to do that. What I underestimated, though, was how much that role means to the public at large. For me, it was a really fun job, but for them—the world is looking for heroes, and it's hard to let go.

In retrospect, I sometimes think that right after *Superman* I tried a little too hard to experiment. It's not coincidental that right after *Superman* I played a gay Vietnam veteran with no legs in *Fifth of July* on Broadway, a psychopathic homosexual in *Deathtrap*, a crooked priest in *Monsignor*—I went into a kind of denial of the hero side of me. I played a lot of people you had varying degrees of sympathy for, but you probably didn't want to be. It was not my conscious strategy. It was what I needed to do. Everybody has a basic need to define himself for the world, not the other way around. Why is it, for example, that Gerard Depardieu, as soon as he's proclaimed a great romantic French actor, suddenly puffs up to 250 pounds? He has another idea of himself inside. Very few people—only Arnold Schwarzenegger that I can think of—will say, "Yeah, I'm exactly the way you think I am, and I'm going to cash in on it."

Superman is nothing more than a popular retelling of the Christ story, or Greek mythology. It's an archetype, watered down and made in vivid colors for a twelve-year-old's mentality. It's pop mythology, which extends to the actor, then seeps over to a demand that that actor reflect the needs of the worshipers. The worship doesn't only go on in the temples—it goes on in the streets, in restaurants, in magazines. But, you know, I'm from New Jersey, I'm not from Olympus or Krypton, so back off 'cause I can't take the responsibilty. The theme of my life at that time was: Screw you, people, for needing me to be more than what I can be. By all means, pay five dollars and go see the movie, but leave me alone. I do think that's fair.

How much does your being tall have to do with your becoming an actor?

I'm very naive on that account, because of my father. My father is a very well-rounded individual, somebody with a very, very strong intellect who's physically imposing as well. Today we think of the intellectual as a sort of reedy, dusty type with a pipe who's not able to cross the street very well. And we think of the athlete as being thick-headed. When you find both those aptitudes in the same person, it can be disorienting. My father had that problem for ages. He just doesn't look like somebody who's a Russian scholar and a major poet. So to some extent he impressed on me that you are not responsible for the way you look. I'm not complaining—I'd rather be attractive than ugly, for sure. But you can't stand back and say "That's my identity" and just get a free ride out of it. And this culture does give a free ride to good-looking people. Because of his work ethic or his own needs, my father communicated to me that you must find something more difficult and go chase it.

But being a writer or scholar doesn't depend on how you look, while being an actor does.

Somewhat, but not as much as you think. I look at Vanessa Redgrave, a strikingly beautiful woman who's never been limited by her looks. There's nothing she can't play. All that really matters is your ability to communicate the truth as you understand it. And this will transcend appearance. Unfortunately, you don't often get the chance. Richard Dreyfuss once said to me, "If your nose is on sideways, they think you're a better actor, because they sympathize with you more. But a guy like you, you don't look like you need help. So if you come out and play a character who's in pain, we're going to doubt it unless the acting is so good that we can't deny it." That's the challenge for all "good-looking" actors.

You can make a lot of money just looking good—that's the Robert Redford story, I think. He has a lot more talent than he lets you know about, and he never plays anyone unsympathetic. He's decided to be the fair-haired boy. I'm bored by that, and I'm condemned to this fascination with seeing what else I can handle. The real challenge, which very few physically attractive actors accept or care about, it to see how deep I can go, to get people to forget what I look like. The actor is a ball of Silly Putty—you twist it, put cookie cutters in it to make whatever shape you want. This, combined with the teaching I got from my father, convinced me that you're not limited to your physical shape. You can move forward.

When the interview was over, we left his building together. It was the middle of the afternoon, and the elementary school on his block had just let out. Suddenly we were engulfed by kids yelling, "Look, look, it's Superman! Christopher Reeve, Christopher Reeve! Hey, Superman!" Chris turned bright red, trying to ignore them. Finally he wheeled around and yelled "Boo!" at a bunch of kids. What none of them noticed was that, on his way to the chiropractor to deal with his bad back, Superman was limping.

KEVIN
BACON

Kevin Bacon

By the time Kevin Bacon became a movie-poster icon in Footloose, *his stage experience had already put him years beyond the category of PYT (Pretty Young Thing). His Obie Award-winning performances as the protective street hustler in* Forty-Deuce *and as a supercilious Whiffenpoof in* Poor Little Lambs, *among others, established him as one of the young actors you most looked forward to seeing on the New York stage.*

He called to ask if we could meet after he took his cat to the vet (his house in Connecticut is a veritable menagerie of cats, dogs, and horses), at five o'clock at a restaurant on upper Broadway. When I got there, he was standing on the corner looking great, though not immediately recognizable. He has tiny facial features, and he was wearing sunglasses. He had a beer while telling me about the film he'd just done, Quicksilver, *and the one he was about to do,* The Rites of Summer.

Most people in movies think of me as a New York stage actor. Crews are surprised I live in New York, because most people in the movie business live in L.A. When you do plays, it gets around—fifteen producers will say they saw you in something. Theater has a mystery and a fascination for the movie biz—it lends credibility. People don't understand why you spend so much time for so little money.

Why are you an actor?
I think it's the cliché—to be the center of attention. I was the youngest of a large family (four sisters, one brother). I had an active fantasy life as a child. I wanted to be a rock star. I still write songs and sing—in the shower. My mother had a box of old clothes, and I would dress up as characters with costumes and props. It was so silly. I didn't want to have to read or write. Mostly, I wanted to be famous. My father, Edmund Bacon, was pretty famous as a city planner—he was on the cover of *Time* magazine when I was little.

I came to New York from Philadelphia when I was just turning eighteen and studied at Circle in the Square for a year. My cousin directed an Equity children's theater, cast me in it, and that's how I got my card. Then I signed up for an Equity Library Theater showcase called *Glad Tidings*. I got an agent—this is in 1976, '77. I knew when I moved here that I loved this place, working on the stage, breaking into this circle that exists, the New York stage scene. It felt like a home. I did a lot of plays where I was the youngest actor around. I got introduced to a lot of actors I hadn't ever heard of. I'd thought that you were either a waiter or a Broadway star. Suddenly I was coming in contact with actors who had this tremendous body of work, who could handle all these dialects, who had a tremendous range, but they weren't really well-known. This was very inspiring—if I could just work like these people, I'd be happy. So I didn't move to L.A., didn't take a couple of TV series.

On *Animal House*, I got $785 a week for five weeks—I thought I'd never have to work again. I made a lot of mistakes, spent almost everything before I got back. I'm a WASP, we don't talk about money, I just didn't know. When they said, "You'll be getting scale," I didn't know what "scale" was. That was my first movie. I could have had the series, but I was offered *Getting Out*, a showcase that paid $100 a week. I knew I should do it. Ultimately, it was the best thing to do. The show ran for a year, gave me a small salary, and I had a place to go. The nice thing about *Getting Out* is that I could leave after the first act and come back for the curtain call. I'd go have a beer, walk around the Village in my costume, which was technically a violation of Equity rules.

I also did a soap and *Friday the 13th* during *Getting Out*. *Friday the 13th* was a horrendous experience. We were filming out in New Jersey, a two-hour bus ride. The producers would say, "You'll be back in time for a half-hour call for *Getting Out*"—and they'd drive me to the bus station at 6 o'clock. I'd have to call the stage manager and have my understudy go on.

Do you have a ritual you perform before going on?
I used to do a workout—sit-ups, push-ups, jumping jacks. Then I'd do a vocal warm-up, stretches. For *Slab Boys*, I did quite a bit of dialect, a Scottish burr, and you had to have your tongue rolling. I did this play at Ensemble Studio Theater, *Men Without Dates*, with John Turturro, who's from Yale—he does warm-ups up the wazoo. He'd sit in the dressing room going "Mi-mi-mi-mi-mi-mi" and I'd make jokes—"Listen to what he's saying: me, me, me . . ." He embarrassed me out of doing any warm-ups. I'd do a big number with my hair, get in costume, walk around the room straightening my clothes, picking off lint. Start bantering in the Brooklyn dialect. If it works, I use it.

What do you do the moment you go offstage?
I listen to hear the applause. I either get very happy or very depressed, because I have a very definite idea of how it went. When someone says, "I saw that show," I want to say, "What night?" I had one bad night during *Men Without Dates*. My girlfriend Tracy's my best critic, she can really call me on a bad show. One night I started off bad and stayed bad. Right in the middle of the show, I'm thinking, "I can't believe how badly I played that line . . . John's great . . . Can't believe how bad it is tonight." Tracy thought it was the greatest.

My whole dilemma is I find myself uninteresting, not worth watching. I have to create someone else—different voice, different heart, different soul. It's difficult to let *me* through. But obviously your best work comes from being yourself.

I don't think of you as someone who transforms himself.
Well, let's put it this way—I don't gain weight for a role. You'll never see me put on thirty pounds. But I can't tell you how many hours of angst I had over such a piece of fluff as *Footloose*—how to play a scene, changes in dialogue. I was really worried about the age. I was twenty-five, and I was afraid people would say, "He's a senior in high school? Come on!" So I went to check myself into the school in the town we filmed in, and when I went in to register, they gave me a lot of shit but not about my age. The teachers and the kids never recognized me.

You mean you actually passed as a student?
Well, this was all arranged in advance—it was for me to see what it feels like to be an alien, to get a sense of what kids this age are like to be around. The new kid in school: it was scary. A lot of kids were really hostile. They shouted things at me like "Faggot!" and "Comb your hair!" Just like in the movie. They would gather outside the classroom to see me come out. They'd never seen a punky haircut up close. They'd seen Bowie, Sting, Boy George in magazines, but the kids themselves wore jeans and cowboy shirts. And the girls looked like hookers.

How do you learn lines?

Just by rehearsing. If I have a speech, I sit down and learn it. It gets harder as you get older. Movies are easy—you only have a page and a half. The night before I shoot a scene, I read the script again up to that point. Then I read the scene a couple of times, work with Tracy on it. I tend to change every take. It keeps me alive, fresh, and it gives them a couple of choices. If it's something I don't want there to be a choice on, I lock it in.

My favorite scene in *Diner* is when you're watching the quiz show.

A lot of people mention that. We shot about twenty minutes for that scene. I studied the show—had to learn the answers to all the questions. They were ridiculously hard questions, I had no fuckin' idea of the answers. I had an earphone in my ear running down the back of the sofa, because we couldn't record with the TV going.

[Barry]Levinson hadn't developed any kind of approach to actors, didn't know how to talk to them. He said, "Just do a little more . . . a little . . . uh, do a *thing.*" To me he would say: "Do less, do less, do less." It's a cliché about movies, but you still have to be told. He would listen to us banter, or start the movie rolling before a scene and keep it rolling after—some of the best stuff in the movie came that way.

Do you ever get scared as an actor?

I get scared about my career a lot. I get scared that I won't be able to handle a role. If I don't work on it enough, halfway through the picture I freak out. But then you get past it. Rehearsal is a process of getting back to your first reading. I don't live the character. The work is so unreal it's nice to go home and turn it off.

I have a love-hate thing with the movie business. I love the work, being on the set. I don't like parties. I get wrapped up in the possibilities of developing things, but another part of me despises it. I see all the lies, and I want to run off to Connecticut and not come back.

On the other hand, I feel so lucky. Sometimes I think about it and catch my breath.

KEVIN
KLINE

Kevin Kline

Kevin Kline is the kind of actor who thinks out loud with his body. And what his body says is usually funny, whether he's chewing every stick of scenery in sight as the rip-roaring Pirate King in Broadway's The Pirates of Penzance *or making a silent entrance in the dark in John Malkovich's production of* Arms and the Man, *whether he's addressing the world from the Brooklyn Bridge as the near-psychotic Nathan in* Sophie's Choice *or merely cocking an eyebrow in Larry Kasdan's deadpan western,* Silverado. *The most celebrated veteran of the Acting Company, the Juilliard School's touring ensemble directed by legendary actor and teacher John Houseman, Kline in many ways epitomizes the generation of young actors who rejected the Actors Studio's Method that dominated American acting in the 1950s and sought an all-inclusive training that would make them adaptable to the full spectrum of experience as an actor—musicals and dramas, theater and film, Shakespeare and Lanford Wilson.*

In person, Kline projects little of the dynamic and flamboyant persona that is his trademark as an actor. He's unassuming, down-to-earth, almost bland, particularly when he's clean-shaven after a series of dashing beards and mustaches. When we met, he was two months away from starting rehearsals for Hamlet *at the Public Theater, and champing at the bit. To occupy his time, he'd agreed to return to Juilliard to teach an acting class, from which he'd just come.*

The criticism so often leveled against Juilliard actors is that they're all technique and no heart. The problem with acting shcool is that it breaks things down so you think that acting has to do with speech and voice and movement and how to wear a period costume. The fact is those are only tools that can aid and abet what is more important—all-important—which is the acting. The instinct. That's why I'm there, to make sure that where those things have become impediments, the students learn to make them only tools or to throw them out altogether.

When you were at Juilliard, did working actors come in and teach you?

Some. In the first year, we were guinea pigs. They would try a class, and if it didn't work, it would just stop. We had classes in learning how to bow in every period, how to use a fan, use a cane, take snuff, how to put on your wig, how the women put on that Restoration makeup—the white stuff with the black dots to cover their syphilis sores or whatever. All that stuff is a luxury. You think, "What use, pray . . . ?" But in fact, years later, when you're doing Shakespeare or Restoration comedy, it helps to know what the cut of that coat meant and what it meant to stand with your foot out this way and how to show your calf.

Of course, when you're in school, you'll be doing a Restoration production, and the teacher will be saying, "No, you should be doing *that* with your foot," and the speech teacher's saying, "Mmm, darling, you're still splashing your T's, and you're biting off your G's." All these things become impediments to the acting when, in fact, like any technique, they should be learned to be forgotten.

What made you interested in acting?

I had been in the school play in my high school, which was an all-boys' Catholic prep school in St. Louis run by Benedictine monks from Appleforth

Abbey in England. And I really had fun. Friends of mine were throwing up, and I was enjoying it. I felt very calm and rather at home on the stage. Whatever repressed exhibitionistic impulses I had were given vent.

When I went to Indiana University, I studied music the first two years, but I thought: I want to try acting, too. So I took an acting class my first semester and got a D in it. It was at eight-thirty in the morning, and I missed the first half of the midterm exam. But I loved it. I started doing one play after another, and I spent the next summer on the Ohio River. Indiana University had a showboat, and I lived on the showboat. Terribly romantic, wonderful summer.

When we got back to school, a few of us had the idea of starting a company, breaking away from the theater department (which was very staid), and doing exciting, artistic drama to "serve the community." We sat up nights writing a manifesto. We started doing satirical revues. I was the pianist. I would play all the parody songs. Eventually, they let me act more. A playwright joined us, and we thought of ourselves as the Group Theater. I spent three years with this group off-campus doing our own theater. We did an evening of Williams one-acts and *Viet Rock*, which was to date the most amazing theatrical experience of my life. At the end of the play, people wouldn't just applaud or write a good review. They would burn their draft cards. We changed people's lives dramatically. That's what theater was all about in 1969. All of us were potentially draftable as soon as we graduated.

Were you always a good actor?

I was terrible at first. They all encouraged me to continue with music. Eventually, I got better and better. I was certainly one of the stars of the theater department. They'd say, "Kline's auditioning for *Threepenny Opera*—there goes Macheath." I had a certain . . . I don't know, I used words and it just sounded good. I was hot. For my graduation present, my parents had promised me a trip to New York to audition for Juilliard. They were taking only three or four people to enter the third year of this four-year program. I thought I didn't have a prayer but at least I'd get a trip to New York. I almost didn't bother with the audition, but I'd paid the $40 audition fee or whatever it was, so I went over and in a sense didn't care. It helped. I got in. Then the draft lottery was imposed, and they decided to cut off at 195 that first year. I was 196, which was how I got to go to Juilliard.

In one sense, I had an edge over people who went right to Juilliard from high school, because I was constantly acting for four years in college. Whatever the quality, I did twenty-five, thirty plays, Wednesday-night improvisations, original plays, as well as acting on a stage that I helped build. I had more of a sense of who I was as an actor than some other people. Although that was a vintage year —an extremely talented class of very distinct individuals. Remember Houseman had worked with Orson Welles. Houseman liked wild people. I realized as soon as I got there that I was tame. On our first overnight out in Patchogue, Long Island, I got a knock on the door at three in the morning. There was an inch of snow on the ground, and three completely naked, drunken actors were dancing around saying, "Come on out, dance in the snow." I literally pinched myself to see if I was awake. We were at a motel right on the main road of this little town, and here are three of our actors *naked*. They came in and jumped on the bed, saying, "Come and play, come and play. We're the naked runners for God." It became a tradition in the company. Periodically, at a dull point in the tour, someone would say, "There's a run tonight, a naked run for God." We even got Houseman to take his clothes off. He'd heard about us over the years. I never did it.

You were much too mature for this sort of thing.

Mature? [*He starts to say "repressed."*] No. I just wasn't into it. Maybe because I couldn't let go of my first job as a monk.

Did you have it in mind to do movies?

I think every American actor wants to be a movie star.

How did that fit into all of this?

"Oh, gee, someday, maybe, wouldn't it be neat if . . . ?" But I never wanted to do stupid movies. I wanted to do fffilms. I vowed I would never do a commercial, nor would I do a soap opera—both of which I did as soon as I left the company and was starving. I was working Off-Off-Broadway for $25. Actually, while I was doing the soap, I stood by for Raul Julia in *Threepenny Opera*. I had $600 a week coming in guaranteed from the soap, and my day finished at three o'clock, so I could go do Off-Off-Broadway or stand by for twelve weeks. After that, I did *Dance on a Country Grave*, a musical of *Return of the Native* at the Hudson Guild, which got decent reviews but didn't move to Broadway.

Then I auditioned for this small part in *On the Twentieth Century*. My agent, Jeff Hunter, said, "It's not a very good part"—of course, I'd been playing leading parts—"but think of it as paying dues. It'll be good for you to work with Hal Prince." Well, that's what I did. I was still very ambivalent about doing a commercial Broadway musical. But I hadn't worked in four months, 'cause I left the soap.

Were you making more money doing the soap than from the Acting Company?

Three times! I was making $300 every time I worked, with a guarantee of two times a week, but I usually only did one. If I worked five days, I'd make $1500. Broadway was about the same. I worked for $650 a week. In the Acting Company I was making $250 a week, maybe more with the per diem. But $600 a week was unheard of at that time.

Did you find it hard to go into movies? Did it feel like a different kind of acting?

Mm! Yeah. Very, very scary. I feared that everything I'd learned onstage was different. Some people say film acting is right here [*he points to half of his eyeball*], that that's your canvas. Yet some of my favorite roles involve playing someone who really uses his whole body. People say, "You can get away with bigger, phonier acting onstage." I don't think so. You can see it from the last row, you can see it from the first row if someone is bullshitting you, if someone is phoning it in, if someone's missed the point. People talk about overacting on film and automatically categorize it as stage acting. But as a matter of fact, it's just bad acting.

What's your favorite thing about being an actor?

Getting to live for a few hours a day on a very exciting, more intense plane. To get to put myself in those situations that transcend the banality of everyday existence. To get to become the King of England by killing your brother, his son, and your wife. To be so crazed with power and sick with self-loathing that it becomes a positive kind of force, an irresistible force. It's too late to know now if I could find that kind of excitement if we all lived our lives as fully as we should, or whether I need that because I'm not living as fully as I should.

You've just been through this long string of doing one thing after another—
Henry V **in Central Park,** *Silverado, Violets Are Blue, Arms and the Man* **onstage. Is it hard for you to sustain that pace?**

In fact, no. I'm not doing anything now, which is why I'm going stir crazy and why I'm teaching. I'm very particular about what I do. Especially with a film. I still can't get over the fact that when you're finished, it's still there. You have to live with that for the rest of your life. Your kids and their children might have to see it. If it's going to be preserved, it's got to be about something. It can't just be stupid.

How much input do you get or require from a director?

The approach I've adopted in the last few years is—you do it yourself and the director edits. I don't think you go in there and say, "Mold me."

A lot of actors think of themselves as a vessel and wait to see what delightful liquid the director pours into them.

I don't understand that. Because I work instinctually, I resent the notion that I am merely the vessel, "a pipe for fortune's finger to play what stop she please." It's hard enough to reconcile myself to the fact that I'm an interpretive, as opposed to creative, artist. At least let me find my way, find out what I have to say about this character and what this character means to me. I rarely argue or fight with a director. Most directors I work with say, "Show me something and let me fix it." They don't like to spoon-feed you.

Have you ever thought of quitting?

Oh yeah. Sometimes I think maybe I've seen enough of me, and I'm afraid everyone else has. I hate repeating myself. It's inevitable if you're an actor to repeat certain aspects of yourself. But sometimes I get bored with my acting, and I think that I don't have enough in my brain to be interesting every time out. I've always respected people who quit. Not that I'm thinking of retiring this year. A lot of that is neurotic, that fear. It can be good to harness that neurosis. It makes you not get lazy and not be repetitive.

Also, it's an agonizing way of life. You have to wait sometimes six months, a year, two years between jobs. What do you do unless you're an avid fisherman or astronomer? I have a piano, it kind of helps, but I'm not big on hobbies. Unfortunately, I define myself by the work I do as much as the next guy. And when I'm not working, a part of me is dead.

James Woods

The Westbury Hotel on Madison Avenue is an English-style hotel, all dark colors and wood-and-mirror panels—pretty swanky for a sleazebag like James Woods. But hey, how are you gonna keep him out? The man has money. In the mid-1980s, it sometimes seemed as if Woods was in every other movie that came out, exploiting his acne scars and sick-dog lankiness to play a succession of virtuoso slimy characters in The Onion Field, Videodrome, Against All Odds, Once Upon a Time in America, *etc. As is so often the case, he showed a broader range onstage. On a bill of one-acts at Lincoln Center one year, he created two performances (playing half of a quarreling gay couple in John Guare's* In Fireworks Lie Secret Codes *and a young stage director on a day trip with his senile father in Percy Granger's* Vivien) *that were so vivid and distinct that many in the audience didn't realize they were by the same person.*

We met downstairs in the bar of the Westbury while the maid was making up the room. In town for the Christmas holidays, Woods had been on the David Letterman show the night before and had a bunch of people over to watch. He had just finished shooting his heroically sleazy performance in Oliver Stone's film Salvador, *and over coffee he told me about his messy divorce (he'd been living for seven years with a costume designer) and his new girlfriend Sarah, who's a horse trainer. James Woods talks very fast.*

How did Letterman go?

It was good. I was surprised. He's really a terrific guy. I was sort of there to talk about *Salvador*, but I always find it tedious to go on and promote films. You know, the actor comes out and says, "Oh, my new film is great." If somebody came out and said, "This thing is such a piece of shit, I can't possibly imagine why anybody'd want to see it," you'd wake up. So I like to go on and tell funny stories about when you were a young actor, that kind of shit, which I think is more fun. People don't wanna hear about your fuckin' movie.

Do they pre-interview for that?

Yeah, they do. Robert Morton, who's the producer of the show, is very good at it. The worst thing anybody can ask you is, "Can you think of any funny stories you can tell?" Of course, immediately nothing in the world seems funny. This guy had done his research. He said, "I read this strange thing I think Letterman might like, that you worked in a factory packing watchbands when you were a kid?" And in fact there was some very funny stuff that happened in that situation. Looking back now, you don't imagine Robert Redford ever screwing nuts and bolts on car wheels.

The great fact of the cinema is that nobody was born a star. There had to have been some grueling aspect to everybody's rise to stardom. I think it helps for people to appreciate that there's a certain humanity behind the actors they fantasize about. Maybe in the old studio system they had the right idea—don't make people seem human, make them seem larger than life. But we're more sophisticated than that now, we know better, and it's fun to share that we're all in the same boat. We've all had to deal with shitty bosses and pompous schmucks and gettin' stiffed on our paychecks and fightin' City Hall.

You make it sound as if there are these two worlds—the world where you're a working stiff, then this other world, Star World, and never the twain shall meet. You pass from one into the other.

I'll tell you, it is astounding to me that there are two worlds. My mother always says, "Why is it that they always give you free tickets and the first seat in the restaurant and free bottles of champagne, you people who can afford it most easily, and those of us who can't afford it always have to pay more?"

Good question, Mom. Why is that?

Listen, you're supposed to jump for joy because they've given you some perk here or there, and the bottom line is—why do you think Spago, which is a Pizza Hut, basically, can charge you $100 for a couple of slices of pizza and a glass of Moët Chandon? The reason is because Bill Hurt is sitting at table number three and Clint Eastwood is sitting at table number five.

Did you always want to be an actor?

I never even remotely thought of being an actor. Ever. I wasn't one of those kids who sat around singing "There's No Business Like Show Business" with a raccoon boa wrapped around his neck. There was a guy like that in my high school. On talent night, this kid actually did one of Lucille Ball's big numbers from *Wildcat*, but he was a guy, which was really strange. He had a scarf on, he was always throwing it around . . . of course, he wished it were a feather boa. Those kind of guys and girls—you know, little girls tap-dancing with their tutus on, eight years old, in front of the mirror—grow up to be Baby June, I guess. I never wanted to do any of it.

There was a regional drama competition in New England, and a friend of mine said, "You've gotta be in the play, we need guys." I said, "Play? What are you talking about? I can't act, I'm skinny, I have this weird voice." He said, "That's okay, we'll put whiskers on ya, a mustache. They'll never notice." I ended up doing Oscar in *The Little Foxes*, which is a great play.

You know those people who can influence your life when you're young? The girls' gym teacher, a lady named Joyce Donahue, who's since passed away, happened to be the director of the drama club and was in fact fantastic. To this day, she was one of the most perceptive directors I've ever worked with.

What did she say that turned you on?

I was playing a villain in this thing, and she said to me, "This man wants something out of life, and he just happens not to have that little computer chip that tells him there's such a thing as right and wrong. So if he wants it, he's going to go get it; that in and of itself is right." So I learned at a very early age that the secret to playing villains is not to go around screaming and snarling and doing Rod Steiger, but to be a little more subtle and to think of yourself as being morally right. Anybody who thinks of himself as morally right is twice as chilling when he does something that is palpably and obviously morally wrong, 'cause he does it with a kind of ease and grace. I've never been that thrilled about playing villains, 'cause they're really not connected to my real life. I'm a regular person. What goes on between men and women is much more important to me as an issue. I'd like to do that kind of stuff more. It's always easier to play someone who's very, very different from you because it's just making believe, because you're not having to open up things in yourself. But to do romantic comedy and/or serious drama about relationships is a lot tougher, because that's the stuff that really affects most of us.

Did you decide after doing one play that you definitely wanted to be an actor?

No. I went to MIT and was majoring in political science, being a little home-spun genius. But I had the bug. To get away from all those hairy assholes with slide rules and white socks and shirt collars buttoned up to their nose I decided, gee, maybe I'll go over to the theater, because there's women there. All those women looked like Wallace Beery, but it was a start at least. I started doing some plays, and instantly became the top actor at MIT, which is hardly what you'd call a major dramatic feat. But the program there was fantastic. We had a lot of money, because MIT was guilty about the humanities, and we'd do these terrific offbeat plays: Gertrude Stein's *Brewsie and Willie* or a Harold Pinter radio play that we'd put onstage. I did thirty-six plays when I was in college. I'd go to the Agassiz Summer Theater at Harvard, I'd go to the Provincetown Playhouse, go to the University of Rhode Island when the Theater Company of Boston was in residence, and be an apprentice in a play with people who became great stars and great actors. They did a production of *Waiting for Godot* that had Paul Benedict, Paul Price, Dustin Hoffman, and Robert Duvall. How's that for a cast?

Was it clear that you would go into acting when you got out of college?

No, I kept thinking I'd end up working for the State Department or something. But it was the Vietnam war, kind of creepy around there, and you can imagine Boston in the '60s. So I figured, fuck it. I did a summer at Province-town. We worked seven days a week, but again we did wonderful plays. I'd done so much theater by the time I came to New York that I skipped all this acting-class bullshit—you know, everybody else was trying to be a radish or something, or play a tree. I knew how to do accents, how to do age, how to do comedy, how to do drama. I'd done it, I'd been out on the front lines.

I got my first job by lying and saying I was from Liverpool when they wanted real British actors in *Borstal Boy*. I did the accent perfectly and convinced them, and they were from the Abbey Theater! After they hired me, they asked, "When were you in Liverpool?" I said, "I've never been to England." They said, "But we wanted only resident-alien English actors." I said, "Luckily, I outfoxed you and did you a favor, so do I have the job or not?" The play went on to win the Tony award and the Drama Critics' Circle award.

Were you immediately good as an actor?

To be honest with you, yeah, I was. I think there's such a thing as talent. You either have it or you don't. I so don't believe in the Actors Studio. It's such a bunch of boring bullshit. I think timing and observation and sense of comedy and sense of re-creating people through yourself is an innate talent. Jack Nicholson was always good. You look at those stupid AIP movies he made years ago, and he's fuckin' great in them. He was always good. I saw De Niro rehearsing a play at the Theater Company of Boston when I was in college, and there was just something about this guy. He was working for $70 a week, nobody knew who the fuck he was, and you couldn't take your eyes off him. They say that about the young Brando. I'm not saying I have that, but there's some magic. The old movie moguls knew that.

Then we spent twenty years listening to Lee Strasberg, and do you know what the result of Lee Strasberg was? Marilyn Monroe died trying to do self-psycho-analysis through her work, and the studios spent the next twenty years hiring football players and models. "Hey, anybody can act!" Well, if anybody can fuckin' act, tell me why Shelley Hack isn't a star.

She is a star. She has her own show.

Well, TV's different. TV is meat for the house dogs.

How did you get into the movies?

When I was in New York for a six- or seven-year period, I spent more nights than not doing a show on or off Broadway. All of a sudden, I started to realize that I didn't really go to theater much. I'd go, and it'd be bad English imports, revivals, museum Broadway, bullshit Off-Broadway, Actors Studio doing a production of *Three Sisters* that was embarrassing. But I realized I was going to movies every afternoon. I thought, well, if I like movies so much, why don't I do them?

I was a snob about movies, the way a lot of people are about TV. Real actors do *The Lower Depths* by Gorky Off-Broadway with Julian Beck directing. I finally realized that movies were wonderful to watch because there's great work in them. The reason Gary Cooper and Humphrey Bogart were stars is because they were great actors, too. Gary Cooper in *Mr. Deeds Goes to Town* is about as different from Gary Cooper in *High Noon* as two actors could possibly be, let alone one actor playing two characters.

My first break, my first time in front of a camera, was a thing called *The Visitors* for Elia Kazan. It was about a guy testifying in an atrocity case in Vietnam, and they released it in 1970 or '71 when nobody wanted to hear about that. I worked my way up the ranks. I met a lot of resistance along the way; they always found a reason why they didn't want to use me. I wasn't conventionally good-looking or I was offbeat. The easiest thing in the world is for people out there to say no. To this day! They didn't want me for *The Onion Field*—I wasn't right for the part. I had to pay for my own screen test. They didn't want me for *Once Upon a Time in America*—I wasn't right for the part. Every movie I've ever gone up for, I wasn't right for the fuckin' part. Finally, I did *Joshua Then and Now* because the director, Ted Kotcheff, said, "You are perfect for this," and Mordecai Richler, who wrote it, said, "You are the perfect one." He's described as a thin, hawk-faced man who's rough and at the same time very bright. Right? So I did it, and fuckin' Janet Maslin in *The New York Times* writes, "Although Mr. Woods is extraordinarily miscast . . ."

People are so used to you now playing against type.

My theory is, if they were having an actors' convention in Los Angeles and I was the only actor in the world who missed it, and there was an earthquake, and everybody in L.A. fell into the sea—God forbid!—except for the five studio heads, they'd get together and say, "Who can we get to work next year?" Somebody'd say, "Well, Woods is in New York." "Yeah, but there's gotta be somebody else—he's not right for these parts."

What do you do when they say that?

If it's something I really want, and I can tell it might be a little bit of a struggle, I say, "Hey, why don't I screen-test or read for you?" They say, "Oh, you're too big a star for that." I say, "Look, if it's gonna make a difference in getting the part, I have nothing to hide. Why don't you screen-test everybody? Let the best man win." That's how I get it.

You would not believe the people who auditioned for *Once Upon a Time in America*. The biggest stars in the world fuckin' *read* for Sergio Leone. I said, "Just let me do a screen test with De Niro." De Niro had thought I wasn't really right for the part, because the character was described as a blond Hercules. So I read this dialogue, and I said, "I can do this better than anybody in the world." Bobby, because he's a great actor and knows what serves a movie well, said,

"Listen, I don't think he's right for the part, but let's give him a shot." We did this all-day screen test, and by the end of it they said, "You're the guy." I can't tell ya what a coup it was to get that part. Every actor in the world wanted to be in that movie. It was a very important step in my life. You can well imagine my disappointment when three weeks before the movie came out the studio decided to chop it to fuckin' pieces. If they'd left it alone, I'm sure it would have won every Academy Award that year and would have been a landmark film.

What's your schedule like when you're making a movie?

Horrific. You're up at five and home at ten and grouchy and tired. All your friends call and say, "Come on, let's go out to dinner." You just want to go to bed. You don't have time for anything. That's the worst part—you're either out of work and your hands are the devil's workshop, or you're working and you don't have time to take a shit in peace. It's hard to convince somebody that one of the great tragedies of your life when you're working is that you don't have time to read *People* magazine. People don't realize you need to have a day when you're sittin' around in a robe, your dick hangin' over the side of your leg, readin' *People* and saying, "God, Joan Collins looks terrible these days!"

JOHN
LITHGOW

John Lithgow

Of all the men in this book, John Lithgow is probably exactly representative of what we think of as a New York actor—a hardworking, seasoned stage performer who has gradually achieved the level of respect and renown in film that he has had for years in the theater. His film career really picked up in 1982 when he moved to Los Angeles (his second wife, Mary Yeager, teaches economic history at UCLA), though he continued to work onstage in New York, both on Broadway (the short-lived revival of Requiem for a Heavyweight) *and off (a one-man show about George S. Kaufman at the Perry Street Theater). When we met in his publicist's office underneath a poster from the movie* Footloose, *John had just lost the lease on his Manhattan apartment and confessed to feeling strange about not having at least a* pied-à-terre *in New York, the scene of his early triumphs.*

When I first came to New York, I would go breathlessly from one stage job to another, panting and sweating. There were five or six years when I always had another job by the time a job ended. It's like Lou Gehrig or Joe DiMaggio. They weren't all hits, but I was always working. Now I have this nice feeling of pulling back a little bit. The compulsion seems to have finally gone.

What made the difference?
Doing movies instead of plays. The difference is unbelievable in terms of how you're paid, how many people see your work, how you're sought after in both movies and theater. Theater is more substantial, and you have your feet on the ground while you're working in it—theater is an island of sanity compared to the movie business. Still, you're performing for thousands of people. In movies, you're performing for millions of people. It really changes your life.

How'd it change your life?
Oddly enough, acting is no longer the gravitational center of my life. My family is now. God knows, I can't really go very long without doing something. But I'm a less envious person now.

Were you always very envious before?
Secretly, I remember feeling Michael Moriarty had run away with everything. Ed Herrmann. Many of these people are good friends of mine. There's an awful quote, "It's not enough that I should succeed, but my best friends must fail." This business is so insidious in its way. It's never enough. You have a voracious appetite for the limelight.
Actors are kind of heliotropic—we go for the light. This need to be emotionally spectacular onstage, the need to create some sort of sensation—it's a combination of a generous and a selfish activity. They go hand in hand.

Do you remember pulling away from the pack and discovering this way of taking the limelight?
My dad, Arthur Lithgow, was an actor, director, and producer in regional theater. He ran these summer Shakespeare festivals out in Ohio. When I was a teenager, I hung around all the time and eventually started acting for him. I pretty much have him to thank for my career.

One role was really the beginning for me. I played Master Pinch in *Comedy of Errors*, which my dad directed. Master Pinch is a one-scene part, a conjurer who works all sorts of mumbo-jumbo. I had this very tall black hat and a cloak that ran all the way to my feet. I was a real toothpick, very tall. Long white beard, white mustaches, big long nose, and saffron-colored face. It was a real clown act. Here I was, this seventeen-year-old kid, it was my first shot, and every single time I exited, there was applause. So first of all, I had this marvelous rush, anticipating my big moment every night, knowing it was going to work like gangbusters. Also, it was my first time working with a bunch of pros, older actors, many of whom I'd known for years and worshiped. To hold my own on a stage with them and get that scene cooking for them every night . . . that was wonderful. Being up there onstage is this heightened consciousness. It's like this rush of adrenaline when it goes well. When it goes badly, I guess it's the same adrenaline, but it has a different effect. It's like going numb, suddenly being afraid you're going to die.

I remember playing Tartuffe at Harvard. I played him as a very comical character, a kind of stork, very over-the-top. The moment comes when Tartuffe is exposed and humiliated in front of everybody. The big comic character has finally come collapsing down, you think, and Orgon says, "Leave my house this instant." Tartuffe says, "No. I'm in charge here, and you must go." Suddenly, this hilarious character has become evil, and he realizes it all in one word— "No." I had an epiphany there about building up an audience's expectations and jerking them hard—an audience is thrilled by that. I look for those moments: just when they're expecting one thing, you throw them something else.

What was your first movie?

I did a film in 1971 called *Dealing*, one of these *Easy Rider* spinoffs. I thought it would be the making of me, but of course nobody went to see it. Quite a few years later I did *Obsession*—well, three years later, in 1974.

And about 400 plays in between.

Yeah, always lots of plays. But I hadn't yet acted in New York. I was doing a lot of stage directing. After Harvard, I studied acting at LAMDA, and when I came back from England, I worked for my dad at the McCarter Theater in Princeton. After one season in which I was acting, directing, and designing these big English classical productions, Dad wanted me to be his associate artistic director, but it was time to go to New York. It was very difficult to get anywhere. My directing credits got me much further than my acting credits. I was just about to take a job as associate artistic director at Baltimore's Center Stage when Long Wharf offered me a season as an actor. That was my big Rubicon: do I become a director now, or do I become an actor? I decided I'd better give acting a chance. So I went to Long Wharf, and the second show I did was *The Changing Room*. That production moved to New York intact in March of '73, opened March 6, and I won the Tony March 25. After that, I was really an actor.

I did still direct a few things, but year by year, acting really did take over. I still intend to direct. I haven't worked with many directors who are better than me.

Does that cause problems?

No, I'm a good boy as an actor. I really like a good director. Whatever director there is, I tend to hang on his every word. I try to suspend all my directorial instincts while I'm acting. Sometimes it's hard. I came back from LAMDA with this fruity English accent that I had never intended to acquire, and I did *Star-*

Spangled Girl by Neil Simon in summer stock with some dreary director who had a little bell on his desk. Every time I gave a Neil Simon line an English inflection, he would ring the bell. It drove me crazy. He was ringing the bell every thirty seconds, but he showed me just how English I'd become.

Movie directors tend not to direct you much at all. They're much more into staging and the camerawork. More often than not, you arrive, and you're expected to start acting immediately. The director hardly has a word to say to you. You'd be amazed. Some of them are very candid about it. I worked with Peter Hyams on *2010*, and he said, "Boy, these guys who direct plays, and they have four weeks of rehearsal? I wouldn't know what to do." And he doesn't. You arrive, the camera rolls, and you start acting. It's as simple as that. The other extreme is someone like Herbert Ross, who is a stage director also, who wants two weeks of very attentive rehearsal. He really breaks down the script, stands people up, moves them around on taped diagrams. In movies, an actor has to do a great deal more, because directors aren't accustomed to worrying about it, and their ideas are usually not very concrete. So especially if you're going to do anything sort of unusual—use an accent or prosthetic makeup or something like that—I feel much better if I get a big head start.

For instance, for *Buckaroo Banzai* I got these rotting pale green teeth and this shocking wig of bright red hair that I went around astonishing my friends with, and I got together with this very sweet little tailor in the MGM costume department with this fabulous thick Sicilian accent. I sat and talked with him for an hour and tape-recorded the conversation to get his accent down. In *Santa Claus*, I got a wonderful set of shiny, sort of used-car-salesman teeth—great big phony smile. In both cases, I talked to the directors on the phone beforehand, basically asking them, "Will you pay for these items if I get them?" Usually the directors are surprised and delighted.

When I did *Footloose*, I went to a Baptist minister in Provo, Utah, where we were shooting, and pretended to be in a terrible spiritual crisis just so I could hear someone talk in earnest about being saved, someone who really believed it. I felt like a real hypocrite, needless to say, but it was very useful. I'm not like Dustin Hoffman, though, or these people who really dive in and live that way. When I played Roberta Muldoon in *Garp*, I'd never met a transsexual before. I'm not that exhaustive a researcher. Maybe I'm just lazy. But I certainly know what I'm going to do by the time I get to the set.

At a certain point you changed from being primarily a stage actor to being primarily a film actor. How did that happen?

It was a combination of things. I got married and moved to Los Angeles because my wife was teaching at UCLA. There I was, just at the time they released *Garp*, by far the showiest role I'd ever done. All you need is one of those, that extraordinary little moment in a little part where people say, "God, nobody could do that as well as this fellow, he's something." *The Changing Room* did it for me in theater, and *Garp* in film.

A few months later, there came a flood of things—*Footloose, Terms of Endearment, Buckaroo Banzai, 2010, Santa Claus, Manhattan Project* . . . eight or nine movie projects, and I was different in all of them. So I began to get that reputation as this guy who has a character talent and is not afraid to use it.

I never thought I'd be in a movie. Not ever. I never even thought I'd be on Broadway. I thought I'd be like my dad, working at Arena Stage and Long Wharf and the Guthrie, that this would be my life. All these things have come along and astonished me.

TREAT
WILLIAMS

Treat Williams

Treat Williams was having an unusual year. He'd spent eight months, on and off, working with director-choreographer Michael Bennett as a salaried actor in a workshop production of a new musical called Scandal, *written by Treva Silverman of* The Mary Tyler Moore Show *with music by pop songwriter Jimmy Webb. (A similar workshop process had resulted in Bennett's greatest success,* A Chorus Line.) *Treat, though primarily known as a dramatic actor in films like* Prince of the City, Once Upon a Time in America, *and the television production of* A Streetcar Named Desire *with Ann-Margret, has a lot of experience with stage musicals. His first professional job was a role in* Grease, *and he replaced Kevin Kline in Broadway's pop version of* The Pirates of Penzance. *For* Scandal *he had four six-week sessions which included lessons in acrobatics and dance classes every morning. But at the end of the workshop period,* Scandal *was still in bits and pieces, so Bennett abandoned the project.*

Then Treat signed to play the lead in a feature film about Ernest Hemingway. He delved into an extensive preparation for that film, even shaving his head bald for the part. Then, only days before shooting was scheduled to begin, the project fell through for lack of money. So here he was, in the dead of summer, hairless and out of a job. Considering the circumstances, he was remarkably placid, baking in the sun on the patio of his apartment on the Upper West Side. He was thinking about playing Tom in a production of The Glass Menagerie *with Joanne Woodward and Karen Allen, but he was waiting to see if he definitely had the part he'd been offered in the movie* The Men's Club, *which was shooting in Los Angeles. (He ended up doing both.)*

How do you feel when you're not working?

After a while, I get crazy. But I've just spent eight months with Michael Bennett and three months doing research on Hemingway. I consider that working. My career's always been steady. There's been a lot of rest and reading and catching up on myself the last two years. Not necessarily by choice. It's not as if you say, "I think I'm going to do this now"—it just happens. But I have more of the feeling now of working because I'm really interested in something. It's harder to say no when you're younger. When you're younger, you think, "I'll never be out of work." It gets easier, because life gets interesting. Then if you read something, and it excites you, you do it.

I'm planning for the future, for periods of being out of work. I'll be thirty-four in December, and my lifestyle's changed. I don't just do whatever I want to do anymore, flying everywhere. I'm a commercial pilot. I've been flying since I was seventeen. There was a time I felt I would rather fly than act. I was losing the sense of why I was doing what I was doing. *Hair* and *Why Would I Lie* were well-received but unsuccessful. That got me down. My expectations were high. So I quit the business, and I flew for four or five months with a company in L.A. Then Sidney Lumet called with *Prince*, and I realized I could never give up acting.

What made you want to act in the first place?

Originally, it was a feeling of the sense of control. I did my first play in eighth grade—it was called *If Men Reduced as Women Did*, in which a bunch of us guys walked around with pillows tied around our waists. I had this Coca-Cola, and I set it down too hard on the table. It foamed up, I did a take, and there was this laugh. There was such power in that.

So I kept doing plays because I liked the idea, and I got more serious about it. In college, I sought out work as an actor. Eventually my interest shifted to the idea of creating a character, looking at the different ways people breathe or act, seeing the world through someone else's eyes. I began to study mime, and I found that interesting, the physicality. When I did *The Eagle Has Landed*, I played an American Ranger, so I went down to Ft. Stewart, Georgia, and spent two weeks on maneuvers with the armed forces playing war games.

What was the Hemingway research like?

Well, flying into a Communist country with my own plane was interesting. I didn't know if it would be confiscated, or surrounded by soldiers, or what. Cuba's like going on the set of a western after seeing too many westerns. You think you know all about it, and then you see it firsthand. Then seeing Hemingway's home, which is like Beverly Hills . . . well, it was a trip.

Where did you go to school?

Franklin and Marshall College in Lancaster, Pennsylvania. They talked a lot about Roy Scheider—you know, you follow the careers of guys who went to your school. I went to the University of London my last year of college, mainly as an excuse to see plays. The best thing about that was that I realized that there are bad English actors, too. They have a certain facility because of the opportunity to be in regional rep and touring classical productions, which we don't have, but that doesn't automatically make them better actors.

Do you prepare for a stage role the same way you do a movie role?

I always begin with the text. What is he saying, what is he doing, and what is everyone else saying about him? The luxury of doing a play is that you can break it down. You have to attack the scene in every possible way, go as far as you can in rehearsal, because you're going to be doing it a lot. If you don't give yourself a range of possibilities, you're going to get bored. In film, you only have to capture a moment. Sometimes I'm wary of working things out too much in a film—I want to just let it happen.

For instance, with *Hair*, we improvised a great deal. But *Prince of the City* we rehearsed like grand opera. Sidney Lumet did run-throughs for a week at what used to be a Puerto Rican nightclub (now it's the Ritz). It was a very difficult project—my character was a man who had to deal with the fact that doing something he thought was right was destructive to others. I had to find sides of myself I didn't like. It wasn't joyous like *Hair* was, where I flew to work every morning.

Then sometimes it's the same old scene, again and again. Actors who've done a lot of stage work have an advantage in that situation, because they usually have stronger technique. There's a famous story: Billy Wilder told Jack Lemmon and Tony Curtis, when they were doing *Some Like It Hot* with Marilyn Monroe, that they'd better be at their best in every take because "the one *she's* good in is the one they'll use."

What do you do between takes?

I don't like to talk when I'm working. What I do is sit by myself with the script and keep outside influences away. I don't leave the environment. If you walk across the street to buy a bagel, and the guy gives you an argument, it can throw you off. You try to keep your motor running. It's like sitting at a stoplight in your car—you don't turn off the engine and get out.

When you're doing a play, what is the last thing you do before going on?

I'm always very much alone the moment before I go onstage. Whatever gives you the strongest reality. I've seen actors shootin' the shit with the stage manager, excuse themselves, go on, come off, and pick up where they left off. I can't do that.

Do you mind auditioning for roles?

I don't mind if I'm not being taken advantage of, if they're really unsure. Nothing's handed to you. The only things that come easily are the things you've already shown you're capable of doing. In life, you have to struggle to get what you want.

But there are other uses for auditions besides seeing if you're right for the role. The reason you have so many meetings on a movie is often just to see if you're emotionally compatible with the director. After all, you'll be working together five or six months, up to fourteen hours a day.

How do you determine if you're compatible?

First you see their work. Then you meet them. If you go to dinner with someone you've never met, and he starts slapping you on the back and calling you "baby," something's wrong. You're interested in their approach to the work. You're interested in the unspokens—Is he clearheaded? Is he abusive? Is he a drunk? Will he let me take chances? Will he let me use my sense of humor? Will he force me to play the character the way he sees it? Does he have a discerning eye, or will he edit out the good stuff? Does he know what kind of movie he wants to make, or is he just making a movie? None of those things are talked about, but they're all going on.

Are you conscious of being an actor in your everyday life?

"The Actor" is always presented as this flamboyant, Shakespeare-quoting character, the guy who comes through the back door. People think it's a very flamboyant life-style. Actors do tend to be odd in their ways—it makes them interesting. I feel I'm an actor by profession. When I started I was afraid to say it. I've worked very hard to be comfortable saying I'm an actor. Now I'm proud of it.

Are you vain?

I'm somewhat vain. I mean, I wore a hat for two weeks after shaving my head. But real acting is the least vain thing you can do—you're giving up yourself to present what the writer wrote, to play that character without letting yourself get in the way. There's a kind of acting that leads to vanity because it's based on looking good. You see it on TV. The actor may not be vain, but if looking good is what you do for a living . . . On the other hand, if you spent four hours in front of a mirror making yourself up as the Hunchback of Notre Dame, is it vanity? I'm always striving for the medium between false modesty and vanity.

Acting is a lot of hard work. I've been through analysis not to get caught up in the success, which came fast, heady. It frightened me that it was so easy to lose the values that brought me into this business. When you first hit, it's the hardest time because it's out of your control. You're hanging on for dear life. It's frightening emotionally. Luckily, I had a stable family background. A friend of mine who's an interior decorator is going to redo my living room, cover the sofa, all that. He teased me and said, "I know, you want whales and boats." And he was right.

John Shea

John Shea is the epitome of a certain kind of actor. Handsome, intelligent, sincere, eager to please—sometimes too eager to please for his own good. He can also surprise; completely miscast as a sleazy record-company president in Stephen Poliakoff's Off-Broadway play American Days, *he gave a remarkably tough, high-strung, unpredictable performance. In person, he is unremittingly charming, naturally flirtatious, and intellectually curious.*

What's the hardest thing for you to do as an actor?

Wait for scripts. Particularly when you have more energy than you know what to do with and you've been spoiled by your training in classics and the things you've done in the past. Then you're confronted with a television series, and there's no way you're going to do that and ruin your gift. Therefore, you're forced to wait for long periods of time until something good comes along. That's the worst. Being powerless, until you reach a point like Dustin Hoffman or Warren Beatty or Bob De Niro, where you become bankable. I have lots of ideas for projects, but essentially nobody cares right now, because my name isn't going to raise $15 million from a Hollywood studio. The point is to reach that status, if you can, without ruining yourself along the way.

What's the silliest thing about being an actor to you?

(*Long pause.*) The difference between the image you project and who you really are. That's part of the baggage you carry around when you're an actor. Fame is the price you pay for success. Being famous is a tool, not an end. Poetry 101 tells us how fleeting and absurd fame is, and a visit to any cemetery will tell you the same thing. At the same time, in this world I work in, your name carries a certain value, and that name then becomes a tool to reach an audience. They don't teach you at Yale Drama School that you're going to have to work with publicists and go on *The Today Show* and do interviews for *Esquire* magazine and tour Europe, get out there and beat the drums. At first it's very disquieting; it makes you feel unlike yourself. You don't want that fame to go to your head and to change you so you don't relate to your friends the same way. You have to walk this tightrope between the fear of being famous (or well-known or successful) and the need to be that if you want to continue working.

What is your favorite dressing room?

The Public Theater, because they have all these great rooms you can wander around in for your warm-up. There's no such thing as a star dressing room there. You share dressing rooms, people are sharing makeup, throwing things back and forth. I love that. You feel like you're in a locker room before a football game or basketball game, putting on a costume, changing yourself into a character who goes out and plays with these other people in front of spectators.

It also goes back to the religious training I had. I grew up as a Catholic, and I was an altar boy. The priest is the star, you go out there as the supporting cast and, bang, you do this ensemble ritual that has meaning for a lot of people. That was my earliest stage experience.

JOHN
SHEA

Ken Marshall

Growing up as an Army brat, Ken Marshall came from a cultivated household. His father played cello, his mother was a dancer, they didn't own a television, and when they took their kids to the movies, it was strictly Walt Disney. Maybe that's why Ken is clean-cut and polite in person, secretive and imaginative as an actor. A Juilliard graduate, he was honing his chops onstage playing a drunken Irish farmer, an archaeologist, and Camus' Caligula in rep at the Circle Repertory Theater when we met, but his public recognition and his professional experience were still dominated by his appearance in the title role of NBC's ten-part mini-series Marco Polo.

Did you always want to be an actor?

Not consciously. I wanted to be a doctor. I realized after four years of pre-med at University of Michigan I'd like to *play* a doctor—they were wonderful people—but I don't like science. I wasn't good at it, and you don't like what you're not good at.

What made you want to act?

As a kid, I used to read biographies like crazy and act everything out in the backyard. I just loved being inside these people, vicariously living their lives.

How did you happen to do *Marco Polo*?

I'd made another film in Italy called *La Pelle*, directed by Liliana Cavani, with Marcello Mastroianni, Burt Lancaster, and Claudia Cardinale. I got to be very good friends with Mastroianni. He was making another film right after that near Venice. I went to visit him on the set. I was hanging out with a couple friends from *La Pelle* who were working on pre-production for *Marco Polo*. I met the producer at the hotel. As I was leaving, he said, "Will you give me your picture?" That night I got a phone call saying "Would you come back and screen test for us? We think you might be our Marco Polo." I screen-tested for three days and got the part, so I ended up never going home. My wife took a leave of absence from law school and joined me in Venice, and I just stayed and shot for thirteen months.

What was a typical day like?

No day was typical. We were shooting basically in three places, Italy, Morocco, and mainland China. For each place, you'd get into a routine. In Venice it was winter, ice cold; I don't remember ever being warm there. I'd have to get up and be there at five-thirty in the morning to start putting on the beard, 'cause he would do it *pelo per pelo*, hair by hair. So I'd be up at four. By the time they finished the makeup and wig and beard, I'd be on the set maybe by eight, eight-thirty. It took a long time to get shots because the cinematographer was so particular. There's an incredible amount of tedium that goes into making a film. There are so many things draining you; you have to learn to pace yourself, to concentrate, because when they're ready, you've got to be there 100 percent. You'd work until the lunch break at one or two. Sometimes it could be really elaborate and nice, but I wouldn't be able to indulge the way I'd want to, because I would fall asleep if I got too full. Then you'd work until you'd lose the light, sometimes beyond that if it was indoors. We'd usually finish at six-thirty, seven. They eat fairly late, eight-thirty, nine. Then crash.

Did it feel real to you being in these exotic locations?

It's a sort of in-and-out existence. You're there, but you're dressed in character, you're being the character, so really you're living in the thirteenth century most of the time.

What's the silliest thing about being an actor?

Having to talk about it. For any film, if you've got a lead, they'll use you forever to publicize the movie. For *Krull*, I went to Japan, to Paris, to Australia. I like to travel, but they schedule these interviews very tightly. You're eating three meals a day with reporters who are always trying to chip away at you, seizing on anything slightly negative or unusual, which is their job, I suppose, but the strain on your sense of self is enormous. Nobody knows what privacy is until it's taken away from them.

HOWARD
ROLLINS

Howard Rollins

In person, Howard Rollins presents a very different, more casual figure than the severe, angry, well-spoken men he has portrayed in films like Ragtime *and* A Soldier's Story. *So much so, in fact, that when he showed up at the Columbia Pictures building on Fifth Avenue in dreadlocks and a black leather coat to do publicity for* A Soldier's Story, *the guards didn't recognize him and wouldn't let him pass—even though the lobby was full of nearly life-size posters of Rollins as Captain Davenport. When we met for this interview, he arrived at my apartment with very closely cropped hair and little round glasses. It was early in the afternoon, and he asked for a shot of Jack Daniel's and a beer. He was quite guarded and serious at first and became progressively more voluble. He had just finished one television movie, playing a cocaine pimp in* Children of Times Square, *and he was preparing to play an FBI agent in* The Johnny Gibson Story. *He said he was eager to do a stage play, but everything he'd been offered was insufficient.*

When I get onstage, I wanna have my ass kicked. I gotta have something that, when it's over, the only thing I can do is go get a drink. That's what being onstage is about. It's one chance to get a straight-through orgasm—no coitus interruptus like filmmaking is, where just before you bust a nut, somebody says, "All right, hold it." In a play, you can just go all the way through to orgasm. That can wear you out if you get a good one. That's what I want.

Did you always want to be an actor?

No, I really didn't. Growing up, what was there to emulate? I had no desire to walk around in tuxedos with trays. I had no desire to be, as Lena Horne puts it, "the part you can cut out when they get to Alabama." I wanted to be something that was integral to the piece. Acting came to me sort of as a surprise. When I was sixteen or seventeen, I read for the part of Crooks, the stable buck in *Of Mice and Men*, as a favor to a friend. When the director called me back to say I got the part, I didn't even remember the audition. But if there's anything in my life that's come close to perfect, it was my being introduced to theater. I thought it was great. It blew my mind. It gave me a theme.

And no one had to tell me, "Howard, you have to speak this way, don't turn this way, onstage you can't do this or that." It just all made sense—until opening night, when I refused to go on and ran back and hid in the prop room. I said, "You didn't tell me there were gonna be people out there!" The director said, "Don't do this to me, Howard. Come on." He literally, at my cue, shoved me through the door. Luckily, my character could stumble, so I stumbled down the stairs. I was just frightened of people. Then once I got up there it became that strange thing that one enjoys, which is being able to pretend it's very normal to have people looking at the crack of your ass. Then when the show is over, you say, "Okay, you paid your money, you can't see any more, now it's mine." I never stood around waiting for accolades like others did. I was always the first one out of the theater from the very beginning.

When I went to college, it was neck and neck between French and theater. I was gonna be a French teacher, because my sister was a teacher, and I thought at least I can do that. I studied French for eight years, all through junior high and high school and two years in college before I dropped out. I was working at a TV studio in Baltimore doing sort of a public-service soap opera dramatizing the problems of the city, and I was a little disappointed in school, so I thought: Why don't I just work full-time? It kept going from then on.

At what point did you consciously decide to become an actor?

When I did that first play in '67. It was the greatest thing I ever discovered, that I could get up onstage and actually do that. I had no trouble with lines. I learned them very fast, and I understood the act of creating and playing and getting out of myself into somebody else. I knew then I wanted to be an actor.

Why do you think you were able to do that so immediately?

What is this, a therapy session? [*He laughs.*] I don't know why. I guess it's a chance to express things I rarely got a chance to express in my ordinary life except with my best friend. I just wanted to act. I didn't know where it would go ultimately. My sister, who was older, said to me at one point, "Well, baby, black people don't become movie stars." I said "I don't care, I want to be an actor." I never thought about it consciously.

Did you ever study acting formally?

Not really. There was some acting class we had in twelfth grade, but that teacher, all he talked about was his antique store. Then you get to college and you have Acting 1, which is improvisation, playing fried eggs and blades of grass, stuff like that, and Acting 2, where you blow a kiss at Shakespeare. But that's not studying. First day of July 1974 I came to New York. When this public-service soap opera ended after four years, I thought I'd save some money to go to New York. I started substitute teaching, which was not saving money, then I took over driving a bus. I happened to call my sister-in-law one time, because I was gonna visit her in D.C., and she started crying on the phone, saying, "Oh God, I hear you're driving a bus. You're a good actor. Don't be like the rest of the family. Don't wait for years and years and then say you could have done this, you could have done that. Just go do it." Ten days later I was in New York.

I moved into the YMCA on Sixty-third Street and just started walking around trying to learn the city a little bit. I spent a lot of time just sitting around Lincoln Center watching people going to the theaters and stuff. I even saw Patti Labelle with her band rehearsing for their wear-something-silver concert at the Met. I was sitting on the steps, and they were out there taking pictures for this magazine. A feather came off one of her dresses, and I kept that feather for the longest time.

You were in *Streamers* at some point, weren't you?

Yeah, I was in it the last eight months of its run. One day Mike Nichols came back to tighten it up for the Tonys or something. I stayed there while he reworked the whole show. It was really interesting to watch him work. He'd say, "Nope, that's a tape. That's a tape. You're playing a tape. Erase it. Go back to the real thing." The only thing he said to me was, "I hear you're pretty good. I'm glad to meet you." I almost shit on myself.

When you came to New York to act, did you think you would also do movies or just theater?

I really didn't think about movies. I'd done some television in Baltimore, some commercials even—nice commercials, not just advertising Benny's Pizza Parlor. But I didn't come to New York thinking about movies, I came to New York thinking about acting. I figured if you wanna be an actor, you do it in New

York. I never thought about California at all. I only thought of going to New York for the stage. It was the only place to go.

Was *Ragtime* the first movie you ever made?

No, the second. The first movie I made was a thing called *House of God*, about medical students in their first year of internship. It starred some people who went on to get some nice work—Tim Matheson, who always does those get-the-pussy movies. Charlie Haid, from *Hill Street Blues*. Bess Armstrong, Sandra Bernhard, Joe Piscopo was in it. It was directed by Donald Wrye. His other film was a Robby Benson film called *Ice Castles*, about a kid goin' blind or somethin'. I didn't see it. [*He rolls his eyes.*]

So *House of God* got you lots of work, eh?

No, 'cause no one saw it. After that, *Ragtime* came. I went to the Gulf and Western building and met Milos Forman for about fifteen minutes, and we talked. I had just seen *Hair* and I loved the movie. So after talking to him, I got to the door, and I thought, "I don't give a fuck what he thinks," and I turned around and said, "I really liked *Hair*." I thought he might say, "Oh, sure, you liked *Hair*. You'd probably have liked it if I did *Betty Boop Meets Tolstoy*." But I meant it, and he said [*Czech accent*], "Oh, thank you very, very much," and I left. Then I got a callback, and I met him again. I met him three times altogether, and I screen-tested two scenes. Then I went away to do a TV movie in France as Glenn Turman. When I came back five weeks later, I figured I didn't have it. I walked into the agency, and the secretary said, "Hello, Coalhouse." I almost shit on myself. I couldn't believe it.

Did you know other people who were up for that?

Yeah. O.J. Simpson. [*He sticks his finger in his mouth, as if to make himself vomit.*] I saw him in the makeup room before we did the shoot. And [*he does his make-me-sick gesture again*] LeVar Burton was there. There was talk of Lou Gossett, who somebody said was too old. And Richard Pryor, who by that time had burnt himself up with that rum drink that didn't do right. [*He laughs.*] So he was out of the running. Somebody said two hundred guys were up for that part.

What's the hardest thing for you to do as an actor?

To finish a good job and leave and know that it's over. With *Ragtime*, for instance, working with a director like that and a cast like that and feelings like that for five months, it's almost unrealistic the closeness you have to have immediately. For that to be over really bothered me. The last day of shooting in London, I just made it out of the studio up to my dressing room before I burst into tears. If I'm not working, I'm usually alone, and I don't do that well. Acting is fine, but socially I'm not very good. I'm like an octopus on speed in a china shop—all the Waterford crystal comes down to the floor, all the Steuben glass. But if I have a character to be behind, I can have fun with it. That's my world. I'm not good at dating or meeting people. My life is not conducive to normal relationships. There's a part of me that always wants to be normal, and I'm not normal, never have been normal. I've always been a strange little fuck, and I've gotten used to it. When I'm acting, I know how to tie it down, how to use it. When I'm not working, I get really bizarre.

Are there actors that you've looked to as role models or inspirations for your career?

There are actors I look at and say, "Goddam, they're hot," like John Hurt in

1984. Whew! And Richard Burton in *1984*. Those two motherfuckers are incredible. De Niro is . . . MM! That motherfucker must have come out of his mother's womb with a little tee-tiny script clutched in his hand, like those tee-tiny cartoon books you get in Cracker Jack boxes. He had to have! The work that Paul Winfield did used to blow my mind. I think those guys are brilliant. Glenda Jackson is still one of my favorites.

What's the silliest thing about being an actor for you?

Let's see, that's interesting. Let me figure that out. One thing that always strikes me as silly is people who act like they don't have genitals. There's an actress right now in film who everybody wants and everybody begs for, who is technically brilliant. But to me, I think there's, like, a Barbie doll up under that dress. I can't believe there's a vagina there. And this woman has children, too! I cannot imagine her with her legs in the air in the throes of passion. I can't!

The other thing is signing autographs. Walking in to get some toilet paper, and someone says, "Oh, aren't you . . . ? Weren't you in, uh . . . ?" It's silly to me that somebody would want my autograph, because if they knew what I knew, they wouldn't want it.

What do you mean?

OH, I WOULDN'T TELL YOU THAT! YOU THINK I'M A FOOL? SHIT, I AIN'T COMPLETELY CRAZY! I CAN'T TELL YOU THAT! JESUS! HONEY, THAT TAPE RECORDER WOULD BE BURNIN' UP!

LENNY
VON DOHLEN

Lenny Von Dohlen

Lenny Von Dohlen grew up in the tiny Texas town of Goliad, not far from the Mexican border, where his father was a Ford dealer who owned a racetrack on the side. Lenny had his heart set on being a jockey until he turned fourteen, at which point he was much too tall at six feet. His fixation then turned to becoming an actor. The first order of business was shaking his accent. He started by sending away for a record of John Gielgud reading The Ages of Man, *which he played obsessively in his room and imitated at the dinner table—"Pahss the salt." Naturally, when he made his movie debut, the first thing he had to do was greet Robert Duvall with a good ol' Southern "Hah!" as the country-rock bandleader in* Tender Mercies, *a role he got by lying to screenwriter Horton Foote and swearing, "I used to go listen to Willie Nelson when he had a crewcut, man."*

His foghorn bass voice and bay-blue eyes match Lenny's "Yessir/Nosir" Southern-gentlemanly manners, but there's something unexpectedly searching in his attitude toward his work as an actor. When we met, the twenty-six-year-old actor had most recently appeared onstage as British playwright Joe Orton in Terence Feely's The Team *in New Haven, and he'd just finished shooting* Billy Galvin *with Karl Malden in Boston. Throughout the interview, Lenny smoked incessantly, until he was lighting each new cigarette from the butt of the old one.*

My first acting teachers ever were these two Polish women at the University of Texas, who I thought were very glamorous. They'd moved from Warsaw and were living in Austin, Texas, this college town, exuding this incredible energy and hope and this wonderful sense of truth. One of them had worked with Grotowski. They were very good for me, except that (as one of them said) Poles thrive on suffering. There was this sense of "Oh, what we've been through! And we're here to tell you about it." Now, I'm an obedient sponge, and I'll absorb anything around me, and I did not need to absorb any more of that notion that an artist needs to suffer. Before I realized that maybe these women from Poland weren't the great messiahs, I would hear these stories about catastrophic things that happened to people, or I'd walk on Fifty-seventh Street and see some atrocity, and I'd give full rein to my feelings. It's that pain we all feel momentarily when we see something or hear something, but I'd drag it out. It had a lot to do with where I grew up. For a long time, I wanted to be black. Then I wanted to be Jewish. Actually, I didn't want to be black, I wanted to be a black *woman.* I thought they were particularly soulful. Enviable, somehow. They knew something that made them purer and wiser than I was and closer to God and goodness.

Anyway, these two women left at the end of the year to go to different schools. I was unhappy with school, so I was going to go to New York. And this one teacher said [*Polish accent*], "Lenny, if you go to New York now, it's like throwing a sheep to the wolves." She was probably right. I would have been a baby, and I might have gotten eaten up in the teen market. She recommended this small liberal-arts college in Denver, which allowed me to do classics, work hard, learn my craft. I met an Indian woman there in the dance department—all these exotic women in my life!—who taught musical theater and stage movement. I played Romeo at eighteen, which I had no business doing, considering my experience. I had all the passion, I knew what this guy was goin' through, and I thought I got it right a couple of nights because I got an erection in the balcony scene. I thought, "This is it, man! Forget Grotowski, Stanislavsky, whatever—I've got the proof." But I didn't know anything about voice projection, and my body wasn't projecting—well . . . [*He looks down at his lap.*] After she saw my Romeo, this American Indian mystic said two words to me: "Jump rope." I looked at her like she was nuts. What she was saying was, "You can have all the feelings in the world, but if your body doesn't communicate what you're trying to say with your heart—on a stage, or anywhere—then you're sunk."

Are you a vain person?

Yes. When you do movies and see yourself, you want to be true and good and be the part and all that, but then you also want to be attractive. I did a lot of research for *Electric Dreams*, went around to all these architectural firms and got the idea of wearing the bow tie and glasses from watching a Cary Grant movie. All that was part of building a character, but I was aware that it was also me hiding. Because subconsciously I knew it wasn't *War and Peace*, and it wasn't going to be *Mean Streets*. It was not going to do anybody any harm, but it was fluff. I was getting paid a lot of money, and I was going to do it with as much charm and finesse as possible. But at the same time, maybe I could hide behind these glasses while I did it.

So there's less of you involved?

Yeah. And it's braver to be more you. Beau Bridges was directing this TV movie called *Don't Touch*, and he wanted me to play this child molester. I was very encouraged by the fact that it was the first part I ever got offered without having to audition, but it alarmed me that he wanted me for this particular role. An instinct I had was to make him a little bit off. There was a guy I knew growing up in Goliad who everyone was a little frightened of 'cause they thought he might be a child molester. He wore his pants way up around his waist, and he would walk real goofy. You definitely knew there was something peculiar about this guy. So I thought that's what I'll do, I'll play him. Then I realized that the brave thing to do, the right thing to do—and the reason Beau wanted me, I found out—was for me to play myself, because this fellow in the story had to be perfectly likable and unsuspicious, even though he did these terrible things with this little girl. So that was a pretty brave thing, to open yourself up to that. I listened to that Bruce Springsteen song a lot—you know, "Hey, little girl, is your daddy home?"

My parents recorded that movie on their VCR, and the thing that's kind of weird is that my younger brother has two little girls, four and two. They always watch me when I'm on TV or in the movies, but for some reason with this thing, I guess because they saw Bubba (that's what they call me) playing with this little girl and they didn't know the implications of the story, they watched it over and over and over. I said, "Mother, how could you let those kids watch that?" I didn't even want them to watch it once, much less over and over and over. She said, "Because they cried when it was over and they wanted to see Bubba." I said, "Oh, God, that's not good. Mm-mm."

DAVID
RASCHE

David Rasche

David Rasche is the sort of actor who makes you appreciate supporting players—those characters in a movie or a play that you don't pay much attention to until the focus suddenly shifts to them and they become, however briefly, the only thing happening. The actor in that situation has to work harder than the star, in some ways, because he has only a few lines or one dramatic action through which to convey an entire life. Perhaps because of his background doing improvisational comedy in Chicago, Rasche has the subtlety to recede into the background and the substance to make an impression quickly—as when he played the stunt man in Jonathan Reynolds' farce Geniuses, *who suddenly turns and beats a starlet nearly to death.*

You've been working like crazy in the last several months.

I have. I did a play at the Second Stage, then a *Miami Vice*, and then I did a little part in this new movie with Sylvester Stallone. I was an innocent bystander brutally murdered by an ax. Yes, I know. It's a difficult business.

Did you always want to be an actor?

I guess I did. I've always been involved in the theater. My father's a minister, so my whole childhood was involved with the church and politics. I spent a couple of years in divinity school at the University of Chicago. I sort of treated it like a monastery, which it isn't, so it didn't work. It's really for people who already know what's going on so they can learn how to tell other people. It's not for those who are just lost. I had to write a paper on Paul Tillich—eight pages of what Paul Tillich said, and then the next eight pages were supposed to be what I thought. I wrote the first eight, and that's all I could do. I think it's hard to figure out what's going on. Don't you think so? I just didn't have much to say. And I was twenty-five at the time. I had already gotten a master's degree in English at the University of Chicago and taught for a year at Gustavus Adolphus College in Minnesota. Then I came back to divinity school for two years. After that I didn't do anything for a year. Then I started going to Second City and taking workshops. A typical story.

What made you go to Second City?

I wanted to be Mike Nichols. I didn't want to be an actor, I wanted to be him. I like satire. The summer after my senior year, I worked on a boat in the Great Lakes, and I used to rip off Mike Nichols and Elaine May routines, inflection for inflection. In the evening, the college students who worked on the boat gave a little show for the people. I'd corral these waitresses and sit them down next to the record player and make them talk exactly like Elaine May. I really loved Nichols and May. Then I heard you could sign up for workshops at Second City, and I thought, "My God! You mean, they'll take anybody? All you have to do is give them $60?" I was afraid to go alone, so I paid the tuition for a friend to go with me. When I first went, I knew that's really what I wanted to do. I didn't necessarily want to be an actor. At that time, you know, actors were pretty silly at Second City—"Acting? You must be kidding!" But it was a lot of fun. You get to the theater at eight-thirty, start laughing, and continue to laugh until around one or two in the morning. You can't beat it.

What's the best thing about being an actor for you?

Well, you know, sometimes you're forced to climb in bed with women who have no clothes on, and you *have* to do it. You have to, even though you're married. You must do it.

What's the silliest thing about being an actor?

I did this play called *Lunch Hour*, and I was only in the second act, so I had a lot of time to wait. But I used to like to watch the curtain go up. It was such a fascinating thing every night. It's like there was this secret. The people in the audience knew there was something behind that curtain, and they didn't know what it was, but they were willing to pay to find out. So they give $40 and say, "Okay, now, come on, show us." And we're backstage going, "So I said, 'Look, Mike, I have a flat tire, won't you help me with it?'" Then the stage manager says, "Time for the curtain," and you go, "Okay, okay." And then there's a moment where the audience is quiet, and the actors are quiet, and everybody's waiting for the secret. We're going to show them the secret—they gave us $40, right? It's time. The reality of help-me-with-my-car is gone, the reality of people taking off their coats is gone, and they merge. I'd go down there and wait for everything to get quiet, the lights go down, then there's this sound whhhhhhh. The curtain goes up, the lights go on, and something begins. It's fascinating.

EDWARD
HERRMANN

Edward Herrmann

Ed Herrmann has played a lot of starchy WASPs—as F.D.R. in the two "Eleanor and Franklin" TV movies and in the movie of Annie, *and onstage as Kate Nelligan's toweringly repressed British ambassador husband in David Hare's* Plenty. *The image Herrmann projects as more intelligent and well-educated than the average guy is confirmed by his conversation, which is littered with references to Thucydides, Socrates, Emerson, Gibbon. On the other hand, he loves to drop show-biz names and dish about other actors. And the first time he appears on screen in* Compromising Positions, *he's sitting in McDonald's eating a Big Mac exclaiming, "I would love to kill a dentist!"*

The attitudes people judge my work by are what they use to judge the old WASP power group—East Coast Anglo, Northern European. My family is from Indiana, German Middle America: the work ethic, picnics, hot dogs, pretzels. But it's fun to make fun of a WASP, who is necessarily stodgy. Like in England they have jokes about the ruling class. There's always a group it's convenient to bounce off.

How does your size affect the roles you're offered?
Big guys (like Johnny Lithgow) usually play parts where they aren't aggressive. Big guys don't have to be. Newman, Redford, Nicholson, those guys are small. Whereas I wear glasses, I usually speak in complete sentences—that makes people nervous. It doesn't do to be too smart. Actors who insist they're brilliant —that puts you out of the running for half the roles you want to play. Or you have to wrap your intelligence in a brooding, self-destructive persona.

Have you done any brooding, self-destructive characters?
Alger Hiss. But he didn't know he was self-destructive. Siegfried Sassoon in *Not About Heroes*, this play about World War I poets that I just did at Williamstown, was a personal favorite. The review in the *Boston Globe* said, "Herrmann has made a habit of playing gifted, passionate aristocrats." That's the journalist's trap of delineating history while you're in the middle of it. When I was at LAMDA in 1968–69, the sun rose and set on English actors. They went on and on about Olivier's *career*. Yeah, it was great stuff. But he made a lot of stupid mistakes, too. The business has changed so much since I started out in 1970. The way it's structured now, you could play an asshole in a John Candy film, and it would be better for your career than doing this play in the Village about the values that World War I was fought over.

Did you think *Annie* would be good for your career?
It was a disastrous choice, but how else would I get a chance to meet John Huston? And I met Albert Finney. But it was a horrible experience all round. It's best not to make choices based on that mentality—that if that's what's selling, it's good because it gets you considered for pictures. "Oh, he's in the hit."
But you see, I'm cowardly and frightened, I'm basically a nervous person, and I'm reluctant to initiate my own projects. I had been with [agent] Robbie Lantz for a long time, but I couldn't get him on the phone. When I did John Guare's

play *Gardenia* at Manhattan Theater Club, I tested the water with Sam Cohn. The great fear for an actor is not to have access to your agent, and in Sam Cohn's office there's a needlepoint pillow that say's "Tell him I'll call him back." I couldn't make up my mind, and a guy in L.A. who really wanted me to sign with him flew three thousand miles to meet me. But I said no, I'll try this.

The first thing Sam advised me to do was *Plenty*. Of course, he handles Kate Nelligan too. The day after I said yes to the play, I got offered this wonderful TV movie with Blythe Danner. It sounded like a good movie, and I needed the money. I really wanted to do it, and Sam said, "TV movies are like Kleenex." I said, "I know, that's what's great about them." He said, "*Plenty* will be the play of the season." So I thought to myself: I knocked on this guy's door, and now I'm going to turn down his advice? So I did *Plenty*, and like almost everything else Sam has advised me to do, it was on the money.

And do you have access?

He'll get back to me one out of three times—I guess I'm part of the charmed circle. He's eager one minute and indifferent the next. Don't misunderstand—once he has you, he'll talk for an hour. No one can make things happen faster than Sam Cohn. He's not traditional in any sense. The people he represents have reached that point of "Let's do something we like."

But his inaccessibility teaches you to do a lot for yourself. He taught me you are responsible for your work. You can't think of yourself as a victim of some Tarot-written fate. If you don't do it, who will? Sly Stallone. Warren Beatty helped me with that, too. When I did *Reds*, one day we were shooting down on a dock, me and Warrren and Diane Keaton. It was a light day—only fifty takes on one close-up. I asked Warren how to proceed with a script. He said, "Do it." I said, "No, no, I mean, who do you call?" He said, "Just do it."

Why did you want to act in the first place?

To act out feelings too intense to articulate. To release pain or elation by acting it out. In high school, I emulated my athlete brother—I was a trainer. I stayed away from the theater crowd. Everybody thought they were pansies, and weird. I'm glad I stayed away from them—they *were* pansies, and weird. If you go too soon into the hothouse, you develop attitudes that make you unfit for other things. The best actors are inclusive of experience, not the ones who are overly specialized in theater.

When you're an actor, you tend to draw parts to you that are essential to working something out in your life. There's something crucial in that character's dilemma that you can apply to yourself. It's the most creative therapy under the sun. But it's not just therapy. I've often found parts allowed me to experience things I didn't have to go through in life.

I did *The Great Waldo Pepper* with Robert Redford in which I had this relationship with this megastar where I had to put him down all the time and call him an asshole. I didn't do it very well; I was obsequious. We mythologize other actors. They don't need it. When we were doing *The Betsy*, Olivier found out I was from Michigan, and he came over and asked, "How's the accent?"

How do you get over being starstruck?

You don't get over it; you learn to control it. The first thing to recognize is that it's something *we* do—it comes from us. Stars are primary psychological images. Actors forget that the profession depends on the tribe mythologizing us into the image they *need* in order to be healed. Fonda's a healer. Duke Wayne, Stewart—they express something that needs to be expressed. Right now, unfortunately, it's Rambo. It may be horrible, but it's a fact.

But the profession doesn't recognize it. All those towers on Sixth Avenue, those solid edifices, are built on nothing. They're built on what happens between one actor and another, an energy that passes through performers from a writer, a series of ideas with no substance that draws the interest and need of a community. If television executives knew how those images affect the community, they'd become monks. They're responsible for the psychic health of the world, and they turn out images of lust, cruelty, greed, violence, and meanness twenty-four hours a day. It amazes me that people still talk to one another.

The only thing to do is to do the best TV possible. If you play a wicked man, show why he's wicked. Cosby's doing a good job; *Love Boat* isn't. I believe in the eighteenth-century idea of enlightenment. You can't have a society with healthy values by creating images of destruction. The way our society works now, if a man wants to have feelings and express them, you're forced to be gay. If you want to hold to the masculine values, you have to join the NRA.

JOHN
LONE

John Lone

"Pay attention to the way you walk," the director is telling a young actress. "You were going like this," he says, hiking up his jacket to show off the sensual sway of his hips as he walks across the rehearsal room. "That's too sexy, too contemporary. Your character is very protected. She's simple and innocent. She walks like this." He goes back the way he came, this time in a more contained posture, bowing his head, tucking his hips under, and slightly bending his knees as he walks. An observer watching this demonstration might think he had just seen two different people, a gum-chewing flirt in stretch pants and a humble, kimono-clad maidservant. Yet both were enacted by a tall, unshaven man in red sweat pants, a plaid hunter's jacket, and a black-and-white-checked beret.

His physical grace, his dancer's sense of movement, and his ability to transcend age, sex, and culture make John Lone an extraordinary performer by any standards. But he has proved uniquely useful as a performer and director to Chinese-American playwright David Henry Hwang, whose work attempts to combine Asian myths and theater styles with contemporary American characters and realities—a combination that finds its ideal embodiment in John Lone. His ability to express his quick imagination through his body also won him the title role in Iceman, *Fred Schepisi's film about a prehistoric man found frozen in the Arctic ice and brought back to life. Lone, whose English is fluent if heavily accented and at times ungrammatical, says he spent five months in Canada working up to seventeen hours a day under heavy makeup. He found the challenge exhilarating, the camera experience invaluable, and the company of Timothy Hutton and Lindsay Crouse enjoyable, even though he points out that, given the disparity between his salary and Hutton's, the film should have been called* Rich Man, Poor Man.

Lone is keenly aware of the limited opportunities for Asian actors in America. He doesn't express a lot of bitterness about facing discrimination on the basis of his looks, but when I asked who his role models were, he said Stevie Wonder and Bette Midler.

I was born in Hong Kong, but I grew up in the theater. I grew up in this old world, this secret world, this religion of perfection: Peking Opera. It's a total theater form with no psychological reason behind it. They teach singing, acting, tumbling, acrobatics, form, symbolism—everything except psychological understanding. It was always presentation, presentation. If tears come one night, I'm criticized: too emotional, not supposed to be emotional.

After I'd been with Peking Opera school for eight years, I realized there's a world out there. I started going to two or three films a day—it was like getting out of prison. Mostly American films, all sorts. Movies affected me in such a way, I sense some kind of truth somewhere. I like it. We were having problems in the company, and I thought, "All these other things are happening, everything is James Bond—who wants to sit here and watch this serious art form?"

I did kung fu movies for one year for Runrun Shaw—you know, the empire run by two brothers that makes all those kung-fu films in Hong Kong—and they offered me a ten-year contract. I was only about seventeen, too young to be a star, but they wanted to groom me because they liked my look and all that. But those films are just awful, no substance, just cheap cheap thrill. Again, I don't intellectually understand what's going on in my life, but instinct leads me not to go to Brussels to dance with Maurice Béjart. I didn't want to be a dancer. Somehow instinct leads me to America.

I was eighteen when I went to L.A. First three months I just stayed with the family sponsoring me. I went to Disneyland, I did all that. Then I went to night school to learn English, because I didn't speak a word. Spent three years in a community college, just drilling my English. Since I couldn't speak, there was no point in even studying acting, so I did some dancing. I signed with an agent in L.A., and I thought, "Oh boy!" It took me years to realize I wasn't going to make it immediately.

When I started studying Method, the Western acting, I loved it. Now I understand there's a reason why a character behave. The approach is much more immediate knowing the thoughts behind the character, the history. I was so excited, I can't tell you. What I did before was important [*clapping his hands over his heart*], but this [*pointing to his head*] is also so important.

ANTHONY
HEALD

Anthony Heald

Anthony Heald had twelve years of experience in regional theater when he moved to New York at the age of thirty-five, but he still felt insecure about finding his place in the marketplace. "I'm not handsome enough to be a leading man, I'm not ethnic-looking, I'm too old to be in the brat-pack category but I'm not old enough to be a character actor. And people who are familiar with my work tend to think I'm British." Despite his fears, he has established himself as one of the most versatile and hard-working actors in New York. Within the space of two years, he played a gibberish-spouting outcast in The Foreigner *Off-Broadway, a Madison Avenue super-Yuppie in* Digby, *the bellicose Fluellen opposite Kevin Kline's* Henry V *in Central Park, a roller-skating revolutionary in Andrei Serban's staging of* The Marriage of Figaro, *and a jailbound journalist in* Principia Scriptoriae. *When we met, he had just returned to the long-running production of* The Foreigner *after going on a honeymoon—his first break from nonstop work in years.*

I always swore I'd never come to New York—it was not the place for a serious actor. I grew up in the '50s on Long Island, where people brought the worst parts of the city with them. A lot of kids I grew up with ended up in prison or strung-out on drugs. I loved the Midwest; working in regional theater is what I thought serious actors did. In New York, you did commercials, soap operas, maybe one play a year, and took a lot of classes. At the BoarsHead Theatre in Lansing, Michigan, we do a new show every three weeks—*Blithe Spirit,* then *Macbeth,* then *Cat on a Hot Tin Roof.* I teach from ten in the morning to twelve, rehearse from one to five, then perform at night. It was a great laboratory.

But after four years, I was making $130 a week. And it becomes a dead end, because nobody sees your work except people in Milwaukee or Hartford. Most actors won't admit this, but a lot of times you phone it in. It's a Sunday matinee, the show's been running for six months, you don't feel so hot—who cares? But here you never know who's going to be out there. In New York, at any performance Mike Nichols could be in the audience, or Robert Whitehead, or Helen Hayes. Actors say every job contains the seeds of a dozen more jobs.

Still, you end up losing money doing theater. I'm taking home $280 a week doing *The Foreigner.* I just came back from California where I got $2500 for a day's work in film. I'll be forty-one in a couple of weeks. I want to have a family, and if I do, my wife will have to stop working, so I'll have to double my salary. We have an apartment in Brooklyn for which we pay $275 a month, my wife works, and we split expenses. I don't dress expensively. I never go to expensive restaurants. I don't have a penny in the bank. It's literally a hand-to-mouth existence. Lately I've had a continuing role on *All My Children.* That pays $700 a day, and if I'm on a couple days a month, that helps. I've done a couple of small things in movies and episodic TV. I did a *Miami Vice.* You get $400–$500 a day. That helps. But I need to do a series for a couple of years. This is the thing—I'm not going to get the big Broadway roles without some film experience. Broadway has to appeal to out-of-towners, who don't know from New York actors. They know TV and film actors. So I'm really thinking about going to L.A. for a while, see what happens there.

What's the silliest thing about being an actor?

Going to commercial auditions where they want you to face-act. You'll go and they'll say, "Now, you have no lines, I just want you to respond to what I say with your face: 'Do you want a hamburger made with this oooold . . . *dried-UP* . . . beef—or do YOU want BRAND-NEW Yummyburger?'" And you're supposed to do this. [*He pulls his face into a deepening frown, and then immediately puts on the insanely excited face of testimonial commercials.*] The other day I went in, and they said, "Just dance around and look happy." Uh-huh.

What makes it the silliest thing is that if you get a couple of those commercials, you can send your kids through college.

JOHN
TURTURRO

John Turturro

Barely two years out of Yale, John Turturro had already made a name for himself in New York. He won an Obie Award in 1985 for his howling performance in John Patrick Shanley's Danny and the Deep Blue Sea. *William Friedkin gave him a plum role in* To Live and Die in L.A., *which brilliantly exploited the edgy, streetwise, nearly psychotic veneer of the Queens-born actor. Lest he be typed as a permanent bad guy, he took small parts as a librarian in Michael Dinner's* Off Beat *and as a television scriptwriter in Woody Allen's* Hannah and Her Sisters. *When we met, twenty-nine-year-old Turturro was about to leave for Chicago to do* The Color of Money, *directed by Martin Scorsese.*

I haven't been doing leading roles in films. My first role was in *Desperately Seeking Susan*. Then I did *To Live and Die in L.A.*, and I got single billing on that. And I just finished Ron Howard's new film, *Gung Ho*. *The Color of Money* was a smaller role, even though it's the third male lead. My agent didn't want me to do it, and the studio wouldn't give me what I would be worth for that amount of time. Eventually I decided to take the role.

Did that cause trouble with your agent?
He considers it a step down. He wants me to make money, but he lets me do what I want to do. He has taste, and he knows I've always wanted to work with Scorsese. When I was in undergraduate school, I did *The Tooth of Crime*, the Sam Shepard play, and De Niro came to see it with Cis Corman, who was casting *Raging Bull* at the time, and my friend and I were called in to meet Scorsese and De Niro. I was twenty-one, and I had never gone on an audition before, professionally. So we prepared a scene from Jake La Motta's book—we rehearsed it like mad. It was only a three-page scene, but wherever we were we would rehearse the scene. We rehearsed it rowing in Central Park, running, playing basketball, boxing, just to see what would come out. When it came time to do the scene for them, I remember Scorsese didn't want us to do it: "What scene? We don't even have a script." But they liked it and called us back. I auditioned for months. Finally they said we were too young, but we each got one line.

When did you get interested in acting?
When I was real young, eight or nine, I used to make scrapbooks of movie stars. I liked Burt Lancaster and Kirk Douglas. I would tell my mom I was sick and stay home from school so I could watch *White Heat*, because I'd see it was on at one o'clock in the afternoon on Channel 5. I did impressions for a while with my cousin in high school. I worked at the Improv, and I would perform at banquets and weddings, doing Ratso Rizzo from *Midnight Cowboy*—serious stuff. I played basketball, and I boxed for a while. Then I broke my hand, and I started realizing I was always doing these impressions or entertaining my friends, and that's probably what I wanted to do.

I didn't read plays in school, except for Shakespeare, so when I auditioned for colleges, I did this monologue from *On the Waterfront*: "I coulda been a contender." I didn't do it like Marlon Brando did, I did it my way. That was at New Paltz State College. At NYU, I did a scene from *Midnight Cowboy*. When I think about it, how did I get this material? I never taped it, I didn't have a VCR. I guess I knew the movie so well I would write down the dialogue. *On the Waterfront* I've seen almost thirty times. I've been watching *The Fugitive Kind* a lot—I do have that on tape—I've really discovered Anna Magnani, who is a genius. The scenes between her and Marlon Brando as a couple are incredible.

Did you think you would do movies as well as theater?

I wanted to do movies. Everybody wants to, 'til you do one and find out how boring it is. Unless you're working with exciting people and you have a large role—then it's stimulating on a whole other level.

Did you find it different acting on film than onstage?

Somewhat. The size of it—I'm just learning to say to myself, "I can do less." You don't realize it at first, so you want to make sure they see everything. But Robby Müller, the cinematographer on *To Live and Die in L.A.*—he's done all those Wim Wenders films—helped me. He's a very sensitive cameraman. He adjusts the camera to what you're doing. Sometimes I'd mark the scene in rehearsal, then when I'd perform I'd give a little bit more. He told me, "What you're doing in rehearsal, that's enough."

What's your favorite thing about being an actor?

I can sleep late. [*He laughs.*] Discovering something. Performance can be great sometimes, but rehearsal is really exciting. When we were doing *Danny and the Deep Blue Sea*, I couldn't get the character. It sounded like me too much. Then one day my whole body started changing. I had the thought of being in a shell, and everything started coming in, my shoulders, my forehead, my back—almost like an ape. People who are afraid turn in on themselves, like a turtle or a crab.

What's the hardest thing you've ever been asked to do?

Sometimes you have to meet the greatness of the play—if you're doing *Hamlet*—and some plays you have to make way better than they are. Doing that long run of *Danny* was exhausting. I felt like the play didn't work on the level I wanted it to work unless I destroyed myself—vocally, physically, emotionally mostly. When we didn't do that, people said, "Oh, nice little play." When we did do that, it covered the play, and people gave it a standing ovation.

TOM
HULCE

Tom Hulce

When he was fifteen, Tom Hulce left his home in Michigan to study acting at the North Carolina School for the Arts. Three years later, he precociously moved to New York with his heart set on landing the role of Rimbaud in Christopher Hampton's play Total Eclipse. *"They didn't know I'd moved to New York to be in this play, so they neglected to hire me." Six weeks later, he landed the job of understudying Peter Firth in the original Broadway production of Peter Shaffer's* Equus; *he eventually took over the role himself, playing opposite Tony Perkins on Broadway and Anthony Hopkins in Los Angeles. After nearly a decade of working in film, television, and regional theater, he was appearing Off-Broadway in* The Rise and Rise of Daniel Rocket *when he learned he'd been cast as Mozart in Milos Forman's film of Peter Shaffer's* Amadeus—*the role that changed his life. It earned him an Academy Award nomination, and he had to hire someone to read the hundreds of fan letters he received each month.*

We met one afternoon at a downtown café. Then thirty-one, Tom looked taller, chubbier, hairier than the wraith-like figure he presents on stage or in film, and he had a slight stammer that made him linger over words beginning with M or N.

There's something incredibly powerful about sitting in a dark room and seeing an image that's very large. You can pin your life to it, or your hopes. There's a part of me that's a soft touch. I get letters from people asking me to come meet them when they get out of the hospital after having an operation—things that just don't make any sense.

Was *Animal House* the first movie you did?

No, the first was an odd movie about college kids in Arkansas when James Dean died called *September 30, 1955.* Then *Animal House,* then *Those Lips, Those Eyes*—a document in depression.

Who directed that?

No one. Just kidding. Michael Pressman. It's an experience I'm thrilled to have had, because what I learned allowed me to make my way through *Amadeus.* Through that bad experience, I started to learn how to take care of myself around a camera. The circumstances are so different from theater that it took three movies for me to get a clue about how to make a structure for myself that I could work in. I learned that the closer the camera got, the worse I got, so I knew I had to do something about that. And no matter what anybody says, the camera doesn't create something that didn't happen. I thought there was this magic thing that happened: no matter what it felt like to me, it was automatically going to be better—or why would these people be accepting what I knew to be only acceptable? I didn't know what to do when they put me in front of a camera to do a close-up and there was a whole scene that was supposed to be there. I literally didn't know what to do, and I assumed that somebody would tell me. They'd be going "Speed!" and "Action!" I'd be saying, "Where should I look?" I learned that nobody's going to do it for you.

Did Milos Forman set the scene for you?

He rarely said anything except for "Oh, disaster!" or "Oh, this is terrible!" He was perfect for me. He said instantly when it was bad, so I had no chance to get paranoid or start wondering if he had a good eye or an opinion. To have all those questions in front of a camera is difficult. It prevents me from doing good work. I get scared. Then it's harder to be risky.

In film you do a performance only once—are there things you can do in that situation that you can't when you're in a play and you have to repeat the performance many times?

Mm-hmm. What I love about working in front of a camera is that it's a machine put there to capture a moment. So you can do one moment extraordinarily, and if you do another great moment, they can put the two together and make a performance you couldn't possibly deliver all at once.

Why?

I don't know. *[He has an emphatic way of saying "I don't know," as if he were saying "I know."]* Maybe because you don't have to do it in the context of a performance and you don't have to repeat it. I can give you an example. In the scene between Mozart and Salieri, when Mozart is dying and dictating the Requiem, the bargain that Murray [F. Murray Abraham] and I made was that we would not stop the scene. I would know the music well enough that anytime he, the actor, got behind, he had an invitation to stop me, to ask questions within the scene. It meant that I knew he would be with me. The scene was intricately worked out in the writing. In the doing of it, I would leave out a piece of information, so he would find out two lines later that he needed it, just to give it the messiness of life, knowing it would make him seem stupid to have to ask for something I'd already gone beyond, d'you know?

There was a moment when we were shooting the scene that I got lost. I didn't know where I was and what we were doing. I was lying in this bed, and I didn't know what was going on. So what you see in the scene is Mozart, in his condition, off someplace else in his brain for a while, and you see Salieri trying to get Mozart back on the track so he can get this fucking piece of music that he's eating himself alive to get. And because the trust and commitment between Murray and me as two people working together was great, he stuck with me, and Milos used the entire sequence. When I saw the movie put together, that was the moment when I started to cry, because it was something that could only happen in a film. It was something that could only happen with an intense connection between two people, as characters and actors and men.

BILL
IRWIN

Bill Irwin

Classic comedy begins with a dilemma, two forces pulling in opposite directions. That's the basis of Bill Irwin's identity as a performer. An intellectual versed in the theoretical underpinnings of postmodern dance and avant-garde performance art, he also has an irresistible attraction to all forms of clowning, and these two extremes, the highbrow and the low-tech, enrich each other. Irwin launches a lofty lecture-demonstration on "the death of the playwright and the rise of the actor as poet" and then pulls some outrageously corny pratfall—a fake smack in the face—that you can't believe you're actually laughing at. Meanwhile, his signature is a comic soft-shoe during which he's inexorably drawn toward one corner of the stage by some supernatural force that ultimately pulls him offstage altogether. No wonder the Village Voice, *which gave Irwin an Obie Award in 1981, termed his style of clowning "metaphysical vaudeville." And in 1985 his unique skills earned him a five-year "genius grant" from the MacArthur Foundation.*

Born in Southern California and raised in Oklahoma, Irwin got interested in clowning partly in reaction to his own All-American good looks: "Even though I look like Sunshine Jim, the nice boy next door, I could make myself into anything I wanted." In college he studied both mime and martial arts; he took workshops in Jerzy Grotowski's hermetic "holy theater" and spent weekends learning the ropes as a street performer. He followed one of his teachers, Herbert Blau, to Oberlin College and spent two years working with Blau's experimental theater collective KRAKEN. Next came the Ringling Brothers' clown college in Florida and eventually the San Francisco-based Pickle Family Circus, with which Irwin appeared in Robert Altman's movie Popeye. *He is best-known for* The Regard of Flight, *a combination clown show and rumination on contemporary theater that ran for six months Off-Broadway to rave reviews and was taped for television by PBS.*

I'm fascinated by the circus. Ninety percent of it is excruciatingly boring, but there are a few moments at the circus—or a gym meet, or the Chinese opera—where people actually fly through the air. I put in a lot of time trying. I started late, in my mid-twenties. I hung out with gymnasts, I paid a lot of different teachers. I was forever starting over again, because that would allow me to come in as a promising beginner. I wanted to be able to do some basic things like back handsprings. I could do them with the harness on, but they'd take it off, and the instructor would be there with his hand at the small of my back saying, "Come on, you can do it." I never could. Flying through the air . . . it's something I really want to do, but there are certain frontiers of fear.

Comic talent has a lot to do with fear of being foolish. I trip walking down the street all the time. What's funny is not the fact that people trip, but the way they react to it, with a surreptitious look backward ("I hope nobody saw that") or pretending to run a few steps. Or the guy—this is actually one of my favorites —somebody who trips and immediately turns around and says, "Uh, people, we have a *very* dangerous place here . . ." People who are vain and paranoid about their dignity are the people who sharpen their observational powers. That makes good clowns.

One of the things I liked about the work with Herbert Blau is that it was experimental in the true sense of the word. We were doing "performance research." There are a lot of really stupid things done in the name of performance research, but good things, too. From Herb I picked up this idea of "The performance is always about itself." You're onstage portraying something, whether it's *Uncle Vanya* or *The Regard of Flight* or *Waiting for Godot*, yet what's actually happening is the audience is sitting there, and it's *that* time, *that* day, either a careless spring day or the brink of World War III. Whatever people bring into the room that day is what's happening. Actors get into real trouble trying to say, "Nothing out there is actually happening." You may have the Uncle Vanya costume on and your gestures perfected, but what's going on in your mind is what's really important. If you're thinking, "I hate that actress over there," if you don't manage to make your hate for her part of your Uncle Vanya, then the audience won't get anything except an actor uncomfortable with someone he's onstage with.

I still feel like a hick as far as theater goes. I didn't grow up in New York seeing plays. I wasn't a movie brat who watched Cagney work. Like any kid brought up in a suburban environment in the 1950s, I didn't see any performance except via the television screen. Watching early television—*Amos and Andy, Sergeant Bilko*—was like learning piano by playing the scales. I got a feeling for comic rhythm and structure, how long you should do something before you let it go for a while and then come back and pick it up. I watched a lot of cartoons, too, and often there were cartoon characters based on entertainers whom I knew nothing about but ended up imitating. I remember in one cartoon, some fish was swimming around and found a pair of barbells, put them within her costume, and became Mae West. I didn't know who Mae West was, but I took it all in. When I was very little, I remember climbing up on something way up high and saying, "Hey, hey, Mom and Dad, look at me. Whyn't ya come up and see me sometime, big boy?"

GRIFFIN
DUNNE

Griffin Dunne

Griffin Dunne is in the unique position of being able to hire himself as an actor —not because he writes plays, but because he produces movies. Before he turned thirty, he had already coproduced three classy pictures: Joan Micklin Silver's Chilly Scenes of Winter, *John Sayles's* Baby, It's You, *and Martin Scorsese's* After Hours. *He didn't plan it that way. Although his father, Dominick Dunne, was a movie producer (*The Boys in the Band*), Griffin started out, like many New York actors, the hard way. He moved to Manhattan as a teenager, studied at the Neighborhood Playhouse and HB Studio, worked at Radio City Music Hall as popcorn manager, and scrambled for roles in Off-Off-Broadway showcase productions like* I Never Cried for My Mother. *"It was a rotten play about Vietnam. I had to cry six times onstage—you know, 'I don't wanna die, I don't wanna die.' I didn't know what to cry about to begin with, and after three times you really have to fake it. Even if you're from the Actors Studio, no one could cry six times in an hour and a half."*

His acting, as Griffin puts it, "was not taking off as I hoped." But he wasn't alone. At a party he met a couple of other frustrated actors, Amy Robinson and Mark Metcalf, and the three of them decided to get together to develop projects for themselves. Robinson brought in Ann Beattie's first novel as possible stage material, but they quickly saw that it could be a movie, and Triple Play Productions was born.

As is the producer's prerogative, Griffin cast himself in Chilly Scenes of Winter. *"I had a tiny scene, but it got laughs. Wilford Leach liked that scene, so he cast me in Wally Shawn's* Marie and Bruce *at the Public Theater, and I've been working as an actor ever since." He's also been in demand as a producer of hip young-adult movies, which gives him a better shot at plum roles. He played the lead in* After Hours. *A dog-eared copy of the latest hot novel, whose goofy-romantic hero is a perfect movie role for Griffin, rests prominently atop a stack of scripts in his production office. And his temp-service secretary tiptoes into meetings with urgent phone messages from people like "David Mammoth."*

The two careers don't always mesh, though. When he was acting in Ted Tally's Coming Attractions *at Playwrights Horizons in 1980, he read Tally's teenage comedy* Hooters *and thought it was so funny he cried with laughter. Two years later he was cast in the play just as* Baby, It's You *was going into production, and somehow the humor had gone, maybe because he spent every rehearsal break off in the wings with a wad of quarters phoning agents, lawyers, and studio executives. "Deal-making on an adult level made it hard to go onstage and play a horny seventeen-year-old."*

After Hours *posed no such problems. It was his favorite acting job so far, partly because he was working with Scorsese and partly because he was in every scene. The latter was also true of* American Werewolf in London—*the inspiration for Michael Jackson's* Thriller *video. "But* American Werewolf *wasn't much fun. I don't like the makeup and the pyrotechnics, the spraying and the fussing. I was a walking sight gag; people always wanted to take me out to lunch. But I took it very seriously, and sometimes I thought I'd made a mistake, that it was bad karma to look like that, to play such a graphically victimized person. The makeup put me in character instantly. It was very depressing. If I thought about it too much, I'd get upset. I thought, 'This is exactly what I'd look like if I died.' "*

Matt Dillon

Matt Dillon was the kind of kid whose favorite movies were the dumb and loud ones: Planet of the Apes, The Towering Inferno, The Poseidon Adventure. *But after he was plucked from the freshman class of Homocks Junior High in Mamaroneck to play a cocky, streetwise kid (not unlike himself) in Jonathan Kaplan's excellent teen-riot picture* Over the Edge, *his taste improved. Under the tutelage of casting-director-turned-manager Vic Ramos, he skipped the boy-pinup-type movies and made his name with a remarkably intelligent series of three pictures based on novels by S. E. Hinton, Tulsa's answer to J. D. Salinger:* Tex, The Outsiders, *and* Rumblefish *(the latter two directed by Francis Ford Coppola). Rather than going for premature star vehicles that would most likely only expose his inadequacies, in almost all his movies Matt has played character roles that helped expand his resources as an actor. Likewise, he made his stage debut in* The Boys of Winter—*a dreadful Vietnam play that closed quickly—but a worthy experiment that allowed Matt to try his wings on Broadway within the safety of an ensemble piece. At twenty-two, Matt is undeniably still a kid, but some unpredictable quality about him makes him more than just another male starlet. His enigmatic youthful beauty made superstar photographer Bruce Weber devote twelve pages of a book to him, and he has an artlessness that made B-filmmaker Paul Morrissey proclaim him "the best actor in America." And although his all-time favorite movie remains* Gunga Din, *the director he most wants to work with now is Roman Polanski.*

Matt Dillon is not an easy interview, partly because he hates interviews. "I hate to talk about myself," he says, knowing that there's not much self yet to talk about. And when he tries to talk seriously about anything besides himself, he sounds so pretentious that even he can't keep a straight face. So he doesn't try.

Matt arrived at the appointed meeting place—a cafe in Chelsea—forty-five minutes late, checked the time and ordered a Spaten Light (never too early for a brew). He also ordered a green salad, which he hardly touched, though he ate a lot of bread and butter, smacking his lips loudly like the Brooklyn boor he played in The Flamingo Kid. *He kept grabbing napkins from other tables and blowing his nose. The conversation was very stop-and-go. I asked him about his mother, and he said, "Let's talk about The Work." I asked him about* Rumblefish, *and he said, "We definitely had the feeling we were making something very odd." What gave him that feeling? "Let me put it in one word—Dennis Hopper." When he was a little kid, he told me, he first wanted to be a Catholic priest, and after that a writer. His current favorite author was David Plante. He said after he made* My Bodyguard *he realized there was more to being an actor than playing yourself, so he studied for a while at the Actors Studio, but he quit because he found the approach "too introspective."*

When I turned off the tape recorder, our conversation became much more relaxed. The United States had just bombed Libya, and we spent an hour talking about Qaddafi. Matt said, "I understand Qaddafi, 'cause he's crazy just like me." Clearly, I had before me the kind of guy who would far rather stay up all night drinking beer and discussing theories of how the world works than do interviews. When I asked him what he would be doing if he weren't an actor, he said, "I'd probably be unemployed."

MATT
DILLON

WILLIAM
HURT

William Hurt

For a relatively young actor, Bill Hurt has acquired a surprisingly powerful mystique as a bruised soul and flaky person. It's easy to see where this impression comes from. He has played a long string of characters who are physically, spiritually, or sexually crippled. He has appeared onstage as Hamlet, Ken Talley in Lanford Wilson's Fifth of July *(with the Circle Repertory Company, of which he is a long-standing member), and Eddie in David Rabe's* Hurlyburly—*all of them wounded creatures, as were the men he played on film in* Altered States, The Big Chill, *and* Kiss of the Spider Woman. *In interviews, he has a habit of talking at great length with excessive earnestness about acting. What some people consider flakiness, however, is often simply thoughtfulness and a refusal to be glib. Besides, when he starts talking about out-of-body experiences, you can simply change the subject.*

Born in Washington, D.C., Hurt was raised in the South Pacific, where his father served in the diplomatic corps. When he was ten, his parents divorced, and his mother went to work at Time Inc., where she met and married Henry Luce 3d, the son of the company's founder. There is an aristocratic aloofness to Bill Hurt that could be traced to his background, but also the self-questioning of someone who doesn't take anything for granted. He was married to actress Mary Beth Hurt and later lived with a ballet dancer, with whom he has a young son. While filming Children of a Lesser God *in Canada, he fell in love with Marlee Matlin, the deaf actress who was his costar, and they were living together when I met Bill in the office of his publicist. He had been nominated for but had not yet won the Academy Award for his performance in* Kiss of the Spider Woman, *and he had been idle for several months since completing his work on* Children of a Lesser God.

What do you do when you're not working?

Whatever occurs to me that day. I have a really good time not working; it's a lot of work to act. I have some hobbies—I fly-fish, I sail. I have a fleet of remote-control boats that I work with my son in the bathtub. I love those things.

Did you always want to be an actor?

No more than I wanted to be a cowboy, fireman, cop, diplomat, statesman, artist, whatever. I never thought about being an actor. I wanted to do something serious. I used to think a lot about religion. I read a lot. I loved the woods. I would love to have lived out in the wilderness and been a ranger or parks department guy or farmer.

Until I was sixteen, I was very chubby and a terrible athlete. My grades were shit. I didn't have many friends. I had real trouble adjusting. One day a teacher named Hugh Fortmiller walked up to me and said, "How would you like to try out for the school play?" I didn't know him from Adam; he was just trying to help a kid. I was fourteen. I was nervous and said, "Okay." I got this part, and I did it. I was playing a boy.

As opposed to the boys who were playing girls?

No, there was a girls' school nearby, so girls played girls. That was another interesting part about it. *Very* interesting part about it.

This we liked?

This we liked. *[He laughs.]* There was something about theater and the women that changed the experience for me. People couldn't dump on me so much when the girls were around. You had to act polite.

When I was around sixteen, I grew six inches, and I began to be physically attractive to people. Suddenly, doors were open that weren't before, and I'd go, "Look, just close the door, I don't want to come in." I had the same heart before I grew—why wasn't I loved for that?

When you went to Tufts, did you study acting?

I started out as a religion major. I wanted personally to be saved, and I wanted other people to be saved. I had lived in many countries with my father and seen tremendous agony inflicted on supposedly innocent beings. I couldn't comprehend how a God I loved could allow these things to happen. I began to ask the question when I was eight and worked on it 'til I was nineteen or twenty. In the center of my thoughts, I didn't really work on anythng else. I became furious. I was also probably furious at myself for lots of reasons.

I was raised as a Presbyterian. I had myself confirmed as an Episcopalian. I learned about ritual and how important it is. If possible, I wanted to belong to a ritual that leaves people their independence but at the same time allows each participant to learn more about him or herself and the mysteries of this existence. A lot of religious rituals are too dogmatic. I guess I wanted to belong to a ritual in which one is encouraged to ask questions. In drama, the order of the day is curiosity about the human condition, not judging it. Your effort is to become more compassionate and to seek compassion.

Is there a relationship between movies and that kind of ritual?

There can be. Making a movie is a tremendously ornate affair; a lot of people you never even meet work hand in hand with you. Your participation is through your work, your job. It's not a surrogate family. That takes a long time for people to get out of their systems. They're trying to assuage their personal fears of loneliness or separation through a communal act.

Where does the satisfaction come from in making a movie?

Acting. Acting is not different when you're onstage or on a film screen. Ultimately, it comes down to this phrase: "trying to find the truth." In acting, I have an opportunity to ask a question other situations don't afford me. Someone else could satisfy himself being a taxi driver or a philosopher. Acting is just my form. That's the way I ask.

I could go on forever about the things I enjoy about acting. I get the giggles sometimes if I'm standing offstage just before an entrance and I'm wearing tights. I think, "What the fuck am I doing here? This is hilarious. I have skinny legs. Why am I about to walk out in front of those people wearing tights?" I enjoy other actors. I especially enjoy not having an excuse to look away from somebody else's eyes or listen hard. I love that. I love the fact that our usual avoidance systems are set aside, and I can just saturate myself and look at another human being.

When I was on the road, I'd be having a cup of coffee and staring at some guy gassing up his truck. So many truckers said to me, "What are you starin' at?" "Nuthin'." I could never say it, but a lot of people say it to me.

When you got out of college, did you set off to be an actor?

I thought I wasn't an actor. I knew I didn't have the technique. I didn't know what technique was. It was just this big word. I could walk out onstage in one act as one character and have a totally different character the next act. I was having a ball, but there was no consistency. So I thought, if I'm going to think about this seriously, I have to have a specific idea of what acting is.

Did you set your sights on Juilliard?

As it happened, I would never have gotten into any other school. I was taking my senior year of college in London. I didn't have enough time or money to get back to America to audition for schools, which meant I'd have to wait an entire year, go back to the States, dick around, wait for auditions, take my chances. I was beginning to entertain the idea of going to an English school when a very dear, sweet boy in my class at Middlesex was killed, and I was on the next plane home for the funeral. I had to stay in the States for five days because of my plane ticket. So I just called schools, and nobody would give me an audition in that short a time except Juilliard. I got hold of them at five o'clock in the afternoon, and they said be here tomorrow at ten with $40 and two pieces. So I worked all night with my stepbrother trying to memorize this speech from the heath scene in *King Lear* because it was the only script in the house. The bookstores were closed. I had been working just for myself on *Look Back in Anger*, so I strung three of those speeches together to come up with two full minutes. I just went in, did it, and wrote if off. No way I would get in.

After that school year, I was in a farmhouse in Gloucestershire with sixteen other people from school mounting a production of Lanford Wilson's *Rimers of Eldritch* on our own. I was sitting at the breakfast table one day, and there was a message that I'd gotten into Juilliard. I asked Mary Beth—we were married then—how she felt about that. She wanted to start looking for work in the States, so we went back to New York. Those were lean years.

How did you get to Circle Rep?

After Juilliard, I went to the Ashland Shakespeare Festival to play Edmund in *Long Day's Journey into Night*. I don't think I've acted well but a few times in my life. In my own opinion, I don't think I've acted really well in a film yet. I hope I do someday. I don't know if I can. I'm not crapping on myself, I just think it's a very serious thing. But as Edmund, I acted well. The following season, I thought I'd get some decent roles, and I got nothing. I asked the director, and he said, "You have to pay some more dues here." I said, "No, I'm not paying those kinds of dues anymore. I want to work." I just got in my car with my dog and took off, drove around the country trying to find a job. I couldn't find a job anywhere. I drove to Seattle, San Francisco, some other theaters around the country. I'd show up and say I wanted to audition. They'd say, "We're sorry, we don't have anything."

I went back to New York, and I couldn't even get a showcase. Then I walked into the Children's Television Workshop, where they were doing *The Best of Families*, and there I was with this great job. The head writer, Corinne Jacker, asked me to come down and read the first act of an unfinished play called *My Life*. I went down to Circle Rep and sat in those chairs with those people. I didn't know Marshall Mason, I didn't know anybody, but I felt like I was home.

So *My Life* was your first role in New York?

No, I played three parts in *Henry V* in Central Park. Paul Rudd played Henry, Meryl Streep played the princess. I played Bates, Scoop, and then an invented role, the French interpreter. I created these three totally different roles, with beards, makeup changes, accents and everything. I was onstage maybe a grand total of half an hour, but I was so busy racing around that I would lose three or four pounds a night.

You liked doing that stuff, changing the way you look?

Yeah, the mask is everything. I do the same thing in film, it's just more subtle. I wish I could take huge physical risks in films. *Kiss of the Spider Woman* is about as extensive as I have been allowed to do in movies. I wanted to do twice as much in *Spider Woman*. I wanted him to start out almost as a harpy, like a Medusa, then become a true queen. I had a whole physical idea in my mind, but I wasn't allowed to do it as flagrantly as I would have liked. I think I could have pulled it off believably, but it's really hard to get people to accept that.

You have an unusual voice; you don't seem to have to do much to get a lot of volume and resonance.

I don't use my voice that well. Some people have a hard time hearing it in theaters. I've been accused of being a mumbler onstage. It has a lot to do with what a person expects coming to the theater. If a guy comes to a Broadway house, he's expecting Jerry Orbach out there, going [*He suddenly speaks in a loud, brassy voice*] "Silver platter? Screw the silver platter! I'm gonna give this to you on a freight train!" [*Back to normal*] Maybe this is selfish, but I think more about what am I doing with another actor on the stage.

When you started acting professionally, did you think you would do movies?

I was frightened of movies, because of the things they do to your life. I don't like people peering at me and prying into my life. So I turned them down for a long time. I was enjoying myself immensely at Circle. I couldn't have been in a better position: I was a member of a wonderful company working on wonderful plays in a wonderful atmosphere. Someone offered me $10,000 if I wouldn't accept a job from someone else for six months, and I turned it down. I knew I wasn't going to accept a job from anybody else anyway. Then I read *Altered States*, and that was it. I knew I couldn't turn that one down.

Did it happen right away, the thing you thought would happen? Did your life change?

The changes were not as severe as I feared. I do lead a private existence. No one can really take that away from you. It takes a while to learn that people are looking at you because they've seen your movie. "What are you starin' at?" "Nuthin'." That's what I'd like them to say.

Are there actors you've looked to as role models or inspirations?

There's a Greek actor Mary Renault wrote about in *The Mask of Apollo*. He was a renowned actor, but he wasn't known as a man. He was himself. He would walk on his own feet between cities. He would do this great thing for the kings and the queens and the people, get a little money and a wreath or something, then he would walk to the next city. He had dust on his feet like everybody else. The mask was important. The comprehension of the ritual was important.

It's hard to talk about contemporaries. Meryl did one of the most incredible character jobs I've ever seen in *Out of Africa*. It was a remarkable, ephemeral, honest job of physical characterization—there was real blood in those very fine capillaries. Olivier had the mask for the better part of his career, as did Spencer Tracy, but the use of the mask there is so different. You could say that one suited his mask to the piece, and the other vice versa.

The best performance I ever saw was Paul Scofield in a piece by Pirandello, where it was as if his thoughts came out of his body. I was just sitting there and I started to tremble. I couldn't believe what I was watching. I was plugged into some mental-emotional organism that wasn't my body but that I recognized. I didn't know if I was going to be able to stay there very long. I kept thinking, "I've got to check out of this, it's too much."

What's the silliest thing about being an actor?
There's nothing about it that isn't silly—that's one of the attractions.

After the interview was over, the receptionist appeared and told Bill he had a call from Marlee. I thought, "This will be interesting—talking to his deaf girlfriend on the phone?" But Bill whipped out a portable computer terminal from a shoulder bag, stuck the cradle of the phone into the computer's built-in modem, and proceeded to have a conversation with Marlee by typing on the computer keyboard. I peeked over his shoulder to see how it worked, and he turned to me and said, "Please! This is a private conversation."

BRAD
DAVIS

Brad Davis

In the original production of Larry Kramer's The Normal Heart, *Brad Davis played a gay activist (closely modeled on the author, an old friend of Brad's) whose own obnoxiousness negates his efforts to provoke public officials into dealing with the AIDS crisis in New York. During the run of the play, Brad stayed at the New York apartment of Billy Hayes, the person whose real-life experiences in a Turkish prison he re-created in the movie* Midnight Express. *When I arrived at this apartment, the door was ajar, and music was blaring. Momentarily, Brad appeared wearing a blue workshirt unbuttoned to the navel—baring the muscular body he'd exposed both onstage* (Entertaining Mr. Sloane) *and on-screen (Midnight Express, Chariots of Fire, Querelle)—and led me into a large living room with blinds drawn against the sunny day, making it as dim as Blanche DuBois's parlor. He seemed to be someone who enjoys shaving the distinction between real life and playacting to an exquisitely thin line.*

I moved to New York when I was nineteen and left when I was twenty-six. All I wanted was to do theater—I wanted to be in a Broadway play. My agent promised me if I went to L.A. I could come back and do anything I wanted. He was right. But I got confused out there and forgot why I went. I was a very sick boy. Drugs, drinking.

I wanted to act from about five. I'm from Tallahassee. I knew that's what I wanted to do, though I didn't get onstage 'til I was sixteen.

What made you want to act at age five?

My mother took me to see *Pinocchio*, and I knew I could play the puppet better than the cartoon. I used to beg my parents to take me to Hollywood. They should have; I would have made a lot of money. I did nothing but perform as a kid. Very precocious. I was skinny, shy, awkward, always big with adults. I didn't like playing with the other children. *[He grabs a huge volume called* The Synonym Finder, *looks up "theatrical," and reels off a long list of mostly pejorative synonyms: affected, mannered, false, campy, overemotional.]* Pick ten of those, and that's what I was like as a kid.

I learned how to act from a man named Wynn Handman. I learned how to be characters as opposed to being sparkling and glittering onstage. People who do that, who are good at performing, usually do the same thing every time. Wynn taught me how to start with the seed of a thought of a character and let it grow until it fills my whole body. I learned about being other people through my own feelings. That way I don't have to fake it or make arbitrary choices or feel desperate or be up there and all of a sudden not know where I am—I'm suddenly just Brad. The thing is, I'm always me. Anyone who says they turn into someone else, they're living some delusion. If you become a chameleon and make people forget you, you're still showing another side of you.

What's the silliest part of being an actor?

[Long pause.] For me, it's how actors who get successful enough to be written about tend to find their validation in what people write about them. Actors allow people they've never seen or met who write about them to affect their—our—lives and egos so incredibly. They believe their own publicity.

My life changed drastically after *Midnight Express*—a door was open to a new plateau of existence. My arena was expanded one hundred times. I was given a lot of lessons to learn fast—why we're here, priorities, egos. It meant I could no longer play like a little kid at the fishing hole. I had to take responsibility.

What did that mean?
You want me to get the book?

Not the dictionary meaning—what did it mean to you?
[*He lights a cigarette, looks at his watch. Pause.*] I had obscurity before. I could be an asshole, and nobody cared. Then this movie comes out, and all of a sudden, I was no longer just a guy pissing on a building on Eighth Avenue between Fifty-third and Fifty-fourth streets, it was, "Look, it's Brad Davis, and I think he's drunk." It's sort of like being born again when you have a hit movie. Everything you do or say is going to have a big effect on your life, because now people are paying attention. You can play the game, or you can say fuck 'em, I'm going to blow snot on the street, throw chairs across a restaurant, none of it can touch me. Which is what I did. I took no responsibility for the result.

I protected my work. I've constantly gotten better as an actor. Theater is where I learned to act. Then I went to Hollywood, and I did *Sybil* and *Roots*, and I was okay. When I saw the rough cut of *Midnight Express*, when I went to London to do the looping, I was blown away. I wasn't embarrassed by my performance, I didn't hurt the movie, and I was happy for that. I showed potential. I was slightly raw, slightly awkward. Then came the period where I was slightly confused—I did *Small Circle of Friends*, *A Rumor of War*, and *Chariots of Fire*.

Then in the spring of 1980 I started to grow up. I was searching in my personal life for some real answers. I wasn't doing drugs of any kind, no drinking. When I did *Chiefs* in 1983, suddenly I was playing men instead of boys. I looked at my performance in *Robert Kennedy*, and that man up there and the boy who had been in *Midnight Express* were so . . . different.

Some actors are artists, not many. Some of us want to be artists—that's enough. It's very rare we're given a chance to make art—the people who hire us aren't very interested in making art.

Are there actors you admire or careers that give you inspiration?
I borrow from everybody. John Hurt gave me some very good advice. When we were doing *Midnight Express*, I took investigating your navel to the limit—that Method acting attitude that if you don't mumble to yourself for half an hour and hit your head against a wall, you can't possibly do it. I was so into that, and he would say, "Why do you put yourself through all that?" I said, "I want it to be real. How do you do it?" He said "I pretend. It's that simple. It's like playing cowboys and Indians when you're a kid." Well, when I was studying acting, the word "pretend" wasn't allowed in the room. I took "pretend" to mean fake, phony, bullshit. At first I was stunned. Then I thought, "If what he's doing is pretend, it's pretending in a way I never thought you could pretend. It's believing."

Is acting a sexy experience for you?
Yeah! No one ever asked me that before, but yeah. It has nothing to do with taking off my clothes. It's sexual, because acting is so physical. One thing I change with characters is how he moves, what he does with his hands, whether he touches people or not. I'm aware of his sexuality, on what level it's expressed. I'm aware of my body, making it different from Brad's.

Tell me about working with Fassbinder.

I was going to do another movie with him, based on a book written by this Italian guy Pittagrilli in the '30s, called *Cocaine*. Then while I was doing *Entertaining Mr. Sloane*, I got this telegram offering me *Querelle*. I said, "Oh, great! What is it?" They sent me the book and the script, and I was terrified. I thought I'd never work again. But I knew if I turned down *Querelle*, his ego wouldn't allow him to work with me again. All this time I'd considered myself this artist of courage, but *Querelle* was another world altogether. I found there was this bourgeois mouse in my head saying, "You can't do that." So of course I said yes, I'll do it. I wasn't insecure about doing it—I worried that I would be persecuted in my professional life.

The movie's nothing like I thought it would be. It was supposed to be three hours long. Now everything that makes it make sense has been cut out. It looks like this guy just gets off the boat and starts killing people and getting fucked. The Jean Genet purity was gone. Gaumont, the largest film distributor in Europe, said he had to cut it down to an hour and forty-five minutes—this man of no compromise compromised on *my* movie! The amazing thing that people don't know is what a private movie it was. It was just Rainer's perspective on his life in those last three months. That's why it was so disturbing.

How did you create that character physically?

Querelle didn't move a lot. He was described by Genet in the book: "He was like something from the grave that came to prey on life, like vegetation. He moved very slowly, through people." Very narcissistic.

How do you play narcissistic?

You feel it. You feel every part of your body, what your right buttock feels like on this chair, your left buttock, the cloth pushing up against it.

What do you think of in that moment when the house lights are out, just before going onstage?

I think, "I can't believe I'm going to do this again." What I do to myself is very intense. I don't cheat—I don't know how. It's hard for me to walk through a play, say, at a matinee and only give three-fourths. If I did that, nothing would come out. I think, "Take a deep breath."

HARVEY
FIERSTEIN

Harvey Fierstein

Harvey Fierstein acquired his ravaged Tallulah Bankhead voice during the run of a play called Xircus, the Private Life of Jesus Christ. *"I had to deliver a five-page monologue over a recording of Kate Smith singing 'God Bless America' at full blast. The director refused to turn the volume down, AND I WANTED EVERY WORD HEARD." At the time, he was completely unknown outside of New York's Off-Off-Broadway fringe, where in six years he had acted in more than sixty plays by such writers as Andy Warhol, Jackie Curtis, Ronald Tavel, Tom Eyen, and Megan Terry.*

A couple of years later, I interviewed Harvey at Off-Off-Broadway's legendary La Mama theater, where he was appearing in his own play The International Stud. *He had written plays before, including* Freaky Pussy *and* In Search of the Cobra Jewels, *but* Stud *changed his life. It was the first of three one-acts which would later be produced together as* Torch Song Trilogy, *a four-hour tour de-force portrait of a gay relationship, and win him Tony Awards for best play and best performance in 1983. In 1978, however, the trilogy was still a fantasy in Harvey's mind. It was a chilly February afternoon when we sat in the theater while Harvey ate his lunch—or breakfast—of potato chips and Diet Pepsi while showing me his scrapbook. Many of his earliest performances were in drag, and I asked him why he liked playing women's roles.*

Have you seen men's roles? They are so *boring.* All of the men's roles in the '50s and '60s are I-wanna-get-laid and I-wanna-shoot-up and I-wanna-this and I-wanna-that. The women get the "Poor Pearl" roles, and the last bow, and the nicer clothes, and the softer moments. Women's roles are always more interesting, because there's more to play with. A lot of them are underwritten so you have to bring your own strength to them, while men's roles are so overwritten that if you want to bring softness to them, you can't. I'd like to play Eleanor in *The Lion in Winter.* She has lines like, "I made poor Louis take me on crusade. I dressed my maidens like Amazons and rode bare-breasted halfway to Damascus. Louis had a seizure, and I damn near died of windburn, but the troops were dazzled." Men don't get lines like that!

When I sat down to talk to Harvey for this book, his life had changed radically since his La Mama days. In 1984, he won his third Tony Award for writing the book of the Broadway musical La Cage aux Folles, *which has toured all over the world and made him so much money that, with wise investment, he need never work again. He had written another play called* Spookhouse *and several screenplays, and he had played small roles in* Garbo Talks, Apology, *and on* Miami Vice. *But* Torch Song Trilogy *continued to dominate his life, for better or worse. On one hand, the play had launched the careers of Matthew Broderick, Fisher Stevens, and Estelle Getty; on the other hand, Joel Crothers and Court Miller, the two actors who played Harvey's onstage lover Ed in* Torch Song, *had recently died, one of cancer, the other of AIDS. Harvey himself was just leaving for London to take over the role of Arnold Beckoff from Antony Sher, who had won the British equivalent of the Tony Award for his performance in* Torch Song Trilogy, *so the difference between American and English actors was very much on his mind.*

American actors go too far with this intense playing of subtext and never reading the script. Like the actor who says, "My character wouldn't say that." I say, "That's fine. We don't want your character. We want the character in the play. The guy says it. So either you got something wrong, or you're the wrong actor for the role, 'cause that's exactly what your character says." In England, all they care about is the written word, and they play it to death. It's embarrassing when you've written a bad line because they say it so nice and clearly. You hear every word.

Is it easy for you step back into the play after a hiatus?

The hardest thing is the third act, those raw fight scenes, the whole point of which is to let yourself get to the point where you don't know what you're saying, and you say things you don't mean. It's hard because I know that I am coming to a dark, dark place in my personality and I've got to show it. I take eight to ten aspirin a performance of *Torch Song*. It's physically painful for me to do it; you don't come through to the other side. The audience does, but the character doesn't. By the time he gets everything gathered together, the lights are coming down, and you have to smile, because it's your curtain call. Nothing in this world do I hate more than having an actor waltz out for his bows with tears running down his face, to show the audience how hard he's worked.

Do you find curtain calls therapeutic?

I don't even remember them. I don't remember anything for a couple of hours after the show, especially in that role. When we first did the trilogy Off-Off-Broadway, I used to take the subway home to Brooklyn. We'd all get on the subway together, Matthew Broderick with his bicycle and the producer Larry Lane. I would get home at one-thirty in the morning, put on the David Letterman show or whatever and cry for three or four hours, because there was no place at the end of that play to dump all that pain and emotion. It's what leaves that lump in the audience's throat, when done right, but it can make you very miserable. In the early days, if I had gone out to eat afterwards, I would have been fine. But we didn't have any money to buy food. I had to borrow money for the subway. The end of the run was an entirely different thing. By then I was playing a split week, Monday, Tuesday, and twice on Wednesday. Four performances a week was a lot easier.

Did the success of *Torch Song* change your identity from actor to writer?

Not in my mind. If someone said to me, "You can't write anymore," I couldn't care less. If they said, "You can't act anymore," I'd have to find some way to get that energy out. That walking the tightrope—which is what acting really is. You got witnesses. Somebody's going to know what you did, and that's very dangerous. It's not like writing, where you can always use the white-out or say "I mistyped that." Writing is for yourself. Acting is not.

What's the hardest thing for you to do as an actor?

Walk out on the stage. After that it's a lot easier. It's like stepping out on a tightrope between two buildings—the first step is always the hardest. I shake like a leaf. I stand back there and curse and cross myself. The hardest thing in an actor's life is a long run. What do you do once all your friends have seen the show, all the critics have come and gone, and you're tired of having dinner every night with the cast? You're back to your routine of coming to work and going home.

What's the silliest thing for you about being an actor?

It has more to do with celebrity than being an actor. In the days when you were starving to death, most restaurants wouldn't let you in dressed like I am today, in jeans and a T-shirt. Now they buy me dinner. That's the stupidest part of the world we live in. In film, the silliest thing is trying to stay sane while you're waiting to do your two minutes of work a day. I've learned how to sleep in a honey wagon.

Honey wagon?

Sometimes you get a regular Winnebago, which is hard enough to sleep in, but a honey wagon is a Winnebago which is broken into four or six rooms down the hall. The door has your name on it, you go in, there's a cot, a toilet bowl, and a sink. That's it. You have to learn to go in, lie down, and go right to sleep.

What's the best thing about acting for you?

Rehearsal. It's the greatest thing, because you're really working. You're trying to find things. You're discussing the text. It's like an archeological dig or like theoretical mathematicians discovering something together. Then you get to opening night, and it's not for you anymore.

Roy Scheider

Although Roy Scheider got his start in the theater and won an Obie Award in 1968 for Stephen D, *his aquiline profile is most familiar from slicing its way across the screen in films like* The French Connection *and* All That Jazz, *both of which earned him Oscar nominations. When we met, he had most recently finished shooting* The Men's Club *and was about to begin rehearsals for* 52 Pick-Up, *directed by John Frankenheimer, with Ann-Margret and John Glover.*

What made you want to be an actor?

When I was in grammar school and high school, I was short and fat, the last guy chosen on every team. That's a pain in the ass, always being last. Acting was something I could be always first at. I was a pre-law student at Franklin and Marshall College in Pennsylvania. They happened to have a theater with a hell of a good artistic director who had been an actor and play reader for the Theater Guild in the Depression. I went to see a production of *Billy Budd* there, and it knocked me out. I tried out for the next play, which was *Coriolanus*. I played an eighty-year-old senator in that. I liked the atmosphere, I liked being there at night. I found a home. Everything in my life changed. All of a sudden, my grades were better, my relationships with everybody were better. By the time I graduated, I said, "Who am I kidding?" I didn't even say I *want* to be an actor—I had a feeling I *was* an actor.

By that time, I had won a couple of acting awards, like the Theresa Helburn–John Opdike Memorial Award. Theresa Helburn was one of the founders of the Theater Guild. I was brought to her apartment in New York, where she would serve these awful martinis. Then when I was in the Air Force, I used to get letters from her saying things like, "I know it rains a lot up there, be sure and wear your rubbers"—like from my mother! I thought, hell, when I go back to New York, I'll walk right into the Theater Guild, and I'll be on Broadway in two weeks. Well, she died six months before I came back to New York.

At that time, the Theater Guild had just had a very successful tour in Europe with Helen Hayes and Mary Martin in *Skin of Our Teeth*, *Glass Menagerie*, and *Miracle Worker*. Now they were planning a tour of South America. Lawrence Langner, Theresa Helburn's partner, was holding auditions, and I couldn't get anyplace. One day I went storming into his office and said, "You mean to tell me that, if Theresa Helburn was alive, the two-time winner of the Theresa Helburn Award couldn't get a goddam job?" They handed me the tiny part of the telegraph boy in *Skin of Our Teeth*, made me stage manager and understudy for about twelve parts, and I was off to a three-month tour. I was twenty-six.

After that, I went back to F&M to do a production of *Richard III*. This English actor in a touring show nearby came to see it and came back raving about how it was the best Richard III he'd ever seen. He wrote a letter to Sam Zolotow, who was doing the theater column for the *New York Times*. Sam Zolotow printed the whole goddam letter. Joe Papp read it, called me up in New Jersey, and had me come over to audition. I did my Richard III and wound up playing Mercutio in a production of *Romeo and Juliet* with Kathleen Widdoes and Richard Jordan. That was my first professional job in New York. My understudy was James Earl Jones. After that, I went out to almost every repertory theater on the eastern seaboard, playing the biggest and toughest classical roles I could find.

Were you always good?

I was good and I was very adaptable. I could play young, I could play old. I could play Irish, I could play Russian, I could play Jewish. Some guys with blond hair and blue eyes are limited. But there was always a job for me.

When you went into acting, did you think you would also do movies?

Come on! I was a serious actor, not a movie actor. The group of guys who were my contemporaries, we were serious. Movies?

Who was your group of guys?

The guys who used to hang around Jimmie Ray's bar on Eighth Avenue, like Pacino and Billy Devane. De Niro, he was younger. Dustin. I did a play Off-Broadway with Dustin called *Serjeant Musgrave's Dance*, and Dustin got fired after two weeks because his North Country accent was lousy. He was devastated. He did *Eh?* a couple of months later. Mike Nichols saw him in that, and a year later he's a fuckin' movie star. Bam! Like that.

Did that make movies okay for your gang?

By then, we were all starting to say, "Well, I suppose I could give it a shot . . ." While I was doing theater in New York, I did a lot of little pieces in things like *Paper Lions*, and I played a summer-stock director in *Star!* with Julie Andrews. The first part that got me anywhere was playing the pimp in *Klute* with Jane Fonda. That same year I did *The French Connection*.

Did acting in movies feel different from what you were used to?

All acting, whether it's television, screen, or stage, is a lie. It's an amplification, an enlargement of life, really. Harold Clurman used to say, "The theater lies like truth." In other words, you create a theatrical conflict, even on film, because it's scripted, directed, and photographed for a purpose. It's not real. You look at your favorite film performances, and you can see where the actors make deliberate, dramatic choices to get your attention or to scare the shit out of you. Those are all theatrical devices. You learn them by being onstage in front of an audience and making them work.

It must have been weird to do *All That Jazz* and have Bob Fosse there to do firsthand research.

It *was* weird. The movie started off being sixty percent Fosse, forty percent Scheider. Then it went to fifty percent Scheider, fifty percent Fosse. But after a while, it became seventy percent the character of Joe Gideon, which was a creation of both of us. That usually happens about the second week of shooting a film. The actor starts to click in to the character. Then the director starts asking the actor, "What do you think your guy would do here?" and you say, "I would do this, but he would do that." You start to talk about the character in the third person. You don't want to be yourself in every film. You want to create something . . . something more interesting than yourself. Which is one of the reasons why you become an actor, right? You want to create something more interesting than what you've got.

What do your parents think about your being an actor?

When they were alive, my father was not delighted by the choice at all. He ran a service station in New Jersey, so he wanted his son to be a lawyer, of

course. When I decided to be an actor, he thought I was out of my head. It wasn't until after I had enjoyed some success on the stage and won an Obie Award and done some films that he got over it. After the Academy Award nomination for *The French Connection*, I started making some money. Parents worry about security. As soon as you start to make some money, they feel better. They know you're not going to starve to death and nobody'll push you around and you'll have life insurance like real people.

Sam Waterston

Sam Waterston is very much the mainstream American actor with a long list of prestigious Broadway and film credits. Few people know that early in his career, around the same time he appeared on television in Much Ado About Nothing *and* The Glass Menagerie *and in the all-star film version of* The Great Gatsby, *he was also seen in cheap "hippie" movies of the sixties like* Who Killed Mary What's'ername? *as well as wild early Sam Shepard plays such as* La Turista *and* Red Cross. *We met for a Japanese meal after a matinee of* Benefactors, *in which he starred on Broadway with Glenn Close and Mary Beth Hurt. He had recently filmed an episode of* Amazing Stories *directed by Martin Scorsese, and after winning an Oscar nomination for* The Killing Fields, *next came an offbeat French film called* Flagrant Desir.

Does movie acting feel different from stage acting, or the same?

It's not that different. You want to be slightly off-balance when you're acting, because in life you're always slightly off balance. There's something distracting over there when I'm trying to talk to you [the cook is chopping sushi a few feet away, banging his knife on the cutting board], and part of your concentration goes to that. You don't know what you might see next, so you're off balance in that way. You want to try to achieve that effect when you're acting, but you have to know what you're going to do next. So you have to fool yourself into not knowing certain things. There are different ways to do that in movies and in theater, so the detail is different, but the result is the same.

John Hurt told me a story about Ralph Richardson. I don't know if it's true or not, but it should be. They were working in a play together, and he saw a little black nose and two little pink eyes and a white face come out of Richardson's shirt and disappear. Then it came out of his cuff and disappeared. He had a mouse in his shirt! John was fascinated to know why, and Sir Ralph said, "It keeps me from thinking about the one thing I must not think about, which is myself."

Do different directors bring out different things in you?

Sure. Good directors define the room in which everything takes place. They define the nature of the surrounding experience. Then everybody freely runs around inside that defined experience, but there are only a certain number of things you can do in a swimming pool or in a deep freeze. I saw this most clearly right at the beginning when I worked with Mike Nichols. When he was doing *The Knack*, I was assistant stage manager and general understudy, so I watched other actors get caught in a web of Mike's making. They all came in, and everybody had a different theory about the play, special tensions, private worries, all that. Mike began talking about college and spring and sex. The actors said, "Well, if that's what you want to talk about, all right. Maybe some other day we'll rehearse the play." Then gradually their minds began circling around these subjects. They would be rehearsing the play, and their minds would also be on these subjects, and solutions would emerge. From the outside, you thought, "Oh, those poor benighted souls, they think they're thinking of this themselves." In fact, they were thinking of it themselves, but what they didn't know was that the world they were living in had been drawn up for them by someone else.

SAM
WATERSTON

SPALDING
GRAY

Spalding Gray

Since 1979, when he moved from the acting ensemble of the Wooster Group into a solo career performing autobiographical monologues, Spalding Gray has become internationally recognized as a unique combination of avant-garde performance artist and stand-up comic. From the beginning, his monologues were nearly pathological in their obsession with self-exposure: witnessing his confessions was like watching someone unravel in public. Gray was clearly on the edge, barely masking his inner turbulence with the polished demeanor of a veteran performer. He was also disarming in his candor, self-mocking in his humor, thrillingly precise in his timing and choice of detail—qualities that continue to characterize his work.

If the early monologues succeeded in keeping Gray from pitching himself into the abyss he circled so precariously, they also bolstered his ego by drawing the kind of personal following rarely seen in avant-garde circles. And when he was asked to play a small role in Roland Joffe's film The Killing Fields, *the experience of spending two months in Thailand, hobnobbing with famous actors and journalists while re-creating one of the most horrifying bloodbaths in recent history, became the basis of* Swimming to Cambodia, *an award-winning two-part monologue that completed his transformation from a borderline urban victim to underground celebrity.*

We met at the Soho loft he inhabits when he's not on the road or at the house in upstate New York he shares with independent film producer Renee Shafransky. It was before noon, and he looked rumpled, like he'd just gotten up; his face was early-morning puffy, red and splotchy. But as he began to talk about himself, a remarkable transformation occurred. His face cleared up, his features became more defined, and he took on a sort of glow. This is a man who thrives in the spotlight.

The idea for the first monologue came to me when we had to stop rehearsal for *Point Judith* because Willem Dafoe went to do a movie. We didn't want the Garage to sit empty, so there was time for me to do something. I don't like the rehearsal process at all, and I tried to figure out how I could work without rehearsal. I had this feeling of impending nuclear destruction, and I wanted to chronicle what I felt was the decline of the white middle-class world as we'd known it. To write it down would be presuming there was a history that would survive on the printed page, so I wanted to do something immediate. I thought I'd take a period of my life and recount it as simply as possible before an audience.

So I sat down and did this thing, and it was about forty-five minutes long. Each night new material would come to me through memory, through my imaginative film of the past, through free association—this was, of course, the psychoanalytic process. I'd been interested in psychoanalysis for years, in the idea that one is simply reconstructing the puzzle of one's life in front of another person. But I trusted the performance process more because I had a community of people—anywhere from thirty to a hundred and fifty—to share the experience rather than one psychoanalyst. Actually, it was reverse psychoanalysis: the audience would be my witness, and *they* would pay.

Since you started doing the monologues, do you feel self-conscious about your life, knowing you may use it in future work?

I don't have a strong concept of self; I feel myself to be an onion. I keep peeling and peeling. A lot of my method comes out of my interest in Tibetan Buddhism, vadrayana meditation—the idea that one watches all experience and says, "This is happening, and this is happening, and then this is happening, and this is my hand," and on and on, so you finally develop this observer. I realized that I was an actor before I chose to be an actor. I was always circling around the outside, and that kind of I-alone-have-escaped-to-tell-you became my signature. That comes out of my terrific fear of death—I'm trying to create my own world in which I am dying all the time and returning from the dead for the last judgment. Always a situation of death and resurrection. All Christians have this fantasy that the supreme moment will be that last judgment with God. When I lost that idea, I had to make my audience God, and the last judgment becomes all the time.

Where can this work evolve to?

Part of me wants to go back and show people in the commercial world of theater and film that I can play a character. It's good for me to read for things, because I've lost the knack of auditioning. Competition is very threatening to me—that's why I went into my own work. When I went to Los Angeles to audition for *Hail to the Chief* with Patty Duke, it was just between Dick Shawn and me. They were auditioning in a good-sized room, like a little theater, and all the producers were sitting in the dark. They pulled me down too early, so I was sitting outside the door for Dick Shawn's audition, and it made me so fucking self-conscious. First of all, they were laughing a lot. Then I had to get his line readings out of my head and try to do something different. The problem is, you can't bring nuance to lines like "I can't do it with you anymore. How can I make love to the President of the United States? You're my commander-in-chief!"

Were you heartbroken not to get the part?

No, because I didn't expect it at all. I took my per diem, which was $100 a day for two days, and I went to my favorite cheap hotel, the Highland Gardens, and took a vacation. I had a good time, but when the plane landed in New York, I felt deflated and depressed. When I come back from any vacation, it's taken so much energy from my own work.

Sometimes I think I should have a motorcycle accident and disappear. That's the cynical part of me talking—I see how that kind of thing works, when people have to line up at a stage door to see me. Renee and I went to see *Death of a Salesman*, and afterwards we were going with John Malkovich to have drinks. I don't know how people recognized him—he had a beret on—but these autograph hounds and people with flash cameras started chasing him across the street. And John, in his inimitable way, turned to me and said, "Don't you wonder why performance artists don't get followed like this, Spalding?"

P E T E R
W E L L E R

Peter Weller

Peter Weller is one of those actors who can change the temperature in a room. Years before he starred in Shoot the Moon *and* The Adventures of Buckaroo Banzai, *I saw him in a mediocre Off-Broadway play called* The Woolgatherer, *in which he created an aura around himself like a held breath. Weller achieves this effect through a combination of silence, stealthy movement, and an odd, glassy-eyed stare—one of his fellow actors refers to it as "Kabuki acting."*

Weller wanted to do this interview on "neutral ground," so we met at a Columbus Avenue restaurant popular among actors. By turns intimate and aloof during the conversation, he kept eyeing a woman he recognized at another table. When he went to the bathroom, he had the waiter deliver a note to her, which made her laugh. A flirtatious conversation ensued, punctuated with steamy kisses, and the two made a date. Two days earlier, Weller had completed work in Toronto on Apology, *a feature film produced by Home Box Office.*

What's your last day of shooting like?

You can't wait to get out. You just want to get your plane ticket and go home. But you have to fight that. We were still shooting a major scene the last few days, so I kept making a mental note not to push it.

Was the last day a typical movie schedule, on the set early?

Yeah. If the call's at six-thirty or six, I get up at four-thirty, quarter to five. I roll out of bed, eat a bowl of bran, stretch out, and run five miles every day. When I come back from that, I'm completely pumped for the rest of the day. Then I meditate in the car, go to the set, vocalize in the Winnebago, do the work, go home, watch dailies, work out.

So on Friday did you watch the dailies and work out afterwards?

No, I went directly home, changed clothes, and went out on a date. My costar Lesley Ann Warren was going to watch the dailies for both of us, 'cause it was mostly her scene. We did a big sex scene, where she's lying on top of me. You can hardly see me at all in this scene. I hate those scenes—sex stuff. I've done three of them, and none of them have worked, which may say something about me. But they'll keep this one in, because it's HBO, and God knows they want all the tits and ass they can get.

How late did you shoot?

Eleven o'clock.

And you were there from six-thirty in the morning?

Uh-huh.

And a late date for Peter.

God bless her. Where is she now? I should call her.

Did you always want to be an actor?

No, I wanted to be a jazz musician. Trumpet and guitar. Highly mediocre at both. I used to play eight hours a day, but I hated it. Now I have fun with it because I don't have to. Now it's acting I hate.

When did you start acting?

When I was about ten, a guy named Robert Jani put me on the stage in *A Christmas Carol*. This was Mineral Wells, Texas. I was born in Wisconsin, but grew up in Texas. My father was in the army. I hated doing *Christmas Carol*. I was sort of bitten by it, but I hated to have these adults standing around telling you what to do.

What bit you about it?

Girls came up afterwards and said, "Aren't you cute?" What really bit me was the immediate acknowledgment of an audience. Everybody loves acknowledgment, and actors get it right away. Maybe I was a little more insecure than my brothers, maybe my parents liked them better—I don't know what kind of psychological claptrap there was, but I liked an audience going "Hurray." I liked performing, and I liked music most.

When did you decide to go into acting?

I was twenty-one, twenty. I wasn't ambitious enough in music; I didn't have the patience to sit on a bandstand for the rest of my life. I wanted to be bigger but I didn't know at what. At this stage in my life, nothing would have given me the outlet I looking for. I was just searching. When I started acting, I did a couple of good things—I came up to New York from North Texas State on a scholarship to the American Academy of Dramatic Arts, and I was picked up as standby to the lead in David Rabe's play *Sticks and Bones*. That was my first encounter with David Rabe. I later went into *Streamers*. The role was originally between me and John Heard. They gave it to John and offered me another part, but I'd quit acting. The things I was not finding in music I was also not finding in acting.

What did you do when you quit acting?

Personal shit. Self-realization stuff, martial arts.

Did that help?

I wasn't looking for help. I was looking for who I was. I didn't want to feel better. I didn't want to be better. I just wanted to know what was going on. There was something I was looking for in my outer circumstances I wasn't finding.

When you went back to acting, what made you decide to stay an actor?

I found out how to let the process of the thing enrich me, rather than just making me famous or giving me money. The only thing I have to communicate is my own particular experience of this planet. This guy I played in this movie *Apology* is a cop who's lost his vision of why he's a cop. He's floundering. I myself know the experience of floundering. If I can communicate through this guy's words my own experience of not knowing what value there is in living, the people who are watching will understand and say, "I've been there." There's no other payoff than this, just contributing the connective tissue to another human being. I do that by taking roles in which I think I have something to say. If it's just a character that furthers a plot, I can't do it. I did some of that shit on television when I was in my early twenties. I not only had nothing to say, but I'm bad at it, because I'm not facile enough to bring the fuckin' thing off.

I came back to acting because Tom Babe wrote this part called Henry Hitchcock in this play called *Rebel Women*, a true story about the three days that Sherman bivouacked outside of Atlanta in a town he did not burn. It had a bunch of unknown actors—me, David Dukes, Eric Roberts, John Glover (who was the most known, I guess), Kathryn Walker, Mandy Patinkin.

A bunch of no-talents.

Yeah, bunch of absolute no-talents. We had a blast. By that time, *Streamers* was a hit, but the rumor was that Mike Nichols was unsatisfied with the thing. I went in and had this great talk with him, and he said, "Why don't you do this play?" He basically let me do what I wanted and let the play redefine itself around me. It was great. I played it for ten months until it closed. Man, I loved that fuckin' play. It was the most unbelievable experience I ever had on a stage, bar none. No one had ever seen anything like that. Big guys fainting dead away, people weeping uncontrollably en masse, no one clapping at the end. When they did clap, it was ungodly. Everybody in the history of show business was coming backstage every night with their fucking hearts in their hands.

I must say, it wasn't just the play—it was Nichols' inspired direction. He took a play full of seeming confrontations and conflicts and directed us never to confront. You read these scenes, and they go, like, "What are you doing in my room?" That's a guy confronting a guy. Nichols said, "You can never do that, or the play is over. It's got to be about survival and dodging and trying to make friends." So whenever intentions would come up that seemed confrontational "Look, Richie, I've had it with this thing"—instead of being threatening, it became a plea, like, "I'm asking you to be on my side." Consequently, the audience kept seeing four guys that they liked. And when the shit started to fall out the bottom of the thing, they'd go, "How did this happen, man?"

Are there actors you've looked to as role models or inspirations?

Cary Grant is one of my favorite people to watch doing anything. Marlon Brando said an incredible thing about Cary Grant in an interview with Truman Capote on the set of *Sayonara* in 1957. He said that the brilliance of Cary Grant is that usually nobody that good-looking has the courage or the presence of mind to make an ass out of himself the way Cary Grant has.

There's a lot of guys I like that don't inspire me. James Dean was good-looking and sort of charismatic, but he didn't inspire me like that telephone conversation by Montgomery Clift in *The Misfits* where he's talking to his mother, which is one of the most brilliant things I've seen in my life. I like Clint Eastwood, I like Arnold Schwarzenegger, I like Burt Reynolds, I like these macho guys. I loved and adored Steve McQueen. But the guy never gave me inspiration like, say, Marlon Brando did, who's probably everybody's favorite actor in life. Marlon is the godfather of originality, the brave guy who took an incredible chance to express what he finds . . . personal in any role. He's a great inspiration.

PETER
EVANS

Peter Evans

At any given time, there is a category of actors who might be called the Best Kept Secrets, and Peter Evans is one of them. An actor of extraordinary range and talent, he has starred in the original productions of David Rabe's Streamers *and David Mamet's* A Life in the Theater, *regional productions of Turgenev's* A Month in the Country *and Sondheim's* Company, *and the Broadway and touring companies of* Children of a Lesser God. *He has given classical vocal recitals and donned a fat suit to play the grotesque title character of Albert Innaurato's* The Transfiguration of Benno Blimpie. *Still, he remains largely unknown outside the theatergoing populace of New York City—a frustrating situation that can either grind an actor's confidence to dust or instill an ironic, self-protective attitude toward the ups and downs of show business.*

How did you get your first big job in New York?

It was November of '75. I was in this lunchtime play called *Foreplay, Door Play,* and I had auditioned about five times for a David Storey play called *Life Class* at Manhattan Theater Club, but they didn't cast me. When the show was in previews, the director called me and said, "Look, we'll probably be firing someone. Could you take over at short notice?" I said, "Sure." Gretchen Rinnell, Juliet's Taylor's assistant—or maybe it was Juliet—came. They were casting David Rabe's *Streamers* at that time, so they called my agent and said, "We'd like to get to know Peter Evans. Since we're an all-woman organization and it's an all-male cast, we need someone to read opposite people we're auditioning. And we'd like Peter to come all day tomorrow." My agent said, "Well, he's doing this lunchtime show, and he won't be free until two o'clock. Could he come after that?" They said, "No, Mike [Nichols] wants somebody for the whole day. Too bad, but some other time." I thought, "It's just my luck. I could be meeting Mike Nichols and David Rabe instead of doing a play called *Foreplay, Door Play.*"

The next day, after the play was over, I did something I'd never done before: I put a dime in the phone and called that casting office. I said, "I know you told me not to come, but I'm finished with my work now, and is there any chance you could use me?" They said, "Thank God you called, because the person we got instead of you turned out to be a real asshole, and we've been trying to find you, so get in a taxi and come down." I was quickly ushered into the room, and I met Mike Nichols and David Rabe. They threw the script at me, and I started reading scenes opposite these people they were auditioning. One of the scenes I read was opposite an actor who was auditioning for Carlyle, the black guy who kills everybody, and the part I was reading was Richie. I said to myself, "This seems like a part I could play. Well, I'm not going to 'not act' just because I'm not auditioning." After the scene finished, Nichols said to the guy who was auditioning, "Well, that was good, Jones," and then he turned to me and said, "And Evans, whoever *you* are, that was good, too." During a break, Nichols said, "Why don't you go upstairs and read the whole script and come down?" They had me read two scenes by myself in the room with Rabe and Nichols. Then they conferred for a couple of minutes and said, "We don't know who you are, but we've been trying to cast this particular role for a long time and we haven't found anybody that has the right combination of qualities, and you walked in the door and you're it." That was all in one day.

As you might imagine, I could barely believe it. The number of coincidences was amazing—if they hadn't fired that guy from *Life Class*, if Juliet Taylor hadn't been in the audience for that particular performance, if I hadn't made that phone call, none of it would have happened.

It was a real lesson about auditions. I was just happy to be there, happy to have met Nichols and Rabe, and happy to be reading a role that fit my talents. When you've had a week to worry about it and prepare, then you walk into the audition and you can barely open your mouth because you're so nervous. It was a perfect kind of adrenaline high. The fact that Nichols trusted me was a great release. He's very cagey that way. He knows how to get people to do that, to release a lot of elements of the personality.

One of the reasons that production was so successful was because of the humor in the performance. It's not innately funny; it's kind of a melodrama. One of the things it's about is bigotry, discrimination of various kinds. If the production hadn't been so three-dimensional, it would have been easy for the audience to put the blame on my character, the homosexual character. The audience could have said, "Well, it's his fault that all these murders happened because he's gay," or "It's the black's fault because he's black." The performance made it much harder for the audience to place blame, because they liked all the guys who were involved. Nichols' great talent is that he gets people with a sense of humor, and he allows that sense of humor to feed into the play.

How do you know that a role you read fits your talents?

If I'm faced with a farmboy from Iowa who's blond and blue-eyed or a sophisticated intellectual from Manhattan, the dark-haired sophisticate from Manhattan is obviously closer to what I am. On the other hand, I had a movie audition yesterday that was interesting; the part I'd gone up for was this rich guy from New Orleans who's got this almost-prostitute as a girlfriend, and he's part of this sleazy cocaine atmosphere, and he goes to New York to hire a guy to kill somebody who's in his way. I read the script and thought, "Fuck, this isn't a role for me." But then when I got in there, the director told me, "We want somebody really intriguing." I wouldn't have been in the room to begin with unless somebody thought I could play this part, so I did far better in the audition than I thought I could. What I'm saying is that sometimes you're wrong about the thing you're right for.

On the other hand, I also think I suffer because I am so versatile. I can play a wide range of things, and sometimes that confuses people, because I'm not easily pigeonholed. When I auditioned for Paul Mazursky for *Willie and Phil*, he said, "You're a real actor. It must be hard for you. Don't worry, it'll all work out in the end. But it'll take a while." A lot of casting, especially in film and TV, depends on what your type is, what you look like. They expect you to *be* the character rather than being able to *act* the character. For film that's necessary in a lot of cases. I just wish that our culture respected the kind of thing that I do more. I don't want to sound like I wish I was English, but when I go to the National Theater in London, where they've got three theaters which employ a roster of a hundred and fifty actors all the time, doing in each theater a repertory of three or four plays, it makes me weep.

What made you want to be an actor?

God, I don't know. It's one of those things I always did from an early age, not knowing it was acting. The house we lived in in New Jersey used to be a barn, and there was this little potting shed I made into a theater—my father and I built a little proscenium arch, got some curtains from somebody's attic and with a couple of friends I did plays that we wrote ourselves. I gave little puppet shows for kids' birthday parties and charged five dollars a shot.

I went away to prep school, which was really a major turning point. Until then, I hadn't gotten respect except from my family. In suburban New Jersey in the late '50s, early '60s, it was "You're interested in theater? That and a token gets you on the subway." But Andover was fantastic; they had an attitude toward the arts that encouraged excellence, and they had this great theater. I did a lot of plays there and was like the Big Man on Campus in the acting realm. It allowed me to see I had talent I would be respected for. If I had stayed in my old school in New Jersey, I would have gotten very fat and neurotic.

What is it that makes you realize you're an actor?

There's an obvious sense of fun in performing that the audience senses. Just loving being out there.

Why is it fun?

That's like asking why is the sky blue. Being onstage in front of an audience and achieving the tasks set out for you in the script, for one. But also controlling the audience—getting them to laugh when they should, getting them to listen. I just love it.

Have you ever done a performance that wasn't fun?

Yes, of course. *Endgame* was one of them. That's not the kind of play you should do eight times a week for four months. It's too intense. It should be in a repertory situation. What else? I was in a terrible production of a play called *Don Juan Comes Back from the War* by Odon von Horvath at Manhattan Theater Club, for which I received the worst reviews I've ever gotten. I hated performing it.

What's it like to be onstage and hate performing?

It's a nightmare, especially if you've gotten bad reviews and you've made the mistake of reading them. After I got those reviews, I felt like everyone in the audience had read them and that they were thinking exactly what the critics had thought, and I wanted to die. I wanted the stage to open up and swallow me.

Do you get tired of the routine of doing a long run?

No. What's the point of being an actor if you don't act every night? That's the creative challenge, to make it new every night. The audience has never seen it before. All those things are clichés, but it's true. In *Night and Day*, it was a tremendous experience to be onstage with Maggie Smith, because she never did the same thing twice. Ever, ever, ever. She would give up whole sections of laughs. Things that were surefire on one night, she'd do it completely differently the next night, and she was just exploring a different aspect of the character. Her mind kept trying to find a better way. That to me is the highest kind of artistry. She could do it a hundred and two different ways. If we'd run five hundred performances, she could have done it five hundred different ways.

Actors sometimes feel that because they're interpretive artists, not primary creative artists like writers or composers, other people put them in a lesser category. But the real creativity comes from that very thing. How much more creative can you be than to do a play eight times a week for a year and make it new and different every night?

What's the silliest thing about being an actor?

Well, in retrospect one of the silliest things I did was to shave my head for *Total Eclipse*. I was so fascinated by the character of Verlaine. I'd seen portraits of him, and I thought I looked like him. I'd already grown a beard for that role, and he had a receding hairline—even though he was twenty-eight at the time of the play—so I thought, "Oh, I'll do a De Niro here," and I gave myself a receding hairline. Then the play only lasted one performance, and I was stuck with this shaved head. I looked like I'd had shock treatment, which in a certain way I had.

Do you ever feel like quitting?

Every once in a while, I think, "Oh, I'll just go to Vermont and write. But that's silly. I love it too much, and I'm too good. No, I never think of quitting. I think more that one has to create one's own opportunities, rather than be at the mercy of Them.

PAUL
McCRANE

Paul McCrane

Paul McCrane was only twenty-four when we met, but he'd already been working in the professional theater almost ten years. Between his debut as Shirley Knight's angel-faced son in John Guare's Landscape of the Body *at the Public Theater and his appearance as the neurotic, prematurely balding Don Parritt in* The Iceman Cometh *on Broadway opposite Jason Robards, Barnard Hughes, and Donald Moffat, he has built up an impressive film and stage career. Short and red-haired, he has small, chiseled features that make him unremarkable on the street yet very striking under stage lighting. During the run of* Iceman, *I met him at his apartment and we went to a nearby café for lunch. Paul was very much the Old World gentleman with his girlfriend Annie on his arm.*

When we spoke on the phone, you talked about "going off to work" with such a workingman's attitude that I imagined you heading to the theater with your lunch pail.

With the show I'm doing right now, it is like that. I'm in the theater about six hours every night. I'm on all but about twenty minutes of the first act and fifteen minutes of the second act, about four hours.

What do you think about when you're onstage that long?

Depends on how it's going that night. Sometimes I'm thinking about how bad it's going. It's funny, this play taught me a lot about acting. I made some mistakes in the way I approached it right from the start which, unfortunately, I'm still compensating for. I was intimidated by the material and the company I was working with, probably because I was out of work for seven months before this. To go through that experience is demoralizing.

How did that affect your work in *Iceman*?

I spent a lot of the early period of rehearsal and performance proving I was a good actor. It got in the way of doing the work of sitting down, looking at the play, and really deducing what this character is about, what he wants, and what's in his way. Instead, I spent some rehearsal time aborting my instincts in the well-meaning but mistaken attempt to do something good *right now*. Rather than following the recipe I know works, I jumped steps. I placed these other people I was working with up there, and I felt I had to keep up with them. So in the first performances, I think it's fair to say that I was making a lot of noise.

I'll tell you the truth—when I read this play the first time, I could feel it, but I didn't understand it. The play is so long, and I grew up not reading very much, unfortunately. Now I'm paying for it. I should have read the whole play three to five times before rehearsal and at least once a week during rehearsal. I worked on the individual scenes, but because I didn't have a really solid grasp of the whole, I would find things that worked in those scenes, but the next scene would come up and I'd be left hanging.

This is the longest run I've done so far, about twelve weeks. Before, I don't think I was able to appreciate the rewards of working on difficult material and a very interesting character for a long period of time. Now I really am aware of the subtleties you can reach, the depth of understanding not only a character but parts of yourself. I think, karmically, that's why film pays so much. You don't get the kind of rewards there are in theater.

In film, you shoot a scene in one day, and that's the last time you do it. Even though you do it over and over again, you're doing it in a span of twelve hours, as opposed to living with material for five months. If I take a napkin and put it over this cup and leave it there, at the end of the day it might have sagged a little bit. Give it about six months, and let all the weather and the rain come down on it, and that napkin's pretty much going to have the shape of that cup. You know what I'm saying? You get the subtler dimensions of the material just from exposure for that length of time.

Did you always want to be an actor?
I did, and then I didn't for a while. I was a senior in high school when I did *Landscape of the Body*, and it burnt me out, trying to go to high school and traveling back and forth to Bucks County. I never saw my friends. After that, I was exhausted. I spent the summer puttering around lawns down in Pennsylvania. In the fall, I got a call to audition for *Runaways* as a replacement. I got that part, so I moved to New York.

What made you decide to go ahead with acting?
To be really honest, I didn't know what else to do with myself. I had registered for college, and I just didn't want to go. I didn't want to stay where I was, and I didn't know what else to do with myself. This offer to do a play on Broadway came along, and I said, I guess I'll do that.

I'd been in school plays, and my dad acts in local theater in Philadelphia, so I ran lights and stuff for them—that was the first exposure I had to the professional theater. I have studied and continue to study with Uta Hagen at HB Studios. She's brilliant, so incisive without falling into the trap of thinking that because we're actors we're superior beings. She's great for young actors to be around, because a lot of us—if we're trying to take it seriously and be taken seriously—can get so self-important. I approached acting like a religion. I really did. *[He laughs.]* You know: The Work. Believe me, I don't for a minute mean to ridicule acting. I know some people who take it so lightly that it makes me angry. But it's not a religion for me any longer.

Why did you want to act in the first place?
I love to pretend. But if I'm really honest, I think I wanted to be close to my dad. My dad loved acting, still does. It was something I saw him doing and knew he liked, and I wanted to be a part of that.

How does he feel about your career?
He's really proud of me. He's a little jealous sometimes.

You've played a lot of gay characters—have you worried about being typed?
Well, you know, it's funny. I've only played three or four gay characters, but I did two films where the characters were gay, and that's what sticks in people's minds. It has been at times a source of minor frustration, I'm sorry to admit, because I'd like to think that it's unimportant. But for instance, I don't often get offered roles outright, without having to audition. Yet the majority of things for which that happens are gay roles. It's to that degree that I'm shying away. Right now, career-wise, unless I played a real queen, it wouldn't be a good idea for me to play a homosexual character. I'm interested in being thought of for other kinds of characters. Time to move on. Even with *The Hotel New Hampshire*, there was some discussion with my agent whether it would be a good career

move for me to do that. I decided to do it finally because I thought it was an interesting character in a really interesting project.

That movie had so many fascinating people in it—why did it turn out to be such a dud?

Who knows? I was too busy *[he laughs]* trying to prove myself as a serious actor.

It sounds like at some point you developed a self-conscious attitude about yourself as an actor. Was there a turning point?

I was always self-conscious, but after *Fame* came out, I became famous for a while, and there's an odd distortion that happens. It's an unusual experience to walk down the street and have strangers stop and look at you with awe, buy you drinks, buy you meals, invite you to their restaurants. It distorts your sense of yourself. I did a lot of thinking about this, and I have a theory—when's the last time in your life when everywhere you went people looked at you as if there was something awesome about you? It happened when you were a little boy, a little baby. When we're little kids, we have a lot of fantasies about the world. Let's say as a little kid I had fantasies that I could fly. As I got older and became more mature, I had to go through the disappointment of realizing that I can't really fly. Well, suddenly, when everybody starts looking at you like that, it triggers all those childhood fantasies. You think, "Well, maybe I can fly! Maybe I really am the center of the universe!" Everywhere I went for a while, it was getting reinforced. That's when I started becoming more self-conscious, because I liked the reflection I was getting, but if I couldn't fly, maybe they wouldn't look at me with awe anymore—and the fact was, I couldn't fly.

One of the reasons *The Iceman Cometh* has been a good experience is that I got singled out in *The New York Times* review as being essentially the only bad thing in an otherwise brilliant production. It was, in some ways, a nightmare come true. There's no question that it hurt my ego. But in some way it calmed the hell out of me. I didn't fall apart. I didn't go to the theater hanging my head and hiding. In a way, my biggest fear was being exposed as the only lousy thing in a brilliant play, and there it was. And look, I'm still here.

MORGAN
FREEMAN

Morgan Freeman

In Lee Breuer and Bob Telson's pop-gospel musical The Gospel at Colonus, *Morgan Freeman played a traveling preacher who went into a trance to play the part of the mythical Oedipus to the assembled congregation. But to the black woman squirming in her seat next to me exclaiming "He's my man!", Freeman was the charismatic star of NBC's soap opera* Another World. *During the two years he toured with* Gospel at Colonus *to Houston, Washington, Paris, and Los Angeles (it was also shown on PBS), he also completed the TV movie* The Atlanta Child Murders *and two features,* Marie *and* That Was Then, This Is Now. *When I met him at his rambling, nothing-fancy Upper West Side apartment, he had just returned from doing* Gospel *in Los Angeles and was taking a break. He was thinner in person than I expected (onstage, he towers), but relaxed and friendly.*

Did you always want to be an actor?

Always, except for a short period between sixteen and twenty, when I wanted to be a jet jockey. When I graduated from high school, I went into the Air Force. It convinced me really quick, "What you really like to do is *pretend* to fly, with the camera sitting right over there, clouds in the background."

What did your mother think about your wanting to be an actor?

She was all for it. She was always telling me when I was a kid, "Boy, I'm going to take you to Hollywood"—I must have heard that I don't know how many times. And she was always my best audience in school, sitting up front laughing and crying.

When I got out of the service, I went to Hollywood. [*He mimes getting a pie in the face.*] I bought a trench coat and a porkpie hat. I had on my brown suit and my wide cable-sole tan shoes. I got on a bus and after about a half-day of riding I wound up in Hollywood somewhere. Paramount had an office up there by Capitol Records at the time, and I didn't know from agents. I walked in. This blond sitting at the desk said, "May I help you?" I said, "My name is Morgan Freeman, and I'm an actor looking for a job." She gave me some slips and said, "Fill those out." I went in this little booth, and there were questions like what office machines can you operate and how many words can you type. I filled out what I could and left. That was my Hollywood experience.

I finally got a job at Los Angeles Community College as a clerk. You could go to school for free if you were working there. I had gotten out of the service in February, didn't get a job 'til May, and didn't have any money. So I learned to deal seriously with hunger. I didn't eat for days. I had some friends, but I went to visit them so often that by the end of April, pride wouldn't let me keep going. It's one thing to have a couple of dollars in your pocket and go to somebody's house and have dinner. But to have absolutely nothing in your pocket . . . I got to where I couldn't eat anything but milk and raw eggs. I'd beat 'em up in a glass, and that'd be a meal.

But nothing comes easy.

So I got into school at Los Angeles Community College. Part of the curriculum was dance movement, and the instructor told me, "You have such a knack for this, you should go into it." In 1961 I dove headfirst into dance, and I was in it for four or five years until it dawned on me that I had branched off the center line. I was in it for acting, not dance. In 1966 I got an understudy part in *The Royal Hunt of the Sun*, along with being in a chorus of Incas. One night one of the stars collapsed onstage, and I got to do the part. It was, like "Yeah! This is right! Acting!" That's what I was supposed to be doing. After that, my acting career just took off.

What made the difference?
Luck. My first job in New York was a play called *The Niggerlovers*. Stacy Keach was in that, and his agent, Jeff Hunter, saw me and liked me and sent me out for some stuff. I went into *Hello, Dolly!* with Pearl Bailey's company. One thing led to another, and in 1971 *The Electric Company* started up and I got a job there. Five years, nine to five, four months out of the year. I had lots of time to play, sail my boat, go skiing, make money. However, I had only planned to do it for a couple of years. When you're young, it doesn't make any sense to do a long series. Your career becomes very finite. But for an actor who's making money, the hardest thing to do is walk away from it. I was developing ulcers and a drinking problem, and my first marriage started to crumble over the fact that I was doing something I didn't want to do anymore. But they know all the right ways to stroke you, particularly with money. I'm always broke.

In 1979, Joe Papp started the short-lived Shakey Rep, as we used to call it. Joe had seen me at my absolute best in a Broadway play in 1978, Richard Wesley's *The Mighty Gents*. I was the new kid on the block, and everybody was talkin' about me. So when they started up the Shakey Rep, I went down to audition for him, but I don't audition well, and I just barely squeaked in. I got the part of Casca in *Julius Caesar*. Then the press got ahold of the whole thing. Edith Oliver in the *New Yorker* said, "And Morgan Freeman was playing Casca—*a star if there ever was one.*" The next play was *Coriolanus*, and Clarence Williams III was originally playing the part. But the director was not satisfied, and because of the reviews from *Julius Caesar* they let Clarence Williams go and I got the part and . . . [*He leads me over to his hallway and shows me his framed Obie Award for his performances in* Coriolanus *and* Mother Courage.] Well, it was a marvelous experience, to do a lead role in Shakespeare and get this award.

Was that your first award?
No, this was my first award. [*He picks up a clear glass paperweight, inscribed "Clarence Derwent Award."*] And I got the Drama Desk Award and a Tony nomination for *The Mighty Gents*.

Which played about a week, right?
A week. It just angered me to death. I took it very personally that they closed the show. It made no sense at all to do it on Broadway. When they move something to Broadway, I don't care what it is, they want to Broadwayize it. If it's a nice, heavy, long piece of drama, they're gonna water it down so it fits this medium [*he points to the television*], which is what Broadway aspires to. They have to appeal to the great number of people, which is the lowest common denominator. That's why I have no desire at all to be on Broadway anymore. When you first come to New York, that's the place to be. Well, I've done Broadway now four times. That's enough.

When you moved to New York, did you think that you would also do movies?
I started out to do movies! I was going to be the first black actor to win an Academy Award—my whole thrust was to do that. We were in the movies by then. Sidney Poitier was getting to be a big name, so I knew there was room.

Were there actors you looked to as role models or inspirations for your career?

For my career, no. For my acting, yeah. Gary Cooper. Bogart. And later in life, James Cagney. They go right at the role, and that's all they do. No personality bullshit. I did most of my learning in my first play onstage from Stacy Keach, just watching him prepare.

What did you pick up from Stacy Keach?

Trust. Part of acting is having the security to turn yourself loose and let yourself go in order to reach whatever depths a character has. If your guts aren't hanging out there, you don't offer anything. I'm forty-eight, I've been doing it professionally now for twenty years. Early on, I had to learn the technique of getting into a role. Once you get into it, getting it across is nothing. Audiences believe what you believe. It's a matter of believing yourself. If I believe me, then you've got no choice. None at all.

AIDAN
QUINN

Aidan Quinn

The son of a schoolteacher and a bookkeeper, Aidan Quinn spent a few years in Ireland as a child (his name means "fire" in Gaelic), but he chiefly grew up in Chicago, and he got his start as an actor in the same fertile theater scene that produced John Malkovich and the other well-known members of the Steppenwolf Theater Company. By the time he was twenty-six he'd been working hard for years. When he arrived at my apartment, he'd been playing in Sam Shepard's four-hour A Lie of the Mind *for almost six months, and he was so tired that his glittery blue eyes were rimmed in red, and his husky voice barely got above a whisper.*

I haven't had a break for two years, and I'm sick of working. I did a play in Chicago that won the best new play of 1984, Marisha Chamberlin's *Scheherazade*. Right after that I came here and did *Fool for Love*, then *Desperately Seeking Susan*. I went straight from that to *Hamlet* for five months, straight from that to *The Mission*, straight from that to Sundance for three weeks' work, straight from that to *An Early Frost*, straight from that to *A Lie of the Mind*. And I'm tired. A lot of it's not high-visibility stuff—it's either theater, or movies not released yet—so if you say you want to take a rest, people in Hollywood say, "From *Desperately Seeking Susan?* That was a year ago."

How did you end up being in *Fool for Love?*

Right after I finished *Scheherazade*, I was supposed to do *The Seagull* up in Williamstown, so I came to New York to meet Nikos [Psacharopolous]. That fell through, so I was just hanging out here for a couple of days. Some people from Steppenwolf were having a big party for *Balm in Gilead*, and when I walked in, Moira Harris, who was doing *Fool for Love* at the time, attacked me and said, "You have got to play Eddie! You're the perfect one! They've been looking for months, and they can't find anybody." She was going crazy, because she was doing it with an understudy. I didn't even know what the play was. She gave me the script, I read it that night, had an audition the next day, and I got the part. I went home, packed some bags, came back here, and two days later met the girl I've been with ever since.

How long did you do *Fool for Love?*

Ten weeks. I don't like long runs. I'll do them, but I don't look forward to it. I would love to play Edmund in *Long Day's Journey*. I wouldn't mind doing that for six months or so. That's the kind of role you can grow with. Hamlet I did as long as I could. It was an incredibly physical production. I lost four pounds on Sundays when we did two shows. It was the most exhausting, the most fun, the most challenging, the most physical, and the greatest role ever.

Aidan played Hamlet at the Wisdom Bridge Theater in Chicago in an award-winning production, directed by Robert Falls, whose most sensational moment came at the beginning of Hamlet's most famous soliloquy. Aidan walked onstage with a can of spray paint, wrote on the wall "TO BE," underlined it, wrote underneath "NOT TO BE," turned to the audience and said, "That is the question."

163

Had you ever seen *Hamlet* before you played it?

I saw Olivier's movie, which put me to sleep. I had seen a German version years and years ago in a movie. Once I was in rehearsal, I saw Derek Jacobi's on PBS, which was horribly directed and horribly cast, but he was very interesting. I'd never seen a production of it.

Did you always want to be an actor?

No. I never even thought about it until I was nineteen. I was sitting on the top of a high-rise building I was working on as a roofer overlooking the lake in Chicago. My fellow roofers were passing around the joint and the whiskey at seven-thirty in the morning. For the third morning in a row, I was about to take a slug of whiskey, and I thought, "Wait a minute." I passed it back and thought, "What am I going to do with my fuckin' life?" I wanted to be a writer above all things. I didn't have the discipline for it, so I decided to be an actor. I went home and looked up an ad for an acting class in the *Reader*, which is a free paper in Chicago, and called up this guy. We ended up talking for an hour. I went to his class, and he offered me a scholarship, because I didn't have any money. In two months I was doing a show with him. It was like, boom! I just loved it. I liked the discipline. The attention. I don't know how to explain it.

Did you keep studying acting?

I haven't studied very much. I took classes with this one great guy, Edward K. Martin, who adapted Sanford Meisner's teaching to his own method. He stressed being in the moment, and doing your homework—the character's past life, what you did just before you went in the room, what you want, what past history you had with the person you're doing the scene with. I only had a four-week course with him, but he was brilliant. Since then, I never studied, because I've been working.

When you're in this long run of *A Lie of the Mind*, what do you do during the day?

I don't do much of anything, because we don't get out of the theater until twelve-thirty, I'm so wound up that I don't get to sleep 'til at least four, and I don't get up until noon or one, sometimes two. I love the play, and I love when I'm onstage, but I hate that you don't have any life but the theater.

What do you miss the most?

Living. Experimenting, meeting new people, exchanging ideas, reading novels. I don't read anymore. I cannot absorb myself in anything with content while I'm working on something else. It's been a couple of years since I read a good novel. And I was a bookworm when I was a teenager! On the other hand, it's tremendous discipline. When I was doing *Hamlet*, I had to do an hour and a half of yoga every day just to cool out. Acting can keep you very healthy. I haven't had a cold in years.

When you started doing plays in Chicago, did you have it in mind to move to New York?

I never thought I'd work here, and I don't consider myself to have moved here. I still live in Chicago. I don't particularly like New York City except to visit. It's very easy, by comparison, to live in Chicago, because rents are cheaper, and people aren't so crazed about their careers. Everyone in New York is after something. It's a very invigorating city and very frustrating. Sometimes I love it, but I don't want to live here.

What's the hardest thing for you to do as an actor?

Photo shoots. I loathe them. I'm too arrogant and too humble at the same time to let them just be what they are. I do a little bit of publicity because if you don't and you're doing stuff like I'm doing—theater—people don't hear about you and don't think about you. Today you have these media creations, whose value has nothing to do with either their talent as actors or their actual box office. So you have to do some publicity because, one, you like the attention (any actor who says he doesn't is full of bullshit), and two, because what roles you'll be considered for is determined to a certain extent by your visibility.

The way you talk about working in theater, it sounds like being dropped into the bowels of the earth where people can't reach you.

That's how a lot of people perceive it. For instance, when *Reckless* came out and was a big dud, I was doing *Hamlet*. *People* magazine wanted to do a thing about *Hamlet*, and I said, "Absolutely not. I will not be in that magazine." My agent talked to me very soundly. He said, "Look, here's what's happening. There's a lot of people who were really impressed with you in *Reckless*, and the word on you is, 'What ever happened to Aidan Quinn already?'" It didn't matter that I'd been working nonstop in the theater for a year and a half. He said, "Just do this, because it will fill in that gap for them."

How did *Reckless* happen?

This woman came to Chicago on a talent search, and my agent sent me up for it. She had me do a reading on videotape, she took a Polaroid of me, and that was that. Then in London she met someone who was friends with Jamie Foley, the director of *Reckless*, and because she was well-known in casting, he explained the part and asked if she knew anyone who would be good for it. She said, "I know someone who's perfect," and she gave him the Polaroid with the instruction that I didn't have a phone number and she couldn't remember my agent's name. So he took the photo back to Jamie Foley with this information. Foley laughed and said, "What am I supposed to do, track this guy down in Chicago from a stupid Polaroid? Get serious. It doesn't happen that way."

They had another week of auditions for this role, and Jamie told me later that every night he would come back to where he was staying and he'd see this Polaroid. He kept looking at it. Finally, he got someone on the case, they contacted my agent and got hold of the audition tape that woman had made. They looked at that and then flew me out there to L.A. They sent me the script first, and I read it in the back of a Greyhound bus. I closed the script and said, "I'm going to get this part." I just knew it was going to happen. Then I thought, "Omigod, you can't think like that, you'll fuck yourself up." When I went to L.A., I had a cold . . .

Your last cold?

You're right, I think it was. I went into the audition so sick I was totally relaxed. They showed the audition to all the executives at MGM, they thought about it for thirty seconds, and then they hired me.

Did *Reckless* make you a lot of money?

No. When you're a nobody, they pay you the minimum. I got $18,000, out of which I had to pay taxes and the agent and all that. Maybe I got $10,000, and I spent that. In three months I was back working as a cocktail waiter in a bar in Chicago. I would meet actors, too, who knew I did the movie. They'd go, "What are you doing working as a waiter? We heard you starred in this movie." I'd go, "Yeah, I did. Uh, can I take your order?"

JIMMIE RAY
WEEKS

Jimmie Ray Weeks

Jimmie Ray Weeks has had an unusual life. As a small child, he lived for a while in Alaska when it was still a territory. At eighteen, he joined the Air Force for four years, then put himself through college on the G.I. bill, collecting a degree in abnormal psychology from the University of Oregon. After reading an article about struggling actors in Life *magazine, he borrowed $500 and moved to New York, where he worked on the psychiatric ward at Harlem Hospital by day and studied at the American Academy of Dramatic Arts by night. After his first Broadway success in* My Fat Friend, *he went to Hollywood and spent nearly two years unemployed. Moving back to New York, he became a valued member of the Circle Repertory Company, acting in plays by Lanford Wilson, John Bishop, and Patrick Meyers.*

Does it surprise you that you're an actor?

It does. Not just me. I've had people ask me what I do, and when I say I'm an actor, they look at me like, "You're kidding." People say, "You don't look like an actor." I take that as a compliment.

How did you get interested in the theater?

When I was in the Air Force, I picked up this book by Boleslavsky, then I found Stanislavsky, and I started reading lots of biographies of actors. I'm so laid-back—passive, I guess—that I love to read about people who take control and have the chutzpah to get what they want. This is a crazy business, and one of the things you have to do is get out and meet people and PR yourself. I feel very uneasy about doing it, since I don't come from a family that tells you, "Look, you can get anything you want, all you have to do is go get it." We always played by the rules, always. Then later on you find out that there are people who didn't get intimidated by thinking if you don't do such-and-such you're going to be lonely and poor all your life. I thought if you just studied and worked hard, there was nothing else needed.

I kind of figured I wouldn't be working as an actor 'til I got into my forties anyway. I was prematurely bald, and I had a young-looking face, so what the hell do you do? I'm not a character, I'm not a leading man, there's no other place to go. So it makes me feel better to see that John Malkovich's hair is falling out.

You couldn't get cast because you were prematurely bald?

Yeah. I didn't really want to get a hairpiece. I got my teeth bonded, because there were spaces between them, but I drew the line at a hairpiece. I always had an affinity toward character actors, yet I had the appearance of being a jock or a soldier or a cop. I've always wanted to do eccentric things—not necessarily put a lot of makeup on, but flavor a role with something I got inside of me. I get a kick out of some of Pinter's characters—their raw, self-destructive violence, their whining. I like that crazy stuff.

So there's a different personality inside you that's at odds with your physical appearance?

At least three or four. Part of it comes from not wanting to face what I look like. I never considered myself appealing in high school. I didn't date hardly at all. I never learned to dance. I'm more accepting of myself now. When you're younger, there's so much raw emotion. Now, I'm just me, a middle-aged bald-headed guy looking for work.

Are there actors you look to as role models for your career?
    I don't have any role models. I like this guy Bertrand Russell. Do you know who that is?

Sure. He's a great actor.
    He's sort of my hero.

CHARLES
LUDLAM

Charles Ludlam

Charles Ludlam is one of the flaming creatures of the New York stage. A sensational comic performer—legendary especially for his gender-bending performances as Camille, Maria Callas, and Flaubert's Salammbo—he is also a prolific playwright and the visionary director of the Ridiculous Theatrical Company, which started in 1967 playing midnight shows in the back of seedy bars and now has its own modest home in Sheridan Square. As its name suggests, the Ridiculous Theater embraces outrageousness, parody, camp, and all manner of comic exaggeration, but Ludlam himself is a determined theater artist who brings an extraordinary erudition to each carefully scripted show, whether it's a Molière update, a 1940s melodrama, or a gothic horror story. He has taught theater at Yale and New York University, among other schools, and in 1984 was invited to star in Hedda Gabler *at the American Ibsen Theater in Pittsburgh.*

Onstage Charles is usually elaborately costumed and made up. In person, he is a balding guy in blue jeans and cowboy boots. He was performing two shows in repertory when we met, The Mystery of Irma Vep *and* Salammbo. *The latter had recently opened to vociferously negative reviews from mainstream critics, which Charles attributed to the conservatism that would dismiss the Ridiculous as gay theater for a cult audience. "Most gay theater either apologizes or pleads for mercy. What I do is not gay theater—it's something much worse," he said. "I don't ask to be tolerated. I don't mind being intolerable."*

Are there actors you admire that you've taken inspiration from?

Charles Laughton, Marie Dressler. Those are role models in case I gain a lot of weight. For my thin period, of course, there's always Garbo. You know who I really admire, though? Ginger Rogers. I realized something recently: she's an incredibly good actress. Not just the dancing and being able to do serious things in light comedy: there's always such a clarity.

All those people are movie actors.

That's what I saw growing up. That's why I think I will probably end up in the movies. Theater was probably the most natural thing for me to go to, because I'm a hands-on person and I wanted artistic control.

What made you want to act in the first place?

My mother used to take me to the movie theater across the street from our apartment in Hyde Park a couple of times a week. I had a big fantasy life. I was an only child for a long time—about seven years. Until my brother was born, I entertained myself. Parents worry that you're going to be an actor. My mother always wanted me to be a teacher. That would be a respectable, genteel, intellectual thing to do. Funny, if I'd gone into teaching, I'd probably be unemployed today. But I've gotten lots of jobs teaching because I act, because I have my theater.

I've never really taught acting, just *commedia dell'arte* improvisation. I teach them to be decisive and go all the way and not be critical of yourself. If you edit yourself, it's very inhibiting. There's some point in the creative process where you have to suspend the critical faculty. When I first started, I was corrupted by being overly educated. You learn too many things, then you get confused.

When I was studying Method acting, I started to find it very inhibiting. You know, Stanislavsky arrived at all these techniques from watching actors who didn't know what they were doing and trying to figure out what they were doing. If you go backwards from the rules, it becomes very deadening. It's hard to justify everything all the time and wonder, "Am I playing an intention? Do I have my motivation?" I try to go against whatever inhibiting criticism I feel. Sometimes I will set out to do it wrong. "I'm going to write the most incomprehensible play ever." Sometimes I tell an actor who seems inhibited, "Do it the way you worst-fear that it would come out. Let's see that, and then we'll know what that is."

Are you ever afraid of being bad as an actor?

Everyone is. There are nights when the whole thing seems to be rushing by so fast, and it's over, and I don't feel I even did anything. The audience could be cheering, and it feels like, "What was that?" Or you might hit it on a certain night, and then you go, "That's it, but what was it? How can I make it happen again? How can I make it visible to others that I felt it?" Things felt are not things perceived. That's another problem with acting. You might have a wonderful feeling at the moment, but the audience sees nothing. And you can't *try* to have an emotion. All the slow acting you see is from *trying* to have an emotion. It never comes that way. It's the byproduct of an action. So you really have to set up the action so it produces the feeling.

What's it like to play in the same theater so long?

It's nice to have your own theater, because you can rehearse. The first five years we never rehearsed in the space we performed in—ever. Ever! We would often be given half an hour to bring the set in, set it up, light it, and play. It was a terrible disadvantage.

I always wanted to have a theater in the Village, from the time I was a teenager and saw the Living Theater on Fourteenth Street. Julian Beck is sort of my idol. What they did on Fourteenth Street was really quite different from their later work. It was a theater of poetry and symbol, with literature and real acting, and that was the thing that inspired me. Then I saw them do *The Brig*, where they just tortured the actors for two hours. It was agony to sit through, but artistically it was such a bold step. As a young theater artist, I was in awe of it. Nothing mattered except this production. I knew that everything would have to be like this from now on, but I couldn't go there. My whole generation followed them over the edge into physical, ritualistic theater.

The ritual theater had a lot of credibility in a period when everybody wanted peace. Because it was not representing a conflict, it seemed to embody the ideals of that generation. A drama is a war, a conflict. I realize that I don't want peace. I don't believe in peace. I want war. That made me feel very out of touch during the '60s. I went through a lot of crisis about it, too. It's not easy when there's a major artist whose light is so blinding. To follow is to give up your creative life in a sense, and to try to do anything else seems so stupid. But I wanted to act, and I saw there would be no place for actors in that theater. I wanted to play roles, I wanted the pretense, mimesis—imitation of an action. And I felt there had to be something wrong with a theater that had no place for a major figure, the actor.

An actor has to be hired, and that means that he has to wait for someone else to imagine the role. It's a tremendous handicap. You could work your whole life and never have roles that add up to a career. You could make a lot of money and never really find creative continuity. Also, sometimes you'll have a director who'll want you to tone it down. That might not be what you want to do in your life. Maybe you really want to get violent about it or get really vulgar or garish and overdo it.

Do the actors in your company have the same freedom you do?

They have a lot of freedom. It's not that easy to be free. You don't come that way.

How do you write for yourself as an actor?

With *Galas*, the challenge was to try to create a modern woman who was a real person [Maria Callas]. It had to hold up, because people knew what she looked like. To do a two-man show was a challenge Everett [Quinton, the actor and costume designer with whom Ludlam lives] and I set for ourselves with *The Mystery of Irma Vep*: to change costumes that fast and to play all those characters. I'd just done a show with a huge cast, and I wanted a chance to work on the fine points of my own acting. Videotape has been a tremendous plus. After a certain number of previews, we tape the show. Then I can look at the staging and give myself notes.

What was it like to play Hedda Gabler "straight"?

Fabulous. What I really wanted out of that experience was to be intimately familiar with an Ibsen play. I've read pretty much all of Ibsen's plays, but they're so intricate—actors really know plays from doing them night after night. They know all the places the seams don't quite fit, as well as the great moments. I wanted to have that familiarity; I thought it would be very good for me as a playwright, and it was. For instance, I realized that *Hedda* has the same plot as an early play he wrote called *The Vikings at Helgeland*. The characters in *Hedda Gabler* are gods and goddesses and heroes manqué, reborn into a drawing room, and they're playing out the same plot. It is so weird when you realize it's the same play. In fact, at the end of *The Vikings*, Hjørdis, who is this sort of Valkyrie character who also kills herself, much like Hedda, is riding off into the clouds on a winged horse. And her kid says to his father, "Look, there's Mother! Can't you see her, riding through the clouds on a horse?" Curtain. The first time you hear about Hedda, the aunt says, "Oh, remember when we first saw Hedda riding by the house with her cape flowing in the wind and a feather in her hat?" And you realize that Hedda is galloping out of Norse mythology into the modern drawing room, where she can't possibly fulfill herself, she's so big. These characters are deities who have these huge heroic passions and desires and they're being boxed in.

It was a very difficult role, Hedda Gabler. You could walk through it, say all the lines, be perfectly charming, and never know what it meant. People used to come back and say, "I never knew that's what that line is about." Just to make it clear is the hardest thing in the world to do. In *Hedda*, there are three or four moments where she goes "Ah" or "Oh" or "Ooh." They're very oblique, very hard to play, because you feel that nobody's going to pay any attention to you saying those things. Yet those were the epiphanies, the moments where she makes her mental connection and goes to the next step. If you can understand those lines—the "Ah" and the "Oh" and the "Ooh" and the "Eh"—you have the role.

Have you had a lot of offers to work outside your company?

More and more. I can't do them all, because you have to keep your focus or you become just another person in the world with no continuity. I really do stand for something, and I have certain ideals of what I think the theater can be.

What sort of things tempt you to work outside your company?

Operas. I've done a lot of parodies of operas and people said, "Oh, it's better than the original." I wanted to see what I could really do with an opera. Films I like. I'm making my own movies now. Everett and I were on *Miami Vice*. I was in drag, and he was a gangster.

Isn't it weird to do a little TV thing and use a smidgen of what you can do, yet have that seen by . . .

More people than have seen you onstage in your whole life? Yeah, it is weird. It's tremendously difficult work, TV and movie acting. A tremendous amount of waiting around, tedium. But it's kind of fun to do something that drains you for one day and not have to do it day in and day out.

What's the hardest thing you've ever had to do as an actor?

I was playing Puck in college, and I had to jump off an upper level of the stage at Hofstra. There was all this machismo: "Everybody else jumps off there." I was so afraid, and it was so high, and I had these awful bedroom slippers on, and I jumped down and broke all my toes.

What's the silliest thing for you about being an actor?

The audience can never know what you're thinking when you're acting, and there's a certain campiness to that. If I see someone asleep in the audience, I have a lot of trouble not getting the giggles. Or they talk and don't think you can hear. Or cellophane wrappers. I hope there's a special circle in hell for people who rattle cellophane or have those watches that beep.

One time Bill Vehr and I were playing the scene in *Reverse Psychology* where I'm having an affair with his wife, and I don't know that it's his wife, and I start to tell him things she does in bed. It's a very funny scene, and it's hard not to crack up, because Bill does all those great shocked reactions. He tries to crack you up onstage anyway, if he can. So we were doing this scene, and he had lots, of "Oh, really?" and "Tell me more." Well, every time we started to talk, someone would rattle their cellophane. We were staring at each other in disbelief, because it was so loud. It was unbelievably loud, like it was amplified. Rattle ratttle. You'd pause, it would pause. You'd start talking, and it would start again. You'd pause, and it would stop. You'd talk, and it would rattle. We had tears streaming down our cheeks trying to hold that in.

JOHN
GLOVER

John Glover

John Glover is the kind of actor who's likely to turn up anywhere, playing any-thing—a meaty role in a classic, second-banana in a drawing-room comedy, a minor functionary in a big movie, a scene-stealer in a TV drama, the replacement for the star in a long-running show, the offbeat leading man in an Off-Broadway play. When we met, he'd just finished the HBO movie Apology *in Canada and an episode of* Twilight Zone *in Los Angeles. Two weeks had passed, though, and he didn't have his next job lined up, so he was feeling fragile the way only an actor can. No matter how much you've worked, there's no guarantee that a tem-porary state of unemployment will not continue forever.*

I'm trying to be out of work and only do good things, if I can. I've done two things lately, *An Early Frost* and *White Nights*, that have gotten a lot of atten-tion, and I hope that the two of them combined will stick me up on the next rung. It's hard, though. I don't know how to be out of work well.

Did you always want to be an actor?

Yeah. When I was little, I knew I wanted to entertain people. But then I got mixed up in high school with fears about how I would do it. I came from a small town in Maryland, this very isolated town on the peninsula called Salisbury. I'd never been to New York until I got to college, to see any real theater. So I figured I should just teach drama, be the one who directs the plays or whatever. But I went to summer stock when I was in college, I worked with actors who were making their lives acting, so I figured I could do it.

When I got out of school in 1966 and moved to New York, so many of the people I was competing with for roles had been to all those theater schools. Towson State meant nothing because nobody had ever gone on to be an actor from that school before. That's why I went and worked at regional theaters where I could get jobs.

Did you work in New York at all?

Yes, I worked at the 81st Street Theater—I sold the orange drinks at intermis-sion. I got a job in a children's theater doing *The Adventures of Tom Sawyer*. I was Huck Finn. We had a station wagon with a trailer on the back, which was our set. We left from the Port Authority every morning, and we'd go out to elementary schools in Connecticut, New Jersey, Long Island, and set up our little poles and scaffolds and platforms and perform the show, then take it all down and load it up and drive back. That was my first tour.

What drove you to seek a career as an actor?

I don't know. I was always afraid. Afraid to try out for a play, afraid to be in the play, afraid to say to myself that I wanted to be an actor. But then when I moved to New York, I felt fearless. It was what I had to do, what I wanted to do, so I did it. People I went to school with were always amazed that I did it.

What got you over your fear?

I went to the Barter Theater in Abingdon, Virginia, started by Robert Porter-field. Mr. P always used to say the person who was right for the part would get it, so even though I was an apprentice and still in college, I got to play some terrific roles. That made me feel either confident or arrogant. When I came to New York, I had more confidence then than I have now. "When ignorance is bliss, folly can be wise." I felt like a steamroller, and I knew I had to work, so I went up to those theaters and worked and worked. Which sometimes has been a detriment to my career, or so agents have told me. When I've gotten momentum started here in the city, when I've done a bunch of plays here or started doing films, I would take a great job somewhere across the country because I wanted to play a part. It must have been some kind of fear thing. Do you know Victor Garber? When he incorporated himself, he called the corporation F.O.G.—which stands for Fear of Greatness. As soon as he said it, this whole kind of thing started relaxing in me. I understood that I was standing off from a certain kind of success. Hmm. I'm getting hot and flushed as I say this. Maybe I should go to my analyst and come back and talk to you some more about this.

You seem to have chosen not to go for flashy, visible work.

It's more relaxing that way. I sometimes do the best performance in a play on a matinee with a very small house. So maybe that's why I'll go to San Diego. But also I've gone there because I've been offered four incredible roles to play —a season any actor would drool over. It's incredibly hard work. But the last time I went, my agent said, "Don't go, you're just starting to click now in movies." I said, "Yes, but these four roles!" He said, "Everybody knows you can do that." And I thought, "Well, I don't know I can. Maybe I can't." So I went and did it and had a very successful season and came back to New York and felt like I started over again.

When you started acting, did you think you would do movies?

That's when I was fearless and arrogant. I figured I was going to do everything. After a while I thought movies were going to be impossible. I couldn't figure out how to make it happen.

What was your first movie?

It was a Burt Reynolds movie called *Shamus*. I never understood the story. He was looking for somebody. I was a junkie who maybe knew where the person was, and he broke into a room where we were all being junkies. He fought a lot of people, there were a couple of stunt guys he threw over chairs, then I ran out and he chased me. He was supposed to beat me up and kick me, and Burt decided that he'd been kicking too many people in the movie, and maybe he should do something different with me. It was down in this garbage heap, so they dumped a couple of cans of minestrone soup in the garbage, and he took me by the hair and he pushed my face down into it, pulled me up and asked me the question. There was a lima bean, actually, that rolled down my face while I played this scene. That was my film debut.

I've tried not to type myself, although I know I have in films. I'm trying to untype myself. I guess because I played the schmuck in *Julia*, I got all these parts that were either villains or creeps. I did that for a while, because I wanted to work. Now I'm trying to devote some mystic concentration to make myself unvillainous. That's why I was so excited to do *White Nights*, because the part wasn't a villain, somebody who was smarmy or trying to get somebody in trouble.

What's embarrassing is when people say, "I know you—you're an actor, right?" I go, "Yeah," and they say, "Maybe I've seen you. What have you done?" I've done so much, but none of them has really been successful. You know how they write Kevin "Big Chill" Kline? I don't have one of those. I guess the closest thing to that is *An Early Frost*.

I felt great about that show, yet I never felt so glad when it was over. It was the most frightening thing I've ever done, because it was actually happening. I kept getting mixed up between what was fiction and what was fact. I only had four little scenes, so I rehearsed a week, then came back later and worked three days. Aidan was very upset, because he was with it every day.

Did it feel daring to play a campy queen very sick with AIDS?

I wanted it as real as possible. The director, John Erman, made an atmosphere on the set where anything could happen. The scene where I made my will, I lay in the hospital bed while they set up the lights. The crew was working, and they'd lean on my foot or whatever they had to do, but they worked with a kind of quietness because they understood why I had to lay in the bed before we shot the scene.

Normally you would be in your dressing room while they're setting the lights?

Yeah. It was hard. The medical advisor, an L.A. doctor who works with a lot of AIDS patients, took me to meet four guys one Friday. The last one was a doctor who was in terrible shape. He had not many days left on the earth. It was very upsetting. It unlocked all kinds of fears in me. I knew when I was in the bed I had to find a way to let that come out of me, what happened when he spoke. He was all covered with lesions on his tongue and in his throat, and there were things happening to his body. We rehearsed, but I didn't know until we did it how it was going to be. I had to rely on a kind of mystic thing that I so believe is there. Like Vanessa Redgrave—I believe what comes out of her when she acts is some kind of mysticism. When I was in London shooting *Julia*, I'd sometimes watch her and Jane Fonda shoot a scene, and I saw the ease with which she did it. I'm sure there was an incredible amount of preparation that went into it. But what comes out is mystical to me.

What's your favorite thing about being an actor?

I guess getting to escape. To get to play, pretend.

What's the silliest thing about being an actor?

The same thing. [*He laughs*] Dressing up. Seeing the world in the shitty shape it's in and being so concerned about all those things that go into a role seems very silly to me, but they're my concerns.

For every play and every movie, do you change clothes completely?

No. I keep my underwear on. I try to have different shoes for everything. I did some TV thing where they gave me the wrong pair of shoes, a really cheap pair of shoes for a guy who's supposed to be very expensive. It was difficult. Shoes are very important to me.

Do you generally like to do exterior things in creating characters?

I do, yeah. I start on the outside and find some way I think I should look. It usually happens with my hair a lot. I make it a different color or cut it or do something strange. I feel like I'm a character actor more than a leading one. There are those actors who bring a certain part of themselves to a role. I don't do that. I feel most comfortable when I'm escaping, being somebody else. To really get away makes me feel comfortable. I guess the hardest thing to do as an actor, is to play things that are closest to myself. I think the reason I am an actor is the joy I find from escaping and going to be somebody else. That's what I have fun doing. I have to remember this when I go home and wonder if the phone has rung: the reason I'm doing this is because it brings me pleasure.

RAUL
JULIA

Raul Julia

Bill Hurt was once asked in an interview whether he found it monotonous to make Kiss of the Spider Woman, *a film that takes place almost entirely in a prison cell between two actors. He replied, "What more do you need to go to work every day than Raul Julia's eyes?" Although the Puerto Rican-born actor has played a fair share of ethnic characters and speaks with an unmistakable Spanish accent, he has managed to avoid being exclusively pegged as a Latin lover or a Ricky Ricardo stereotype. He's played everything from Prospero in* The Tempest *in Central Park to Jerry in Harold Pinter's* Betrayal *on Broadway, and as a member of Francis Ford Coppola's short-lived repertory company, he appeared with Teri Garr, Nastassja Kinski, and Fred Forrest in* One *from the Heart and* The Escape Artist.*

During our conversation, when the issue of his age came up, Raul mentioned that he thought an actor shouldn't reveal his age—not out of vanity but for practical reasons.

Unfortunately, the hiring of actors is decided by people with very little knowledge of acting. They just see types and ages. They don't understand that actors have ranges. They can dismiss someone for a part just because of a number. When asked, I usually say I don't believe an actor should say his age, or I say younger. Because if you're thirty, they think you can play forty, but if you're thirty, oh, you can never play twenty-five or twenty. It's really a pain in the ass.

Did you come to New York from San Juan?

Yes. My father was a businessman; he had a restaurant there. He was the first man to bring pizzas to Puerto Rico. At the University of Puerto Rico, I studied history, literature, philosophy, but never acting. My family expected me to become a lawyer. But I decided that what I really liked to do was acting. That was it. I came to New York in 1964.

Was that automatic? To be an actor, you had to move to New York?

No, I was thinking of going to Europe, to Rome. Then I met Orson Bean on vacation in Puerto Rico, and he said, "Why don't you come to New York? I think it would be very good for you." I came to New York for a week or so and I saw all the Broadway theaters. It was so exciting to have one theater after another, all open to the public, with people going like to the movies, by thousands, to many plays the same night. The fact that I could actually make a living at it was exciting.

When I came to America, I didn't want to be typed just playing Latins. Joe Papp saw me playing Macduff in a Spanish-language production of *Macbeth* and asked me to audition for *Titus Andronicus* in Central Park. It was my first Shakespearean play in English; that's how we established a relationship. From the beginning, he saw beyond stereotypes. We had a great time in the park. It's my favorite theater, because the audiences are from all walks of life, from Wall Street to the barrio. It's New York City. People have been picnicking and waiting in line, everybody's in a great theater mood. It's like a festival. It must be what the Globe Theater was like in Shakespeare's time.

What gave you the ability to act?

I don't know. I had it since I was five years old. The first role I ever had to play onstage was the devil. I had a beautiful costume. I looked like Mephistopheles in the opera, with the black tights, the black velvet cape and gold inside the cape, black velvet hat with the plume and two little horns. My entrance had to be really crazy, like "AAAAAGH," rolling all over the floor like this fiend. Right before I had to go on—I remember this clearly—I made the decision that I was not going to allow myself to be out of control. It was the first time I remember taking a chance, really allowing myself to be free and make a fool out of myself if necessary. I just let myself go, like I was having a fit, then got up and started saying the lines, because the devil was trying to conquer this woman's love. My mother says the audience couldn't believe it.

When you came to New York to act did you plan to do movies?

My main thing was to do theater, to do the part every night and have my dressing room in a professional situation where you get paid for it and you go home after the show. To me that's a great satisfaction. If movies came out of this, great. It took a while. I went to Dallas, Texas, to do *Bye Bye Birdie*, and then nothing happened for a long time, almost two years.

How did you support yourself?

Very badly. I had a roommate, a friend from Puerto Rico, Jim Demas, who was an actor, too. We used to buy four chicken backs for a quarter and a lot of bread and grapes—that was our dinner. During the day we used to eat very little to stretch the money. I tried selling pens in department stores, asking people to pay $2.99 for these pens that were worth 25 cents. I couldn't even go through with that. I was teaching Spanish for a while, selling magazine subscriptions and all that 'til finally I couldn't stand it anymore, and I called Joe Papp, which took a lot of guts because I didn't have the relationship with him that I have now. I told him, "Look, I'll do anything, as long as it's in the theater. I don't care. I'll clean the floors, I'll wash the toilets." He called me back and he said, "How good are you as a house manager?" I said, "I'll be the best house manager you ever had." That's how I started working with him again.

Are there actors you look to for inspiration as role models?

The first ones were the cowboys—Johnny Mack Brown, Charles Starrett—in movies that they used to ship to these little theaters in Puerto Rico. We used to see two cowboy movies and an episode of *Flash Gordon* for fifteen cents. The very first movie I saw was Cornell Wilde, he played Chopin. What was it, *A Song to Remember*? I can't even say in words what it was to see my first film. Then Errol Flynn came with *Robin Hood* and *Don Juan de Maranas*. Then came Olivier, Brando, Albert Finney, Alec Guinness—those were all great inspirations to me.

Is acting in film any different to you from acting onstage?

Yes, of course, it's all different. The technology is very different. You don't have the physical freedom in film that you have on the stage. When you're with a camera, especially in the close-ups, it's more like this kind of microscopic search of your soul, a silent scanning into your psychology, into what you're doing as the character. It's very interior. It's almost like being in a confessional —that quiet, that intimacy. Your whole reality is that camera in front of you, and you have to pretend that it's not there.

When I'm acting, I just act, and let the director tone it down. I tend to be very expressive and theatrical. But with Valentin in *Kiss of the Spider Woman*, I did something I'd never done before. I chose completely not to express anything but what was there. I felt I was taking a risk, because my tendency is to do something. If I don't do something, I feel I'm not doing my work. Throughout the years, though, I've learned that the implosion can be as powerful as the explosion. *Spider Woman* was a major step in learning how to do nothing. It was frightening for me to allow myself to do nothing, to say, "Whatever happens, happens." To me, that was a scary choice.

Because you were afraid of being bad?

Being bad, yes! Being bad in front of your director and your fellow actor! That's the worst fear in the world.

ANTHONY
ZERBE

Anthony Zerbe

Anthony Zerbe is a trouper, a supporting player, the kind of actor who never stops working. In three decades, he's done it all. He's acted on screen with Charlton Heston in Will Penny, *Paul Newman in* Cool Hand Luke, *Dustin Hoffman and Steve McQueen in* Papillon. *He's played in a zillion TV Westerns and won an Emmy for* Harry O. *He's toured the country with Roscoe Lee Browne in an evening of Shakespeare's poetry called* Behind the Broken Words. *He opened the Mark Taper Forum in Los Angeles with Gordon Davidson's production of* The Devils, *and he was in the supporting cast when Elizabeth Taylor made her Broadway debut in* The Little Foxes.

Did you always want to be an actor?

In high school, I wanted to be a lawyer. I hadn't seen a play. The first play I saw was *Picnic* in New York here with an extraordinary cast. Ralph Meeker and Janice Rule starred. Kim Stanley was in it, Eileen Heckart, Arthur O'Connell, and a young actor with blue eyes by the name of Paul Newman. Janice Rule wasn't on the night I saw it, her understudy was on. I went backstage and saw Paul Newman talking to the girl who was the understudy, whose name was Joanne.

Joanne Woodward was Janice Rule's understudy?

Yes. Then I came back and saw Janice Rule do it, because I was so struck by the play, the experience. Ralph Meeker was actually perspiring onstage! I had never seen this. They were alive, they had three dimensions, there was sound reverberating in this theater. They were feeling these things and actually doing them. They danced across the stage together and ended in this embrace where he put his hands on her ass and pulled it right into him. I was bringing a seventeen-year-old libido to it; I was dazzled. After that, I went to plays every moment I could. I thought, "I want to stand on that stage and do that." That seemed to me to be the most exciting thing anybody could ever do.

I've always felt very proud to be able to say I was an actor. I don't know why. I remember when I first saw Brando play Antony in that Mankiewicz *Julius Caesar* that I left the moviehouse thinking, "Shit, if I could ever speak those words, if I knew them in my heart, how extraordinary that would be! It would be like playing Beethoven." I don't think anybody in my lifetime has been so massively influential as Brando—the posture of the American male, both physically and psychically, was determined and inflamed by his. He was such a vivid demonstration of how visceral and exciting acting could be.

Did you always make a living as an actor?

Yes. I worked in a department store when I first got here, B. Altman's, but when they got interested in me, I left. I realized that if you had a net, you were going to fall into it. If I got a degree as a teacher in case I couldn't work as an actor, I was going to be a teacher. If I got a taxi medallion, I would be a taxi driver.

Being on the street as an actor is a hustle. I did what I needed to do to get the job. If it meant making something up, I made it up. "Are you in Equity?" "Of course I am." Then you go down to Equity and say, "I just got an Equity job, you've got to give me a card." Or, "Oh, yeah, I've done a lot of Shakespeare"—I didn't tell them it was in Stella Adler's class. You run into another actor, and it's "What are you up for? Oh, where is it? Who's doing it? Is he a good director? Who do you call? What agent do you have? Is he any good for you? Where's the theater? Is it any good? What do they pay?" I still get and disseminate that street information whenever I meet another actor.

We're getting a little more London-ish now; it's possible to take a few days off to do something in film or television so you can work in theater and still make a living as an actor. When I was doing *Cyrano* at the Long Wharf, I was paid three times as much for a scene I filmed in one afternoon with Frank Sinatra for *The First Deadly Sin* than I made during the entire rehearsal and run of the play—though it seemed like one hour of rehearsal for *Cyrano* used up as much creative energy as that afternoon with Sinatra.

What was Sinatra like to work with?

Great. All those guys are great, the Newmans and the Poitiers, Dustin, McQueen. They're not where they are by accident. It's not an easy path. Nobody fell into it backwards. I've always found those superstars are very clear about what they're doing, very conscientious and very concerned about making the best possible picture they can make.

When you're in a show, what's the last thing you do before you go on?

It changes from play to play. You are hunting for that thing that your character has done before he gets into the place you're going to. It's amazing how the backstage environment will accommodate that. Something as bizarre as a certain odor or a certain set of lights will set up the reverberation I need. If there's music playing around a piece, all I have to do is hear the music and I'm right into it. Or you smell the perfume on the actress as she's waiting to go on. Onstage, you see the holes in the rug, the little scuffed corner of the couch, you know the lights, certain gels, the exit signs—you're not conscious of them, but all those configurations come together to make an environment, and when you're in that environment, certain feelings begin to take place. Then you lurch off into what you have to do.

What's the first thing you do when you come offstage?

Those are odd things to articulate. I was playing Macbeth once, and sometimes it would take off on me and start to move into these other places, and I was deeply thankful. So afterwards I would give thanks. I'd close the door and get down on my knees and take a moment and say, "Thank you for letting me be here." [*As he remembers this feeling, tears come to his eyes.*] Sometimes you think, "Boy, how did I get to be in the right place at the right time? How did I get to be so lucky?"

MARK
METCALF

Mark Metcalf

A journeyman actor with a long string of stage credits, Mark Metcalf is probably best-remembered as Nedermayer, the sadistic fraternity leader in the movie Animal House—a role he stumbled into again years later when he appeared as a sadistic suburban daddy in two popular rock videos by the cartoonish heavy-metal band Twisted Sister. It was partly in an attempt to shake his psychotic image that, a few days before we met, Mark had flown to California for the weekend to screen-test for the role of Shelley Hack's successful restaurateur husband in a television series, about which he had mixed feelings.

It's sort of a roll of the dice, because just to fly out there you commit yourself for five years. In the back of your mind, you're thinking, "If they make the pilot, maybe they won't pick up the series. Then I will have made the pilot, and it will give me a certain amount of exposure." At the same time, in the back of my mind I know that I do not want to do a television series for five years. That's not why I decided to not. I decided to act so I could do something *different* every six months.

The thing is that even if it runs for only a year, you can make a bundle of money, and it makes life more comfortable. Then you can go do Shakespeare down on Second Avenue or you can have a house. On the other hand, you become a TV actor. Your agents always say, "Do the TV, do the TV," because it gets you in line for movies. You say, "How does that work?" They say, "Look at Steve McQueen, look at Sally Field, look at John Travolta." Then they stop, because there aren't that many.

"Look at Sally Field"—that's a good one. You must always do exactly what Sally Field has done with her career.

Yeah, move in with Burt Reynolds, get your tits done because Burt says so, take movies because Burt says so. When I was in California, sitting in the Century Plaza Hotel at nine in the morning trying to learn my lines before I went over to meet Shelley Hack, I turned the TV on just so there'd be somebody else in the room, and who was in the room with me but Sally Field doing *Gidget*.

Did you always want to be an actor?

I didn't want to be anything for a long time. When I was a sophomore at the University of Michigan in Ann Arbor, I went over to audition for a play because my roommate was doing it. He said, "Come on, it's a good way to meet girls." I was starting to spend too much time in bars, and I thought it would keep me out of bars. (I didn't realize it was just another way into the bars.) I got cast in thirteen different roles in the three parts of *Henry VI*, changing costumes and makeup all the time. And that was it.

Also, I come from a family of sixteen generations of engineers or librarians or teachers—somewhat stoic, unemotional, controlled people—and the theater was the first place where I'd seen people be furious with each other and ten minutes later be weeping with love and emotion. It was great.

I didn't really decide to do it professionally until I graduated in '68 and became eligible for the draft. Eventually I took the physical and got a 4-F, 'cause I was kind of crazy—a lot of drugs. I was heading back to Oregon and stopped in Ann

Arbor to see some friends, and a man who'd been my teacher—Jim Coakley, now a teacher at Northwestern—talked me into doing a couple of plays for him there and trying to make a living. That was when I decided to do it as a serious profession. That meant going to auditions. I went to the TCG [Theater Communications Group] auditions for regional theaters in Chicago, where about a hundred actors a day, for four days in a row, come and do their standard auditions: two and a half minutes of classical, two and a half minutes of contemporary. You do your Hotspur, you do your Harold Pinter. Out of that, I got a full season at Milwaukee Rep, my first paying job.

It still sometimes occurs to me, especially in the winter when I have a cold and I'm depressed, that this is just something I've been doing for fourteen or fifteen years and not anything that I intended to do. There are much more sensible ways to spend your life than sitting around waiting for phone calls, putting up with massive egos (your own included), and trying to understand your life in terms of other people's perceptions of you, which is what ends up happening. There are still hours during the day when I think that maybe I'll just go to U.C. Davis and study marine biology.

Were you good as an actor immediately?

I was taken to be good, because I had a naturally good voice, moved well, looked okay, and had a brain that functioned well in relationship to literature. Also, there was nothing riding on it. I didn't want a "career" in the theater. I was a hippie. All I wanted to do was have a good time.

Sometime after I was thirty, I realized that it was a little late to apply to U.C. Davis and get a degree in marine biology. I had to admit that I'd probably be bored to death being a marine biologist, and to think that the experience of standing up to my waist in a tidepool looking at a sea anemone would be closer to God than playing Oberon on the Lower East Side was just crazy. It was just a way to undermine myself. I was an adult, and I had to start trying to make a living.

One of his ploys to make a living was to become a movie producer. With Griffin Dunne and Amy Robinson, he formed a company called Triple Play Productions, which produced Joan Micklin Silver's Chilly Scenes of Winter *and John Sayles's* Baby, It's You. *Just as the latter was going into production, though, Metcalf bowed out.*

Producing was a very hard thing to do. It was salesmanship. You have to be an adult to produce. When I decided I didn't want to produce anymore, I consciously decided I didn't want to be an adult that consistently. I wanted to be a kid some more. You do get to experience that childlike part of yourself in the theater—you're required to, requested to. At the same time, you're treated like a child when you're an adult. There's this mythology of the actor being a child, the producer and the director being adults. This role-playing that goes on should stop, so actors won't cushion themselves thinking, "Oh, I'm just a child."

What do your parents think about your being an actor?

They didn't like it at all when I first started, but the first play that I got any recognition for was *The Tooth of Crime*, the Sam Shepard play at Princeton, which got a big review in *Time* magazine with my name and my picture. When that happened, they decided it was a good thing. When I produced *Chilly Scenes of Winter*, that was the best thing I'd done as far as they were concerned. To be behind the desk, to be the adult, the guy who signs the checks for all that money, they liked that. They haven't been quite able to understand why I don't want to do it. I just finished doing about six weeks on a soap opera, *One Life to Live,* and they really liked that, 'cause they can turn it on and see me. They've never understood why I turned down commercials, why I turned down soap operas for fourteen years. I used to think it was because they didn't understand the artist, but really they'd like me to do those things because then they could visit me more often. They'd never turn on MTV if you paid them, but when I did the Twisted Sister video, they watched for days on end hoping to see it.

What's the best thing about being an actor?
Those moments when you have absolute freedom to make up the truth out of airy nothing. It's like Baryshnikov when he leaps and doesn't come down—he goes up, and he should come down, and he doesn't. It looks like he reaches the apex and then just lifts himself a little bit more. Those moments happen for an actor, too, when you're up there and you can just think and go higher.

What's the silliest thing about being an actor?
[He lets out a silly laugh.] Having to do it again and again and again until you die. You should be up there, and you should never come down. But you come down, so you have to do it again.

PETER
RIEGERT

Peter Riegert

As an actor and in person, Peter Riegert is a regular guy—low-keyed, laconic, unfussy. He grew up in New York, his father is in the poultry business—"chickens and turkeys and ducks"—and his mother teaches piano. Peter himself was a teacher and a social worker before his curiosity led him to start auditioning for Off-Off-Broadway shows. He spent several years with an improvisational company called War Babies—"that was really where I got my training"—before his first personal success in David Mamet's play Sexual Perversity in Chicago, *which eventually led to movie roles in* Animal House *and* Local Hero.

When we met, Peter had just spent most of the summer at the Williamstown Theater Festival in Massachusetts acting in one play and directing some staged readings of others. Before that, he'd been in Chicago acting in a David Mamet one-act called The Spanish Prisoner *and Mamet's adaptation of Chekhov's* The Cherry Orchard, *both with the Goodman Theater's short-lived New Theater Company. He had agreed to be in a four-character adaptation of* A Midsummer Night's Dream *staged by the young avant-garde director Peter Sellars at the Kennedy Center in Washington, but plans for the production fell through. So Peter was in a rest mode, a placid portrait of an actor not working.*

Actors' days are freer because they work infrequently. It's only hard when your father says, "What did you do today?" You feel like a kid: "Did you do your homework?" It's odder when you first begin—what do you do with your time? It's very enjoyable to me now. I like to read, I'm always looking for material, and this is a great opportunity.

How old were you when you started acting?

Twenty-three. Before then I was running an after-school program at a settlement house on the Lower East Side, hiring college students in the CETA program to run tutorials for kids and also serve as recreational directors. That was in '71. I stopped doing that when I realized my time was going to be taken up with acting.

What was your first show?

I've blocked it out. It was a contemporary play based on a Shakespeare play —it might even have been *Midsummer Night's Dream*—but seen through the eyes of someone on acid. Think ludicrous thoughts and that's the play. I didn't know better. I did one play in college, one play in high school, and to me this was theater. Twenty-five seats.

Did you go to acting school?

No. I didn't really know what I was looking for. I had a lot of friends who were studying, so I'd go visit their classes. I learned it wasn't anything I wanted to do. One, I couldn't afford it. And two, actors tend to talk a lot. The best part about that is you hear other people's point of view. The worst part is that any inbred conversation starts perpetuating its own myths, and I was not interested in getting stuck in that. After a while, I felt my own stubbornness was what I had to contribute—not being able to speak in actorspeak didn't mean I couldn't act. It just meant I wouldn't be the hit of the party.

What's actorspeak?

Whatever actors talk about that prevents them from seeing a movie or a play for what it is. Who wants to talk about great moments if you've got an interesting play or movie to see? I don't want to sit there and say, "Ooh, great shot, good photography . . ." If I see good work, it inspires me to do good work. When I see bad work, I want to go into the bookbinding business or something.

CHRISTOPHER
WALKEN

Christopher Walken

Christopher Walken has become one of our most idiosyncratic and unpredictable actors, onstage, on-screen, and in person. Few people know that Walken was a child actor who got his professional start as a song-and-dance man in musicals like Baker Street, Best Foot Forward, *and* High Spirits—*so it was shocking when he turned up in the middle of the Steve Martin-Bernadette Peters movie* Pennies from Heaven *kicking up his heels to the tune of "Let's Misbehave." Likewise, after having established himself as a movie star in* Next Stop, Greenwich Village, The Deer Hunter *(for which he won an Oscar) and* Brainstorm, *Walken confounded expectations by taking a cameo role in the 1986 Lincoln Center revival of John Guare's* House of Blue Leaves, *for which he was onstage only for the last ten minutes of the play.*

Walken has crazy eyes—darting and secretive like a Lily Tomlin character. He combs his hair in four different directions and speaks in the oddly deliberate cadences of a Yiddish Theater veteran.

Did you always want to be an actor?

I come from a show-business family, so wanting to become an actor never crossed my mind. It was just a part of my life. My two brothers and I were child actors. In those days there was a lot of live television in New York. All the shows came from Rockefeller Center, and they used a lot of kids. There were agencies devoted to child actors.

What did your father do?

My father's a baker. He had his own bakery in Queens. Curiously, my brothers worked much more than I did. It's ironic that they went into other things, and I didn't work much but stayed in the business.

When did you start thinking seriously about making it a career?

When I was about twenty. I was at Hofstra, in a psychology class, and I was looking out the window. It was a very nice day. I got up, went to my car, and I never went back to school. I started working. I got a job in a musical.

Did you ever study acting?

Yeah, with different people. Wynn Handman, he was good. I became a member of the Actors Studio some years ago and listened to Lee Strasberg and Kazan. The best studying I've done is working with Irene Worth, Rosemary Harris, Robert Preston. Or Bill Hurt, Harvey Keitel, and Jerry Stiller. That's an education. When you're onstage with Irene Worth and Rosemary Harris, you better be on your toes, because they can kick ass.

Were you always good as an actor?

No. Only recently.

What made the difference?

Just time. I was able to control it to some extent about the time I did *Pennies from Heaven*. Something in your biological clock tells you "You better get on the stick." There's a point at which I stopped being naive about myself. Sometimes a certain innocence is good, but not about yourself. It's come and gone since then, but I know what it is now. I've got my eye on what it is I'm for in show business.

When you started acting, did you think you would do movies?

I always hoped to. I've been very fortunate, because I've been involved in things that very often lead to obscurity. I was in some pictures that were not successful whatsoever. I think people admire persistence. People notice that I'm still there.

My first movie was *The Anderson Tapes*, the Sidney Lumet movie. I played the Kid. I was already pushing twenty-eight. By that time, people were already saying "How come you never made a movie?" I had gone up on commercials, which I was perfectly willing to do. But it was like going for jury duty and never getting picked for a jury.

I never made more than $11,000 'til I was almost thirty-five years old. I used to get unemployment quite a lot. I've been married for almost twenty years, and my wife and I always did nicely. She was a dancer. As a matter of fact, we met doing a summer tour of *West Side Story*. I was Riff, the head of the Jets, and she was Graciela, his girlfriend.

Did you find acting in movies different from stage acting?

In the beginning, very much so. I never could get over the absence of the audience. When I did *Pennies from Heaven*—this is why I equate that with a kind of turning point in my life—my dance number was lying there like a pancake. I said, "How are you supposed to do this when nobody's looking? This is a performance for an audience." The great thing about Fred Astaire was that he always knew the audience was there, in his mind. You can see it in his dancing. So I said to the grips, all the young guys with hammers hanging off their belts—in a Hollywood production, there are many people standing around the set, many, many friends and their mothers—I said, "All you people, will you come down when we do this shot and give me some encouragement? Whistle, yell, let me know you're there." The whole number just took off.

Ever since then, the basis of my technique is to remember that the people standing on the set there are your audience. Instead of looking at their watches, I ask them to look at me. It's amazing how people want to help if you ask them. It's not like the guy running the lights doesn't want to look at you—he feels like he has to look away. An audience never does that. An audience is the most dangerous thing in the world, because they paid, and they're looking at you. And they paid! And there's a lot of them! And they cast a cold eye, *because* they paid. To be on the stage, you have to be very secure.

Do you like being looked at?

Very much, when I feel good. Then I feel like my mind is as strong as all theirs put together, and they're happy to be with me. Otherwise, it's a disaster because you can feel their resentment coming, and it makes you shaky. That's what they call stage fright. A good actor is like a racehorse or a Ferrari. If a cylinder is missing on a Chevy, it doesn't matter that much. But if something's not working right on a Ferrari, it makes a big difference. It's the three percent that makes the difference between good and great. It's a fine line. If you're not there, it's very painful.

In *House of Blue Leaves*, you just sit there looking out at the audience—it's one of the weirdest, most Brechtian performances I've ever seen.

I'm looking at them and they're looking at me. That's what I'm here for.

That's what I meant before when I said I'm starting to know what I'm for. A lot of critics object to that, but I do it on purpose. I believe that's what God wants me to do.

God wants you to look at the audience?

I know, you say something like that and people think you sound like the Ayatollah Khomeini. But I look around as an intelligent person and see so many wonderful actors doing the other thing—why would I want to enter that arena? I believe as a performer you have to create your own arena so that in a sense there is no competition.

What's it like to do something like *Hurlyburly* where you're onstage with a constellation of actors like Bill Hurt, Harvey Keitel, Jerry Stiller, Sigourney Weaver, and Judith Ivey?

Absolutely fabulous. It's one of the best things that can happen. It's a ball game of a very special and exquisite, exotic sort. If you're on your toes and they're on their toes, you can cook. It's as exciting as sports. When you work with people like that, there's an element of unpredictability to it which might be called danger. You can't take anything for granted. They throw you curves, you throw them curves. The watching and the listening, the constant reversing of those roles, is fascinating both to the actors and the audience. If I'm not sure what I'm going to do, they sense it, the audience—what's he going to do? It makes *them* not take anything for granted. They don't go to sleep.

WILLEM
DAFOE

Willem Dafoe

Willem Dafoe has one of the strangest careers an American actor can have. In film, his Mephisphelean face has become increasingly familiar from his perfor-mances as various roughnecks and malefactors, most notably in Walter Hill's Streets of Fire *and William Friedkin's* To Live and Die in L.A. *Meanwhile, he is a longtime member of the Wooster Group, one of the oldest and most adven-turous experimental theater ensembles in America. Under the direction of Eliza-beth LeCompte (who lives with Dafoe and their son, Jack), the Wooster Group—whose core also includes Spalding Gray, Ron Vawter, Kate Valk, and designer Jim Clayburgh—favors an extreme style of performing that continually tests the barriers of taste and technology. In a controversial piece entitled* Route 1 & 9, *for instance, Dafoe and Vawter played blind men in blackface constructing a make-shift set; later, they tossed away their dark glasses to perform a wild Pigmeat Markham vaudeville routine and ecstatic dances to R&B music. Meanwhile, on video Dafoe was seen first performing scenes from Thornton Wilder's* Our Town *in soap-opera close-ups and then in a crude porno film having sex with an actress in the company.*

Raised in a small Wisconsin town, the seventh of eight kids born to a surgeon and his wife, Dafoe got his professional start with Theater X in Milwaukee and later joined the Performance Group in New York, which metamorphosed into the Wooster Group. To Live and Die in L.A. was his biggest and best-received film role to date, and you might expect an actor in that position to be hanging out in California hoping to parlay his good reviews into major movie work. But when the film was released late in 1985, thirty-year-old Dafoe was in Washington with the Wooster Group performing three shows at the Kennedy Center, though he was soon to begin shooting on Oliver Stone's war picture, Platoon. *When we met for breakfast near Dupont Circle, I noticed he had blisters on the ends of his nico-tine-stained fingers from playing guitar onstage, and his hands shook from drink-ing too much coffee.*

What was the effect of *To Live and Die in L.A.*'s release for you?

People who had a villain to cast, no matter what kind of villain—whether it was a rat-eating monster or a sleazy guy—were talking to me like they've never talked before. Many of them didn't get that far, because I was interested in trying to do something different. The Coen brothers, who made *Blood Simple*, wrote a screenplay called *Raising Arizona*, which was fabulous. It was a screw-ball comedy, and I wanted to do that very badly. But they thought I was too rough. That probably seems strange to you, because you know me, but I'm always surprised how sometimes I'm perceived as being very rough. Mean. Tough.

Did you always want to be an actor?

Pretty much, since I was thirteen. I was always in school plays as a kid. I was the kind of kid who had a facility for accents and that kind of thing, so I tended to play character roles. What I did in those days made me queasy even then. I always had a kind of love-hate relationship to being an actor and to theater. I don't like the mythology around it, the idea of what an actor is, and the classic neediness of an actor. That embarrasses me.

When did you decide you were going to pursue acting as a career?

I really never decided anything. Still haven't. I went for a little while to University of Wisconsin in Milwaukee, which was essentially a suitcase campus for kids from blue-collar families who would work and take six years to get a degree—but they also had this theater department that was quite large. You got a little bit of everything. You had the crazy guy from California, who'd have you write journals and do bioenergetics and that kind of stuff. On the other hand, you'd have some schlocky meat-and-potatoes guy from the South who wished he was at Carnegie-Mellon and just wanted to turn out "the ffffinest Actors," the best instruments. It ran the range.

All I wanted to do was perform, so I really submerged myself in the theater department. I slept, ate, did nothing but theater. When it was time for anthropology or whatever, I didn't go. When I look back on it, I had a terrible education. I think I prided myself on being anti-intellectual.

That's one of the mythologies about actors, that if you're anti-intellectual you're a better actor.

Exactly, and I bought it, and it makes me sick. It's another thing I love and hate about the theater. Just like any other kid, you read bios on James Dean and Marlon Brando, and you're really going right for the pose. Those are your models. Even though Brando always wanted to be something of an intellectual, with the bongo drums and the Schopenhauer, still, that wasn't his prowess, you know what I mean?

So when I left school, I felt totally annoyed. I wanted to be tested somehow; I was going to join the army or something. Just on a lark I saw this little note about auditions; some sleazy guy in Scottsdale, Arizona, was running seven companies doing the same show, *Little Lord Fauntleroy*, with cheesy sets, removable mustaches . . . it was a schlocky children's theater, but it involved a lot of travel. I had Company C. We did the deep South: Mississippi, Louisiana, Alabama, Georgia, Virginia, Tennessee, Texas, Arkansas. I did that for six months. It was like vaudeville. You'd drive around in this little van, do three shows a day, sometimes a hundred miles apart. Sometimes you'd play these big state theaters in junior colleges, other places you'd be playing in some library in some rich day-care center. You were always flying by the seat of your pants. Just to perform that much is really exciting.

How did you end up joining the Performance Group?

It happened in a men's room, Don. Literally. Through Theater X, I met [Performance Group founder] Richard Schechner at a theater festival in Baltimore. We were both at a urinal, and he turned to me and said something real simple like, "Oh, I hear you're coming to New York. You look good, and I think you'd be good in my play." So I said, "Sure." I wanted to be challenged, and I was also having a falling-out with Method training. My training was basically Method—Stanislavsky and Lee Strasberg books and things like that in school—but what we know as acting, the kind of acting you generally see in any theater in New York, I'm not so interested in. I'm interested in something more than emotional recall and crying on cue. And the Performance Group represented that.

At that point, though, Richard was kind of running out of steam as leader of the Group, so when I went to a group meeting and he said, "This is Willem, he's going to be playing the killer in *Cops*," everybody blew up. This was at Liz's loft. I remember first meeting Liz when she said, "I don't know who the fuck this guy is, but get him out of here! You said Ronnie was gonna have that role!" I had to pay a lot of dues before they accepted me. Eventually, I started to hang out with Liz, and Liz and Spalding asked me if I wanted to work on this new piece, which was to become *Point Judith*.

We did a lot of improvisation and a hell of a lot of dancing. We would put on schlocky disco music and just run around. At one point we got a chain saw, and I remember one rehearsal where I was in a jockstrap with this big chain saw, cutting up logs and doing the dialogue. It was always different, thank God. It's one of Liz's geniuses—she's a person who can't stand still. Once something's hot, she tears it up and tries something else. I'd just show up every day.

I get into almost a religious frenzy about my work sometimes. It's all about devotion to the task. The Wooster Group does these structured pieces that don't have a recognizable psychology, and the beauty of them is these people moving around in this structure. To put myself in that structure and become part of the landscape keeps death away from my door the same way some virtuoso psychological performance might make other people feel they're doing important or truthful work. In *Route 1 & 9*, I'm just tickled by how everything looks. It's like being an animal. There's a kind of submission involved that's attractive to me. "Submission" is a funny word to use, because nothing about me is submissive —that's why I use words like "devotion."

Is it weird to go from doing that kind of work to a movie like *Streets of Fire* or *The Loveless*?
It's the same. Performing for a camera is so abstract, and things are so fragmented. I've never done anything with extended scenes, so really you're dealing with tiny littly moments of standing *here* looking over *there* and trying to invest "I'll have a beer" with something. You know? That's what so many films break up into. So it's kind of similar to the Wooster Group work, in that you've got that task thing, and you're not sure what you have to invest it with—it's not necessarily psychological realism.

What's the hardest thing for you to do as an actor?
Talk fast. My rhythms are very slow naturally.

When you started acting, did you think you would do movies as well as theater?
I had no idea. I remember going through a very romantic period when I was younger thinking that theater was really it, movies were just junk, but I don't feel that way now. It was funny—someone that I used to work with in Milwaukee came backstage at the show here and said, "I saw the trailer for that *To Live and Die* you did. I hope you got *paid* well." She just assumed it was schlock and that I wouldn't be proud of it. I couldn't help myself. I said, "Fuck you." You know, I'm not saying any of the movies I've done are great, but it's so much a part of me that I'm proud of them.

JOE
MORTON

Joe Morton

Filmmaker John Sayles had a lot to do with making Joe Morton a movie star, but the actor made a reciprocal contribution. After achieving some notoriety playing twin brothers—a boring ophthalmologist and an androgynous rock singer—on a popular soap opera, Morton was on location in Harlem shooting Sayles's film about a black extraterrestrial when a passing stranger called out, "Hey, ain't you the brother from Another World?"

When we met, Morton, thirty-eight, had just returned from honeymooning with his second wife, Nora, a sculptor who had designed the sets for The Brother from Another Planet. *He was appearing onstage in William Mastriosimone's* Tamer of Horses *at a small theater in New Jersey, and he was very excited about having a major role in Alan Rudolph's film* Trouble in Mind, *which he'd finally seen a screening of the night before.*

What made you want to start acting?

I entered Hofstra University as a psychology major. You know how on your first day they have orientation skits? Well, Hofstra has a wonderful theater, and when the skits were over, I just sat there thinking. I'd been writing music and I liked that and maybe I could act. So I left the theater, walked over to the registrar, and changed my major from psych to drama.

I liked to sing, but I'd never really performed. I didn't even see my first play until I was a senior in high school, and that was *Purlie Victorious.* But I'd never been onstage as an actor. I simply thought maybe I could do it. When I was a kid, I used to go to the Apollo with my parents to see people like Sammy Davis, Jr., and my fantasy was that he would stop in the middle of his performance and say, "Ladies and gentlemen, we have a very special guest in the audience tonight—Joe Morton. With a little persuasion, maybe we can get him down onstage." So when I saw this skit in college, it all clicked; I went to acting classes and loved it. Never looked back. I had some wonderful teachers, and when I left school, one of them helped me get an agent. I walked into a job immediately and have been working [*he knocks on wood*] successfully for seventeen years.

Did you think you would also do movies?

What I really wanted to do was classical theater because that's how I'd been trained. I loved Shakespeare, I loved the Greeks, I loved straight drama. When I left school, I found out that there wasn't a lot of that available. This was 1968. So since I could sing, I thought, fine, I'll do musicals. My first job was a thing called *A Month of Sundays,* which lasted about two days, but it got me my Equity card. From there, it was *Hair* and *Two Gentlemen from Verona* and *Salvation.*

Eventually, I decided what I really wanted to do was film. Musicals were a dead end; you were either going to become Jerry Orbach, George Hearn, or one of the Hines brothers, or you were going to become Melba Moore and go into recordings. After *Salvation,* I made an album which never came out, and I hated the music business. It's a sleazy, prejudiced armpit industry. I knew I wasn't interested in going to dance classes every day. That's when the classical training started to rear its head again. I thought the only way to get into film is to have a dramatic résumé. If I go to an audition, and all they see is a list of musicals, I'm not going to be taken seriously. After I got the Theater World Award and the Tony nomination for best actor for *Raisin*, I decided the thing to do now was go into the boondocks and beef up my résumé. For five or six years, that's what I did. My agents had a fit. "Omigod, he doesn't want to do musicals anymore."

Was it scary to leave New York?

It didn't seem there was an awful lot I was leaving. I could make as much money outside as I could in New York. I also wanted to be in a place without the pressure of having to get great reviews all the time, where I could fail and get a bad review so I could learn. What it did was increase my reputation inside the business. It doesn't make things easier—there still isn't a plethora of roles for black actors in that category.

My luck with film wasn't very good at first. They were still looking for people who sounded as if they were just coming in off 125th Street, and although I could put it on, other people did it better. It's kind of ironic, considering that I have a good voice and I speak well and have all this classical training, that the first big film I get is a character that doesn't speak at all. In a lot of ways, *The Brother from Another Planet* fed into things I felt about who Joe was. I grew up as an Army brat. My father was a captain in the army, so most of my life was spent in Europe and Asia until I was ten. When my father died in Europe, we came back to Edgecombe Avenue, which is near 155th Street and St. Nicholas Avenue. I'd never lived in Harlem, so I was like the character in the film, someone who looked like he should know what was going on but didn't.

What made you want to pursue films?

I've always loved movies. I was the kind of guy who'd sit up and watch all the late movies. Also, I hated the black exploitation movies that were beginning to be made in the early 70's. I was doing *Raisin* on Broadway and getting reviews like, "If this man were white, they would be pounding on his door to give him scripts." I started watching Sidney Poitier's movies and began to realize what position he was in. He came up at the time when he was the only one, therefore he had to play every black man conceivable, from *The Defiant Ones* to *Guess Who's Coming to Dinner*. It just wasn't possible. His forte obviously was things like *Guess Who's Coming to Dinner*, this very clean-cut individual, or *Breaking Point*, where he plays the psychiatrist. So I began to think there was a niche to be filled, and that's to have a black dramatic actor, because there's nobody like Pacino or Brando or De Niro or Hoffman.

WALLACE
SHAWN

Wallace Shawn

Ever since his movie debut as Diane Keaton's ex-husband in Manhattan (*whom Keaton describes as "a sexual animal" and Woody Allen refers to as "that homunculus"*), *Wally Shawn has become familiar as a clownishly malevolent character actor in dozens of movies. But his acting career is a happy accident cultivated to support his true occupation, which is writing plays that catalog in comic-poetic language the nightmares that lurk beneath the placid face of everyday life. Although he is highly regarded by his peers and supported by mighty impresarios like Joseph Papp, Shawn's plays (*Our Late Night, Marie and Bruce, Aunt Dan and Lemon*) are performed infrequently and invariably provoke outrage and walk-outs from a startling proportion of the people who come to see them. Shawn's big breakthrough came when his movie-acting and writing careers converged in Louis Malle's film* My Dinner with André, *which Shawn wrote and starred in with André Gregory. They essentially played themselves: a flamboyant, avant-garde director disillusioned with the theater and the Kooky Actor relishing the cold cup of coffee that no cockroach has died in overnight. You would never know from this or any of Wally Shawn's other movies that he is a history and philosophy scholar with degrees from Harvard and Oxford or that his father, William Shawn, is the editor of the* New Yorker. *This inverview leaps off from the tantalizing opening monologue of* My Dinner with André, *in which Wally says, "I grew up on the Upper East Side, and when I was ten years old I was rich, I was an aristocrat, riding around in taxis, surrounded by comfort, and all I thought about was art and music. Now I'm thirty-six, and all I think about is money."*

In the schools I went to, it was taken for granted that you could do anything that you wanted to do. If you got it into your mind that you wanted to be a novelist, nobody ever told you that you might not have the talent to be a novelist, that your novels might not necessarily be published, and you might have to work as a waiter in order to make a living while you wrote your novels. Of course, the teachers themselves were all struggling and living on small salaries. I suppose the first glimpse I had that everybody in the world was not reasonably well off were these hints that you would get about the teachers. Still, I don't recall that they ever said, "Children, you will have to earn a living one day. You'll have to make money."

I often think that the main thing a good piece of art can do is make the person looking at it more intelligent. It sharpens the brains of the person who's experiencing it. Most films or plays or articles you read actually leave you stupider than you were before you experienced them and leave you on a sort of low, ignorant, monsterlike level somehow. If you see a mindless movie where the plot makes no sense, the characters are incoherently written and self-contradictory, the observations of life are lazy and false, it harms you a little bit, and if you watch six hours of it on television every night for your whole life, it may make you really into an idiot. Whereas last night Debbie *[Eisenberg, Wally's girlfriend]* read me a few pages of *The Ruined Man* by Kobo Abe—he was describing a man who was sitting in a café getting drunk—well, it was so vivid and so exciting that I honestly felt that after hearing those few pages that I was just a better person. It was like someone had turned on the electricity inside me.

Reading your early plays, I have the feeling that they were written for a theater that doesn't exist.

[He laughs.] My first five plays were all written before a single word of mine had ever been spoken by a professional actor. I had had no involvement in the theater. I had been a student of acting at the HB Studio—immediately after teaching Latin at the day school of the Church of the Heavenly Rest, I spent a year pretty much studying full-time. I studied acting because it seemed like a good idea, that playwrights should know about acting. I had no intention of being an actor. I also thought that maybe I would direct one day.

Did you go to the theater all your life?

Yes. What influenced me the most, I suppose, were things I saw when I was thirteen and fourteen years old. That was when Jason Robards did *The Iceman Cometh*, they did the original production of *Long Day's Journey Into Night*, Alan Schneider did *Endgame* at the Cherry Lane, and Eli Wallach did *The Chair* and *The Lesson* at the Theater de Lys. All those things were happening when I was just at that formative period. I was not aware that you'd have to invent a whole new way of going about things in order to do my plays. I wasn't even aware that writing a play for eighty characters was problematical.

So you quit teaching to study acting full-time?

Yeah. I took classes every day for a year. I also studied voice and movement. Katharine Sergava was my acting teacher. She taught straight Stanislavsky school. She was Russian. And I had a wonderful time.

Did you like acting?

Oh, of course. I loved it. It just never crossed my mind that one could do it professionally. The other students all planned to be professional actors, but I sort of thought it was like being a knight or a lord in England. You didn't choose to be an actor, you had to be chosen. It never occurred to me, "Maybe I'll go to an audition. Maybe I'll get a part."

How did you actually begin to act professionally?

Wil Leach had the idea that I could translate *The Mandrake* for Joe Papp, so Joe commissioned this translation. Then Wil had the idea that I should be in *The Mandrake*. That changed my life. I learned there was something I could do to make a living. At the time I was completely broke, and I was considering becoming a taxi driver. Debbie thought it would be dangerous for me, particularly because at that time I hardly knew how to drive at all. So Wil said, "Why don't you act in the play?" I said, "No, I don't think so." He said, "Well, we'll pay you." It was only supposed to be a workshop for three weeks, so I did it. Then it became a hit and played for six months. It was great—I had two checks every week and an acting lesson every night. I loved working with the actors.

Did you take to acting instantly?

I found it difficult, but I enjoyed it from the first day.

I would think speaking your own words would be the most natural thing in the world.

It was, although it was hard for me. I had a lot to learn. It was a little bit outrageous to suddenly be performing a part in a play without really knowing how to act. I did get a lot of extra coaching from the people in the play.

Then you became part of the casting pool?

Juliet Taylor saw me in *The Mandrake*. She called me in to meet Woody

Allen. It was a shock, but a totally pleasant one, like a dream, really. Not having been an actor, I didn't even know quite how amazing it was, to suddenly be called in to meet Woody Allen and to be called back the next day and then to be in this wonderful movie. I think *Manhattan* is one of the best movies ever made. I loved doing my scene with Diane Keaton and Woody Allen; I felt totally comfortable. I felt like I'd known them for years. Then when I saw the movie, I couldn't believe I was privileged to be in such a wonderful movie. I forgot that I was about to appear in it, because I don't show up until fairly late in the movie. I still find it fairly amazing that that happened.

Then Juliet Taylor brought me in to see Alan Pakula, who put me in *Starting Over*. I began to realize that instead of being a Xerox-machine operator or a shipping clerk, I could be an actor.

You've acted pretty much non-stop since then.

Not really, but I've had it better off than most people. I don't know how long I can spin this out. Character actors wear out their welcome. I'd be happy to be a leading man, but no one has hired me to be one. Except Louis Malle.

Why are you reluctant to do interviews?

It's just that the truth about anything personal is so unbelievably complicated that when you try to present a public face of your private life, you're lying. I myself have an enormous interest in other people; you might say I've devoted half my life to reading interviews. When I meet people who are interesting, I think nothing about asking about their private life; I'll ask people anything I can get away with asking. But none of the things I would ask someone when I meet them would I answer if you asked me.

The truth is, I'd like to know everything. I would like to know what the lives of other people are like in their quietest and most intimate moments. What their relationships are like and what they feel about each other and what they feel about themselves when they're sitting alone in a room and what they do after the company has gone home and what suffering they may experience in the middle of the night. In our society all those most interesting things are hidden. You meet people and everybody seems to be leading this sort of sensible life. That's the impression most people try to give you. But really people's lives are much more different from one another than that, and behind the closed doors there are a lot of very strange things going on that are more interesting and moving and a lot stranger than what people would like you to think is going on.

So I totally understand how in our society, there's this crazy explosion of interest in personalities and in what other people are doing. But there's a danger in that. If you are one of the guinea pigs, you have to be very careful how much you want to reveal.

What are the limits?

I'm guided by what has nauseated me in interviews with other people. It's almost impossible not to seem vain. Say there's an article about a writer, and he says, "Well, my favorite thing in life is to lift weights and practice boxing with a punching bag." Well, it's probably true, just a fact about his life, but by the time you get it in the article, particularly if it's illustrated by the guy standing there with his boxing gloves and no shirt on, you think, "This guy is boasting that he's some kind of hero, that he's not only a writer but also a real he-man," and you're nauseated. He wasn't trying to make any particular point, but by the time he's telling the world about it, it's boasting—that's just the way it comes off. I don't want to be that guy.

JEFF
DANIELS

Jeff Daniels

When Jeff Daniels describes himself as "just out of the cornfield," you know exactly what he means. He looks like a cornstalk—tall, straw-haired, healthy, rural. Onstage, as a member of the Circle Repertory Company, he has been closely associated with the plays of Lanford Wilson, the poet laureate of small-town America. His role in Fifth of July *as the lover of a crippled Vietnam veteran (played first by William Hurt, later by Christopher Reeve and Richard Thomas) was written specifically for Daniels. A muscular blond in a tank-top and blue jeans, he had almost nothing to say, but he was a haunting presence—the conscience of the play. And he earned the best reviews of his young career playing Wilson himself in a revival of his early autobiographical play* Lemon Sky. *When we met for this interview, he had just come off a dizzying string of major movies (*Terms of Endearment, The Purple Rose of Cairo, Marie, Heartburn*), and he was nervous about doing a play for the first time in a while. The opening of* Lemon Sky *was only a few days away, so we started off talking about—what else —reviews.*

I used to not care. Now, you hope that Frank Rich loves it. When he likes it, people line up at the box office, they come in with a smile on their face, they're glad they're here. If he doesn't like it—and I've been in those shows, too—they come in pissed off, because they'd bought their tickets before the review. And you cannot get them to laugh—you know, a chuckle here and there, where before it was holding for five seconds so you could be heard in your next line. But if Frank Rich loves it, man, there ain't nothing better. No movie experience can beat it.

You've had some pretty exciting movie experiences.
Well, every movie I've done has been with megastars. Meryl Streep or Debra Winger or Shirley MacLaine or Woody Allen or Mia Farrow or Jack Nicholson.

Did it feel weird to go from Circle Rep, doing shows downtown, to doing these movies with mega-super-household names?
Well, on *Terms of Endearment*, I was very scared. It was a huge break. Put me in a movie with Winger or MacLaine or Nicholson, but not all three. And a major role. I was afraid it was going to be, "Three superstars—unfortunately, the movie sags every time Daniels come on-screen," which could easily have been.

Was the work intimidating on a daily basis?
No. See, ever since the first day I got here in New York and went down to Circle Rep, there was Lanford Wilson sitting in the office. He was a star to me. I had just done his play *Hot l Baltimore* out in Michigan. To make some money, Marshall Mason [artistic director of the Circle Rep] had come out to direct a repertory of four plays at this college theater, and I got cast in two of his plays, *Hot l* and the lead in *Summer and Smoke*.

You were still in college?
I had a year to go. I was going to Central Michigan University, which is up in

Mt. Pleasant—out in this cornfield. I read in the paper that Eastern Michigan University, right near Ann Arbor, was having this rep thing, where you could go audition. I'd been doing well at Central the first three years, and I wanted to see how I'd stack up against kids from all over the Midwest. I got the lead in the best play. It was kind of annoying, because I had tickets to a hockey game that night, and I had to go to callbacks. It was like, "Shit!" I just wanted the audition experience. But one of the guys who came down from Central with me said, "I think you better go to the callbacks, because the guy who's directing the play that you're up for is from New York." So I stayed and we did the play.

Before the first performance, Marshall took me out for a drink. I didn't know what he would say to me. All I was going to do was ask him, "Should I try New York, or should I not waste my time?" Before I could say anything, he goes, "Well, you know what you should do with your life, don't you? You should be an actor." That was it. He said, "I want you to come to New York if you'd like, and become an apprentice at Circle Rep." So I did. I went the following September. There I was just out of the cornfield, holding the *Hot l* script, and there was Lanford. He's the first star I ever met. And I started meeting these people who come to this theater, and they're good people. Bill Hurt came into the company, walked in a star.

You mean everyone knew he was a star?

Apparently. We did this play called *My Life*. Bill and Chris Reeve and I shared a dressing room. Bill was waiting to hear whether Ryan O'Neal was going to turn down *Love Story II*, because if Ryan did, then Bill would consider it. Ryan didn't. Then Bill said, "Well, I didn't want to do it anyway." Chris Reeve, the last week of the run, flew to London to screen-test for *Superman*, and he got it. Bill told him not to do it. "Don't do it, don't do it." Chris said, "I think I will." Meanwhile, I was just broke.

So I'd been around stars, and I'd watched. Especially when Chris came back to do *Fifth of July* on Broadway, I saw the good and bad stuff about being a star. There's more pressure, people expect more of you. They expect you to do what they're familiar with. When you try to do something different—like Chris was trying to do—it's hard. But also I saw all the people, the big names, come back just to say hello, like Robin Williams. So it's not like I walked onto the set of *Terms of Endearment* and had never seen a superstar before. I'd seen 'em. It still doesn't prepare you to meet Woody Allen, but it helps.

Tell me how *Purple Rose of Cairo* happened.

Wednesday morning I got up, and on Monday morning I was shooting. That's how fast it was.

Had you ever met or read for Woody's other movies?

Never met him. Michael Keaton had apparently done the role for two weeks, and whatever the reasons were, it didn't work out. I didn't care, and I didn't ask. Anyway, Woody had to replace his lead guy two weeks into shooting, so he called Juliet Taylor, his casting director, and said, "Find somebody." They had a lot of hot young movie stars coming in. Juliet said, "Woody, you should meet this guy," and I got it on the screen test.

Did you get a script, or did you just go meet Woody?

No. My agent, Paul Martino, calls up that night and says, "(*Gasp*) You're going to meet Woody Allen tomorrow." I went, "Oh." *Terms of Endearment* had been out ten days or two weeks, and it had been a big hit.

What were you doing? Lying low? Riding high?

I was . . . well, trying to get in on *Mrs. Soffel*. So I went and met Woody. I was told it won't be a long meeting, so don't worry about it or be offended or take it personally. It wasn't. It was two minutes long. He was very pleasant. He asked me, "What have you done?" I said, "Some Broadway, Off-Broadway."

He didn't know what you'd done?

Well, he wanted to hear me talk. And I didn't talk very well. And it was Woody Allen. You'd think all the *Terms of Endearment* star-stuff would have mellowed that a little bit, but no. It was *Woody Allen*. I mean, you respect and admire him, and he's interested in you, and you can't believe it. I'm working on this, but at that point it was like, "This can't be true. Woody can't be interested in me and, please, don't be. This isn't funny anymore. Stop this." So he took a Polaroid of me, and out of that two-minute meeting he said, "I think maybe we'll do a screen test. We'll get the scenes to you, and I'll let you know."

This was about eleven in the morning, first week of December. I went out to do some Christmas shopping, and I got back about one-thirty. There were seventeen messages on my machine, all from Paul, the agent, saying, "Get down to Woody's office, you're screen-testing this afternoon." So I went down there, picked up the two scenes, the teamster showed up and took me out to the set in Piermont, New York. I'm memorizing in the car on the way out there. There had been, like, a revolving door of name young actors going in for screen tests and coming out every hour and a half or so, and I was the last one. I went in there, there was Woody and everybody, Mia Farrow. I read the two scenes, and there was a lot of huddling between Woody and the producers. Then Woody came over and said, "All right, thanks a lot. We'll let you know tomorrow by noon." I looked at him and said, "Th-thanks, Woody"—you know, like I never expected to see him again. I was just thrilled for the opportunity.

I found out later that one of the other two guys they looked at was so horrible, they didn't even print his test. They just got him out of there and said, "Thanks a lot." *[He lingers over this point, obviously tempted to tell me the name of the actor and exactly how "horrible" he was. But as happened throughout the conversation whenever he started to say something nasty and critical about another actor, he restrained himself and dropped the thought in mid-sentence.]* Anyway, it doesn't matter, it's the old competitive thing coming out . . . So the next morning Paul Martino calls me up and says, "The screen test is fabulous and Woody wants you. He's just got to convince the studio that he can do this with Mia Farrow and a no-name male actor." That took some doing. The meeting started at five in the afternoon. I went to Paul's office, and we expected to hear at five-thirty. At seven-fifteen, I'm bangin' off the walls of his office. I said, "It's obviously a problem. The joke's over, I'll go home." I was walkin' in the door, and Kathleen, my wife, was hanging up the phone. She turned around and said, "You got it. You start Monday."

Did you always want to be an actor?

I just have always been one. I haven't always dreamed of the marquee and the lights and all that stuff. I stumbled on a stage in high school in this musical because the director needed guys for *South Pacific*, and I was funny. I knew what to do to make 622 people laugh.

What did you do?

I played a sailor, and there was a guy in a grass skirt doing a takeoff on those Bali Hai girls. I just looked at his ass and said, "Look, it moves," and I don't know, it got a big laugh. The director had me do it four times in a row. She laughed every time. You know, usually you've got jocks up onstage in high school, just standing there in their costumes. So she started throwing me onstage in these huge roles. El Gallo in *The Fantasticks*, Harold Hill in *The Music Man*, Fagin in *Oliver*, even Tevye in *Fiddler on the Roof*—this eighteen-year-old blond in the Midwest? I was totally, totally wrong for it. But you glue on a beard, do the hair, it's like college theater. After all, you ain't going to find a sixty-five-year-old Jew in Ann Arbor who can sing and act.

What do your parents think about your being an actor?

They were really supportive. They were the ones who said it's all right to skip your last year of college and go to New York. These are parents who own a lumberyard in a small town. There are thirty-five hundred people in this town, and no actors. What do they know about New York? It was very brave of them to say, "I think you better go." It was hard to go, and it was hard for them to let me do this. They would come see the plays, they would be there for the occasional phone call when it wasn't going well and you weren't making money. They tried to help as best they could when TV pilots were sniffin' at ya, and they're talking $100,000, and it seems like ten million, and you're broke, but you want to do movies, and if you do this TV series and it sells, you've got to move to California and all this stuff. They were very good about saying: "Stick to what you believe in and what you want to do."

Did you make a living as an actor as soon as you came to New York?

Yeah, commercials. I wouldn't work as a waiter or drive a cab. I'm glad I did commercials. That was 'cause ICM signed me and had a commercial department and threw me right into it. It's really great, especially if you live cheaply, one room with hot plate. The check comes in, and it's just enough, and you can still do your small role in *My Life* or whatever play they're doing at Circle Rep and study from ten to four or five in the afternoon.

How did you resist doing TV pilots?

I did one because it was really bad, and I really was broke, and I said, "No way this can sell." So I got the bucks, and two months later it was dead. It was a terrific experience. It's got to be what I want or I'm not going to do it. I wanted to do films, good films if I ever got the opportunity, and Jim Brooks gave it to me with *Terms*. If I couldn't do that, then I probably would have gone back and been a teacher and been perfectly happy. I wasn't going to be a whore. I wasn't going to be a game-show actor. I just wasn't going to do that. As it was, I almost left after three months anyway. I hated it here.

Where did you live when you first came to New York?

Twenty-third Street and Seventh Avenue in an old hotel, right next to the Hotel Chelsea. I had one room, a closet that was also a kitchen. You couldn't open the refrigerator and the oven at the same time. I was there because Marshall had said, "You know what you should do with your life, don't you? You should act."

By the time of the Broadway run of *Fifth of July*, I kind of knew what I was doing. I'd added up all the things I'd been studying at Circle in workshops and all that stuff. Then I did *Johnny Got His Gun*. That was probably it. It was a one-man show at Circle Rep. It was just me and seventy pages of writing and every emotion a human being can go through in ninety minutes. *The New York Times* didn't like the script, so it died in three weeks, but I won an Obie Award for it. But you had to have studied, you had to know what you were doing technically as an actor to pull it off, so that the audience felt this descent into hell, which is basically what it is.

Elly Renfield, the director, said, "Keep it under control, keep it bubbling, don't have a nervous breakdown onstage." I said, "Yeah," but the Method actor in me . . . I tried it once in previews. I sobbed, I was all over the place, I was just streaming tears. She said, "I watched the audience, and they didn't feel much of anything." Other nights I would go out there and almost lose it but fight it back, hold it back—and the audience was a mess. I hadn't known that before, that ability to control an audience. Sometimes you don't know that stuff 'til you try it out.

Who are the actors you've admired as role models or inspirations?

I've always liked Spencer Tracy's honesty. Alan Arkin did some great stuff in the seventies. I saw Pacino in *Dog Day Afternoon* six times. I'd just go back and back and back and study him. There's no way I could be Pacino. But if I lean toward actors that I'm not, it gets me away from just playing me. I've always wanted to be a character actor. I try to make everybody a little different so that at the age of sixty or sixty-five, whenever I hang up the skates, I could invite all these guys I've played to a big party, and each one'll be a little different. I don't want to be a personality performer, the same guy in every play and every movie. Some actors stop going to their psychiatrists and go through all their crap onstage every night. Show me something different.

How does an actor deal with the transition from living in one room with a closet-kitchen to making big money?

I haven't made any big money. I keep reading about these twenty-three-year-old actors making a million a movie, and I just want to shoot 'em. I'm makin' a living. I haven't had to do anything I didn't want to do.

Do you have a ritual that you perform before going on?

One of the tricks to keep you honest, especially in films, is thinking that the guy really exists. He's alive, and he's going to come see the show, and he's not going to tell you when. But after the show, he's going to come back and say, "Let's go out for drinks, I want to talk to you about what you did." And you're going to hope he likes it.

ROBERT
JOY

Robert Joy

For some reason, Robert Joy has a long history of playing characters vastly unlike himself. Onstage, for instance, he played children's parts well into his thirties; once he appeared as Leonardo da Vinci in a spacesuit in a synthesizer rock musical. He's best known in movies for assassinating Norman Mailer for the love of Elizabeth McGovern in Ragtime, *though he's played everything from a mean-looking petty coke dealer in* Atlantic City *to a wild-haired rock musician in* Desperately Seeking Susan.

In person, he seems terribly straitlaced and clean-living—a Mormon, you might think, although his clipped, determined manner of speaking betrays his upbringing in Newfoundland. When we met at the cozy, quilt-lined apartment he shares with his actress wife Mary, Robert was thirty-four and was collaborating on a screenplay with a friend while waiting to begin rehearsals for a Broadway revival of Noel Coward's Hay Fever. *He had rescheduled our meeting once in order to see a chiropractor, so we started off talking about chiropractors, masseurs, nutritionists, and other quasi-medical practitioners that actors tend to patronize.*

I was a vegetarian for about eight years, until about twelve months ago. My agent gave me a lot of flak for being too thin and having dark circles under my eyes. He sent me to this clinic, which cost a lot of money. I got a computer analysis telling me what foods I'm allergic to, which was an incredibly long list, then saying I should be on a diet where I couldn't eat anything, hardly—nuts or grains were out and most kinds of beans. They warned me, "It's going to be hard to stick to this incredibly strict diet because you don't have motivation. You don't feel bad, so why should you change your life?" They were absolutely right.

Were you concerned about looking thin or circles under your eyes?
I was concerned that my agent didn't seem to want to represent me until I got "shaped up," in his eyes. I indulged him and went and did it, and since then every time I go in, he says, "You look great," so I assume he's back on track as far as my career is concerned. Maybe it was some kind of weird, $800 placebo that I administered to him by going. I respected his concern, though. A lot of agents would never say anything if they saw their clients deteriorate. They'd just say, "Well, the product is wearing out." But he seems to be concerned—as I am—that I have an interesting career, not just a lucrative career.

Occasionally, when I'm really low on money, I'll take a job that I consider . . . not terrible or sleazy but not as interesting. Like *Amityville 3-D*. Once you've done a movie like that, you can never feel smug or self-satisfied about your career, because you'll open up the TV listings in the *New York Times*, especially around Halloween, and they'll say "*Amityville 3-D*· Tess Harper, Tony Roberts, Robert Joy, Candy Clark. More horror-house hooey. Please, not again!" It really keeps you humble.

Actually, it was very enjoyable to do. When I read the script, I thought—as did most of the people who were in it—that it would have some real good horror twists. It seemed like a really clever, who-is-real-in-this-hall-of-mirrors-type horror story. When I finally saw it, I was very disappointed. After a few clever turns, it became very derivative. The whole last half was a *Poltergeist* ripoff.

Was that your most lucrative movie job?

Quite a bit more lucrative than the other jobs I've done.

You've had interesting parts in wonderful movies: *Ragtime, Atlantic City, Ticket to Heaven.* Yet they didn't pay as well as *Amityville 3-D*?

When *Ragtime* was being negotiated, the line was "We have no money. We think it's a prestigious film, and you should want to be involved." That line comes at you from a lot of different angles when you're an actor in New York. Someone offers you a good role to play in a new script for no money at all, and says, "Well, it'll be good for your career." Sometimes people with lots of money are trying to shave your salary down on a film and say, "We can't afford it, and it'll be good for your career." *Desperately Seeking Susan* cried poverty all over the place. It *was* a low-budget film, but what happens when a film like that makes an awful lot of money, where do the shares go?

Has it helped in getting other projects, that you were in *Desperately Seeking Susan*?

I go on auditions now, and people say, "You were great in *Desperately Seeking Susan*," and already I can relax a little bit. Just for the increment of relaxation, I'm glad that I did it—aside from the fact that it was actually a fun film to do, and I was proud to be in it.

What made you want to be an actor in the first place?

I didn't always want to be an actor. In high school I was interested in basketball more than anything else. I had never gone to theater as a kid. At school we had a glee club, though, so when the principal of the school was directing *The Pirates of Penzance*, he more or less forced me to play Frederic because I had the highest tenor voice. I remember when he first made me get up onstage and say something, I was inconceivably upset by it. It seemed like a very unnatural place for me to be. I guess I stayed there because of my respect for this teacher, and after a few times I got comfortable. It's like jumping in cold water—you get used to it. But I didn't take to it naturally.

Then the summer after my second year of college, I saw a local production of *The King and I.* I was enjoying it, thinking, "I could do a better job there," and, "Boy, I'd really like to be up there." I just assumed that everybody wants to be onstage, the same way that everybody wants to be a movie star. I asked my brother afterward, "Don't you just ache to be up there?" He said, "No, not particularly." That's the first time I ever thought seriously that maybe I should follow up on this desire.

Did you always assume you would come to New York?

No. I had a very negative image of New York—that if someone attacked you on the street, pedestrians would walk by. When I came to New York with the Eli Wallach-Anne Jackson revival of *The Diary of Anne Frank*, I didn't even give up my apartment in Newfoundland. I assumed that when this was over, I'd go back. But I got good reviews, and people suggested very strongly that I stay and follow it up. So I did, and I'm still here.

I had a bad year in '81 or '82. At one point, I had three movies come out at once—*Atlantic City, Ragtime,* and *Ticket to Heaven*—and people thought I must be very rich. But the money they had paid had long gone, I was facing unemployment, and I couldn't make my rent payments. It was a weird experience. If it had gone on much longer, I would have gone back to Newfoundland, because I became an actor to be an actor, and I didn't particularly care at the time where I did it, as long as I could make a living.

What gives you the edge over another actor for a role?

I don't know. I don't consider myself the ultimate actor. I don't think I've tapped all the emotional resources I've got. I say this partly because I've always found it hard to cry onstage, and I keep thinking to be a really good American actor, you have to know how to cry. I'm jealous of that skill. I know it's a symptom that I've still got some relaxing to do. I'm always aware that I'm onstage, and I'm always calculating to a certain extent. I don't consider this a bad thing; your mind's a very important part of acting.

One thing that directors respond to when I act is that I don't indulge just what I want to do. When I read a play, I take into account what it should be from an audience point of view. I see what the writer wants, and that's what I go for in rehearsal. Whereas I think some actors get involved in the character that they extract from the play and say, "What is this person's past? What are this person's problems?" and sometimes forget about the world the person is in—the play—leaving that up to the director. I can't do that. Not that I'm standing outside like a marionette, but I'm using my intelligence as well as my emotions.

Is it different in films?

A little bit. Sometimes I make what I consider a film choice, like in *Ragtime*. My instinct with Harry K. Thaw was to let him simmer and let it be a sort of inner-directed "film performance." Milos Forman wanted him very much out on a limb. He said, "You can't possibly be too big." He kept telling me [*Czech accent*] "More eyes, more crazy!" It was the direction some actors cringe at— "Bigger and louder!" But it made sense for the character. It was actually thrilling, because he put me in a situation where I was either going to be absolutely brilliant or a real fool. I enjoyed walking that line.

What's the silliest thing for you about being an actor?

Hiding from the audience. I like to hang around in the lobby before performances, but even when I was up at Ensemble Studio Theater for the Octoberfest, which is just a festival of readings, you'd get a half-hour call, and if you were standing around the stage or the auditorium when the audience came in, someone would come up to you and whisper, "We've opened the house now," meaning it's time for the actors to clear out. There's the whole thing in "legit" theater where the actors are not supposed to associate with the audience, it will ruin the effect of the curtain opening and there being these people fresh and pure and new onstage. I always find that very disturbing. It just feeds the we/ they dichotomy to keep yourself apart. It's bad enough once the performance starts—then you have the we/they so strongly. But I'd just as soon have the we/ we experience before it starts.

GREGORY
HINES

Gregory Hines

It was Valentine's Day—Gregory Hines's fortieth birthday—when we met at his gym and walked to the West Village duplex apartment he shares with his wife, Pam Koslow, and their son Zachary. (He has a teenage daughter from his first marriage.) Having recently finished shooting the detective comedy Running Scared *in Los Angeles with Billy Crystal, Hines got the idea from Crystal of joining a gym and lifting weights to add bulk to his slender dancer's body. At the age of two, he started singing and dancing with his brother Maurice and his father in an act called Hines, Hines, and Dad that performed together for nearly two decades. Although he is best known for appearing in musicals such as* Eubie *and* Sophisticated Ladies, *he began taking small nonmusical roles in films like* Wolfen *and* Deal of the Century. *Before long, roles such as those he played in* The Cotton Club *and* White Nights *began to be tailored to his special talents as both actor and musical performer.*

How did *Running Scared* happen?

I read the script, and I knew it was a good part. It was written for a white actor. That's what I'm up against—I have to try to make roles happen for me that aren't written black. The roles written black are the "cool guys," and I don't want to play the cool guy. I did an episode of *Amazing Stories* directed by Peter Hyams, and I knew he was allied with *Running Scared*, so I hit on him. He went to bat for me and fought for me to get the part.

Is it up to you to introduce the idea of casting the character black?

It's incumbent upon me to go after things, because nobody's going to say, "Why are we just looking at white actors? Let's look at everybody." They never do that. So once I know about a property, I'm aggressive just to the point of being obnoxious.

Do you like acting as much as singing and dancing?

I love to play vulnerable men. It's so rare that you get to see a black man be something other than in control of his emotions. Superfly, Shaft, now the character on *Miami Vice*—these guys are always in control. A black man gets into a frightening situation and he's not afraid. When he's with women, he's always got more experience. That's why in *The Cotton Club* it was great to play that type of character, because the woman had so much more experience than Sandman.

How did you start acting?

I got cast in a movie called *Wolfen* because I knew the director, Michael Wadleigh, from when we were hippies together. Once I got the part, I was with Albert Finney, and I was hooked. Just a small conversation with Albert Finney is like Acting 101. I remember one time when we were supposed to come through this doorway, walk through the morgue, and have some dialogue. I was back there trying to figure out how to do this thing. Wadleigh wasn't the type of director who'd really talk to you, unlike Francis [Coppola, director of *The Cotton Club*]. If you even look like you don't know what you're doing, Francis will say, "Wait! What do you need?" Or he'll just start talking to you about the way you should be feeling. Anyway, Albert was sitting down, waiting for our cue, and he said to me, "If I were you, when I go through that door, I'd feel anxious because I'm late. I have someplace else to go, yet I'm intrigued by the possibility that this will be an interesting case." It was like a light bulb going off in my head. Then I knew exactly what to do.

Wolfen was the first time I ever did any kind of a job where I didn't dance. Once we were working at the Persian Room at the Plaza—me, my brother, and my father—and Dustin Hoffman came to see the show. He told me he thought I had some ability as an actor and that I should try it. So I did. I read for a basketball movie called *The Fish That Saved Pittsburgh*, and a movie that was never released called *House of God* that Howard Rollins was in. I wanted to make a movie, because the whole life of the movies appealed to me. You work hard for three or four months, then you don't work at all for a couple of months. I also like the idea of doing a movie, then doing a play, couple of movies, then a play. Also, if you do a movie, you can go see it.

Did you always want to be a performer?

No. I didn't choose to be in the business. I don't remember not dancing. I could always do it. When I got to be about twenty-five, I became very disenchanted. We were in the slick part of show business, the nightclubs. [*He sings.*] "Things are great, dah dah dah." Once I got to be about twenty-five, I got interested in the music of the time. I started smokin' dope, I started drinking, I started slowing down and trying to find myself. I didn't want to work in nightclubs. I didn't want to do *Fiddler on the Roof* medleys. I didn't know what I wanted to do, I just knew I was miserable. I moved to Venice [California], and Pam supported me for a couple of years. It was a great time. I think everybody at some point—especially if they've been working their whole lives—should take time out and think about what they've done. That period of reflection meant a lot to me. I grew up a lot. With the family, I always had a buffer. After a while, I didn't know how to take care of myself. I was twenty-seven years old and very immature. During that period in Venice, I found out how to take care of myself.

How did that period end?

It was like a story out of a movie. The divorce came through with my first wife, and in the custody settlement I got reasonable visitation with my daughter, and I wanted to move back to New York to be near her. I thought I would teach karate to make money, because I was a black belt back then. My brother said, "Come to New York and live with me. I've got an East Side apartment, and I just auditioned for the road company of *Pippin*, and I'm going to make $1200 a week. I'll take care of you." I said, "Great." I came back to New York with $40 in my pocket, my guitar, and my backpack. My brother was in the apartment when I got there—he was supposed to be in Miami with *Pippin*, but he didn't get along with the director and he quit. The place was a dump, an East Side sublet with cockroaches all around. He had to take the mattress off the box spring and put it on the floor for me to sleep on. I had $40 to my name, and he had $120. He said, "Well, I had my agent submit you for this play called *The Last Minstrel Show*." I went down and auditioned the first day I was back in New York, and I got it. It was amazing.

On a really great week in Venice in five years, I made $40. When I auditioned for this show, the agent said, "Yeah, you got it, and they've offered $650 a week, but that's not good enough. I'm going to try to get $750 and get your name in a box." I said, "Are you kidding? I don't care about $750, I don't care about a box, I just want this job. Man, if you blow this for me, I'm going to tear your office apart." But he did get $750 and my name in a box.

And the show closed in Philadelphia.

Yeah. By then I was used to the income —naturally, it came to about $280 a week after they took everything out. I bought my daughter a dress, I sent for Pam to visit. Right away I auditioned for the Broadway musical *Eubie*. They didn't give me the job. I called up the producer, Ashton Springer, and said, "There must be some mistake. I was great at the audition. You've got to give me another audition." He said okay, which probably pissed off the director, because she still didn't cast me. They wanted Larry Marshall, who was in Paris doing *Porgy and Bess* and didn't want to come back. My brother had already been cast. The choreographer was Henry LeTang, who had taught me and my brother to dance. So I kept calling the producer, and finally the second day of rehearsal they said, "You've got the job."

After that, I was really aggressive, 'cause I figured it paid off. *Cotton Club* was another *Eubie*, 'cause I heard through the grapevine that Robert Evans was going to direct *Cotton Club* and he was interested in me for the Cab Calloway part. I went over to my agent and said, "I've got to see the script." He said, "No, Evans won't let anybody see the script." But the script was actually in his office, so when he was called away, I took the script in the men's room for about an hour, and read it. I could see that Calloway wasn't the part for me. I wanted the main black part. I asked for a meeting with Robert Evans—the easiest way to get something is to get directly to the guy—and I went with my hair slicked back, wearing a '40s suit, and told him I wanted that part. He said, "But the part of Cab Calloway . . ." I said, "I don't want that part. I won't do it. I want this part." He said, "I've offered it to Richard Pryor, and if he wants it he's the man. I can get another seven to ten million dollars of financing with his name. With you, I can get maybe $1500." I could understand his point, but I said "You're making a big mistake."

After I left his house, I did as much research as I could on Richard Pryor, and I found that he'd already committed himself to doing *Superman III* and *The Toy*. Once I found that out, I instituted a reign of terror on Robert Evans. I called him every day. I went over to his house twice again, uninvited. It got to the point where he was actually yelling at me over the phone, "Stop calling me! I know you want the part." At first, he liked it. Then when I started calling every day, his people would answer the phone and say, "You can't talk to him." I would say to them, "Look, I'm going to get this part. And after I get this part, he's going to love me, and I'm going to tell him how rude you were to me. So you get him on the phone and let me talk to him. Because if you don't and I get this part, you're out and I'm in."

Gregory, you told me your aggressiveness stopped short of obnoxiousness.

Well, I got close on that one.

FRANK
CONVERSE

Frank Converse

Frank Converse is probably best-known for his regular roles on such TV series as Coronet Blue, NYPD, *and* Movin' On, *though he is a classically trained actor who has worked at the American Shakespeare Festival in Stratford, Connecticut. When we met, he'd most recently been on Broadway with Raul Julia and Jill Clayburgh in Noël Coward's* Design for Living. *He is married to actress Maureen Anderman.*

Were you surprised when you got out of Carnegie Tech and discovered that the jobs that were available had nothing to do with your training? That you ended up doing a TV series instead of Brecht?

I wasn't surprised that the opportunity to work in television and commercial things existed, just that I could be acceptable to them. When I first came to New York, I had two children only eleven months apart. So there I was, trying to support a family of four. When my agent would ask what I wanted to do, I said, "I don't have any choice." I think that's why I got into TV. I'm not in a position to pick scripts and say, "I'd rather do this than that." I don't have the power. I'm still just an actor who wants to survive. I have a new family, I have a two-year-old daughter—this is my third and last attempt at marriage. I'm not as pressed for dough as I was when I first came to New York in the early '60s. But it's always a dilemma.

The best way to be an actor, to be an artist, is to be unattached, or to be attached in very simple ways, so you don't have a lot of bills to pay. Your obligation is to yourself. If you want to do Shakespeare, new plays, good plays, that usually means Off-Broadway or regionals, therefore no dough. It's a sort of gypsy, on-the-road-without-much-baggage lifestyle. I didn't do that. I made this hetero, heavily encumbered choice. But I still won't move to California, which is the obvious place to go if you need a little more income.

What do you think is your most valuable resource?

I'm cheap. *[He laughs.]* I'm big. I haven't lost my hair. For television I'm an obvious type, so I get some mileage out of that. It's a funny thing about TV—in theater I'm not typed too much. The wonderful thing about being an actor is the range of what you can be, how broad the horizon is. If you only think of yourself as one thing, in one tradition, that's boring. In movies and TV, though, there's money to be made in doing one sort of thing. In television I'm encouraged to play a nice macho guy. Now that I'm a little older, I'm encouraged to play a nice macho father.

I saw you onstage in *The Shadow Box* in Boston. Did you feel comfortable playing a gay character in that?

I felt comfortable about every part of it except the last scene, where the two men embrace. To be hetero and playing that felt awkward. I have as many gay friends as hetero friends, so I know that their relationships are very similar to my own in their demands and their problems. But that was something I felt uncomfortable doing.

People often assume that straight actors who play gay characters will have some trouble making that leap. I wonder if you've ever felt uncomfortable playing a romantic scene with a woman?

I think you feel more comfortable because the convention of hetero behavior is so much stronger. Even if I don't like this actress, if her breath is terrible or she's a bitch or I know that her behavior offstage should make you very cautious when you kiss her onstage, it doesn't occur to you to question it the way you would playing a homosexual. The real problem is to find the particulars in hetero relationships onstage, so that they're not clichés. How are these two young star-crossed lovers going to be different from the five hundred others we've seen onstage and in the movies?

When you're standing offstage while the houselights are going down, waiting for your cue, what's going on with you?

I have a little flash of panic. I remember Henry Fonda saying he never had stage fright, because he always knew exactly what he was going to do and say. I never really believed him. It's nice to panic. A lot of energy and spontaneity come from panic. I'm always worried if I don't feel a little trickle between my arm and my shirt.

What's the first thing you do when you come offstage?

You talk. Your subconscious is scribbling all the time you're on, and it's useful to pour out these peripheral impulses with other actors. You walk silently by three actors until you get to your buddy, the one person you can trust, and say, "You know where I say . . . ?" In just a few minutes onstage, you can bottle up more things to talk about later than you said or did onstage.

JEFFREY
DE MUNN

Jeffrey de Munn

Jeff de Munn grew up in Buffalo, where his father worked as a contract coordinator for Sylvania Electric. Jeff planned to be an electrical engineer or lawyer, but loneliness and disappointment with college drove him to the theater department, and almost by accident he wound up studying at the Old Vic theater school in Bristol, England. Despite several juicy character roles in film (Harry Houdini in Ragtime, *Clifford Odets in* Frances), *Jeff is an industrious stage actor whose most sensational work has escaped major attention. When the original Broadway cast of Martin Sherman's* Bent *left, he thoroughly refreshed the role of Horst, one of two gay prisoners conducting a love affair in words under the watchful gaze of Nazi guards. Those who caught his performance as a child-abusing father in an Off-Broadway play called* Total Abandon *still talk about it. And for years, Jeff was a mainstay at the Eugene O'Neill Playwrights Conference, where every summer a core company of actors breathes life into a dozen new plays after intense three-day rehearsal periods.*

When we met, the thirty-eight-year-old actor was living in Westchester with his wife and two small children.

What is your way of working in rehearsal?

I try to come in without having done any homework, but with as much energy as I can pull together each day. Often I will walk to rehearsal. I'll look a lot at the people around me, occasionally as an information search—"Where is he? I know he's down here in one of these people. There's his walk. He'd wear that tie." Or "He wouldn't wear that tie." But the overall thing is just excitement about this wonderful variety of human life you can see in ten blocks. It's a very pleasant feeling of being related to every one of them. As opposed to, "I'm angry . . . the fuckin' taxi . . . Jesus, I hope that guy doesn't do that same shit in rehearsal today . . . My career is shit." Those kinds of things tune you right out, you can't look at anybody really. Then you carry that right into rehearsal, and you don't stand a chance.

Is preparing for rehearsal different from preparing for performance?

It's similar, but more difficult. It's a little bit like if you're in love with somebody. At all hours, even if you don't see that person, there's a part of your brain that's on a state of alert because that person exists. In the best of times, that's the feeling of working on a play.

Did you always feel being an actor was a worthy occupation to pursue, or did it feel a little silly?

Silly and wrong and very much against the Protestant ethic. It took a long time to be proud of being an actor. Part of me was ashamed of it. When someone would say, "What do you do?" a feeling would come over me of apology. "Well . . . I'm an actor." As opposed to simply saying, "I'm an actor. What do *you* do?"

You felt apologetic because it didn't seem like work?

It's *not* work. What do you do? You dress up in clothes that aren't yours and go around saying words that aren't yours—in a *play*? Are you acting all the

time? Are you acting now? All those things that are associated with being an actor: 'The beggars are coming to town.'" There was a lot of discomfort with relatives, people who knew me when I was going to be a lawyer. "You're doing *what*? When are you going to get a *real* job?"

Was there a turning point, when you were happy to say "I'm an actor"?

There were a couple of turning points. First I had to recognize that I was uncomfortable about it, and that happened in a weird way. I was doing my first union theater job, and one of the guys I was working with read palms. He looked at my left hand, which is apparently what you're born with, and my right hand, which is what you do with what you're born with. He looked at my left hand and said, "Holy shit, I've never seen anything like that! You have an incredible talent. Let me see your other hand." He looked at that for a while and said, "You're going to have to learn to accept it before you can do anything with it."

The other turning point was when I found I was able to make a living at it. When I initially came to New York and started going to open calls, I'd watch some of the older men sitting there waiting. The door would open, and they'd sort of pull their insides together and smack on a smile and walk in. When they came out, I'd see the tail end of their smile, and I'd watch them deflate again. I'm looking at a man who's fifty or sixty years old, and I knew that I didn't want to live that way. That looked *real hard*. So I said, "You have ten years of this, and if at the end of that time you haven't got yourself a viable profession going, get out. Do something else."

Those first couple of years were just terrible. All my insecurities, which I think most actors share, ruled me. They ruled me. It wasn't just something I had to live with—they were the boss. I lived in Staten Island the first year; it's always been important for me to get away from New York. Those wonderful boat rides, which were a nickel at the time, were very therapeutic. Looking back at six or six-thirty at night, I'd see the city that an hour before had looked like the worst hellhole on earth to me, and suddenly it was a magic town again, the buildings bathed in the sunset glow.

Was *Comedians* your first big show?

It was my first Broadway show.

A lot of Off-Broadway shows are big shows. Is there a difference?

There's a huge difference. It's night and day. A lot of it is negative. People go crazy when they get near Broadway. The tension level triples, in part because there's so much money involved. For me, there was a sense of "My God, I've finally arrived—now I'll work." You get treated differently by people in the business. It's not all it's cracked up to be; it's a business. But I wouldn't take away from anybody the joy of that first time of thinking that it's the snow-capped peak, because I think everyone should cherish that event, that fantasy. Broadway!

Do you ever feel like quitting?

Yeah, but the worst of that was in the first four or five years, so it's a very old argument that I have inside my head. The other guy immediately says, "Yeah, all right, so what else are you going to do?" And I'm stumped.

MICHAEL
O'KEEFE

Michael O'Keefe

Although best-known as a sort of all-American male ingenue in films—he won an Academy Award nomination for The Great Santini, *in which Robert Duvall bounced a basketball off the back of his head—Michael O'Keefe has had quite an adventurous stage career. He was in the original production of David Rabe's* Streamers, *and Off-Broadway he gave fascinating, unpredictable performances as a bisexual father in Harry Kondoleon's lunatic comedy* Christmas on Mars *and as a child molester in a revival of Miguel Pinero's* Short Eyes.*

I met Michael on the patio of the Kennedy Center in Washington, where he was appearing in Peter Sellars' extravagantly avant-garde staging of The Count of Monte Cristo. *Sellars later told me that when Japanese theater master Tadashi Suzuki brought his company to the Kennedy Center during the run of* Monte Cristo, *Michael joined the company every morning for their rigorous warm-up exercises—the epitome of a serious young actor.*

I was taught to think of myself as an instrument, and I learned to play my body, my voice, my spirit, my individuality. What I aspire to is to have an instrument that can adapt to any style. I've done a lot of contemporary, naturalistic drama; *The Count of Monte Cristo* is the first avant-garde thing, and it's a whole new challenge. The biggest danger is complacency, which leads to mediocrity. Especially when you're successful and young, there's a tendency to indulge yourself and think "I've done it." At times I thought a lot more of myself than I deserved to. But a consistent image in my work is growth. There's never a resounding chord at the end.

How does actor training prepare you for movies?

I instinctively understood film. I like movies. Doing them is like getting behind your dreams and finding out what makes them work.

What made you want to act?

I can't remember wanting to do anything else. When I was three, the girls in the neighborhood wanted to put on *The Wizard of Oz* and they needed a wizard, so I played the wizard. A bunch of us kids used to put on murder mysteries in my garage. It was a way of getting things I couldn't get from life. Camus says, "Actors get to cheat the absurdity of existence," because you get to play all these different people. When I did *The Slugger's Wife*, I spent four months with a hitting coach and went into spring training with the Braves. It was infinitely more interesting than doing the movie.

Most actors I know look back and think they weren't getting enough attention. As a kid, you're not taken seriously. I guess I still feel that way. I like being taken seriously as an actor—I don't like to be thought of as a commercial entity or a star. My life is largely informed by what I didn't have as a child, those deeply rooted desires that come from dissatisfaction. It's very useful; whatever happened to you remains with you in the form of sense memories.

What do your parents do?

My father is a lawyer and professor of law at St. Thomas of Villanova University in Florida. Mom used to be a professional tennis player—Stephanie "Red"

Fitzpatrick—and she's done a lot of work for the Westchester Council on Alcoholism.

Do you have a routine you perform before going onstage?

I meditate. I create images I'm going to use in my performance. For example, in this play the themes are Finding My Father and Freeing My Mother's Spirit. I create those archetypes in my mind, let go of my conscious mind—it's like being drawn into a well. The world around me disappears. Once I'm there, I create images of my own father and myself as a very young boy wanting love, ideal love from a father. Then I create this image of a longing mother in a great deal of pain. I let those things wash over me. Then I put it all out of my mind. There's no time or place for thinking onstage. What's required is action. I go on my instinct, my discipline, and my training.

What's the first thing you do when you come offstage?

Wash my face. I really like it when people come back after the show. It's an immediate message about what you're doing. When I did *Short Eyes*, though, I wasn't eager to see anyone before or after. I'm not so indulgent or possessed as to think I am the character, but you do live with it. While doing the play, I wasn't aware of the emotional burden, but after it was over, I felt the release.

What's the silliest thing about being an actor?

Wearing other people's clothes. In *Slugger's Wife*, I gave him really bad taste —I wore loud checked jackets. It was pretty silly going to Barney's with the designer Ann Roth and saying, "Do you have anything *a lot uglier* than this?"

Being recognized is pretty silly. Or it's like this: At the premiere of *The Slugger's Wife* in Atlanta, I'm talking to Neil Simon in the lobby. There must be fifty pictures of me all over this lobby, and Neil Simon is one of the most recognizable writers in the country. This photographer comes up and says, "Can I get a picture?" We say "Sure." Then he comes up and says, "And, gentlemen, you are . . . ?" I say, "Timothy Hutton." And Neil Simon says, "Woody Allen."

PHILIP
BOSCO

Philip Bosco

Philip Bosco is one of the most industrious actors in New York. He never stops working. When we met, he had recently returned from making the movie of Mark Medoff's play Children of a Lesser God *with Bill Hurt in Canada. He had just completed six days' work playing a judge on* The Guiding Light, *and he was about to go into rehearsal for a short-lived Off-Broadway comedy called* Be Good to Me. *Earlier in the afternoon, he had driven in from his home in Teaneck, New Jersey, for a meeting with Robert De Niro, who was trying to cast a production of Brecht's* The Resistible Rise of Arturo Ui. *He described De Niro as "a very short guy with a ponytail": "It was nice talking to him. My kids said, 'Daddy, bring him home to dinner.'"*

What do you do when you're not working?

I have a big family—seven kids—and we have a pretty good-sized house which requires constant upkeep. But I'm almost always working. I worked at the Repertory Theater at Lincoln Center for seven years when Jules Irving was in charge. When he left, the theater closed, and I was out of work for the first time in a long time, for eighteen months. This was 1973. My wife then went to work for the first time as a waitress. She really kept us together.

I got very desperate. I did some outrageous stuff to try to make money. I sold magazines over the telephone, which is the most degrading thing to do. Have you ever done anything like that? It's not like going up to the door and ringing the buzzer. You call up and give this prepared speech. It's very dishonest. They had these sponsoring organizations who actually got a very tiny part of the money. If you sign up for a subscription for $20, they might get a quarter. You knew that, and you had to give this performance. It was loathsome.

What made you want to be an actor in the first place?

The first time I can remember acting was when I was in eighth grade, and I was in some dumb play. I have this clear image of being twelve years old and people saying, "Oh, you were so good." I must have gotten the idea then that I'm good at this. Why else would I have continued? Nobody in my family was in the theater. I certainly didn't do it for money, because I never made any money until three years ago. I started making a few dollars because I did some movies. Up until that time, I was working myself to the bone, working virtually fifty weeks a year, and the most I made would be $35,000.

What kept you doing it?

It's difficult to put into words. It pleases me to do it, and I really need it as a way of expressing myself. I like it principally because I like language—that's why I enjoy doing Shaw or Shakespeare. It's very satisfying to wrap yourself around those words.

When you decided to be a professional actor, was it obvious you would move to New York?

Sooner or later. But even before I went to college, I was absolutely fascinated with the theater. I would come to New York all the time and go to plays. The first play I ever saw was in 1944—the original *Arsenic and Old Lace* at the

Hudson Theater on Forty-fourth Street. That same week I saw *Angel Street* with Vincent Price and Judith Evelyn and Leo G. Carroll. I'd hang around stage doors. I was absolutely enthralled by the theater. I went to see Ingrid Bergman in Maxwell Anderson's *Joan of Lorraine*, one of the first things she did when she came over here onstage. I went to a matinee—I'll never forget it. There were so many fans hanging around, they blocked the whole street, and Bergman couldn't get out the door to go to lunch. Finally the management came out and made a speech saying, "Miss Bergman has agreed to meet you all in the theater." They opened the doors, we went in, Bergman came out onstage in a beautiful robe and made a little speech saying, "You're lovely but I really must go to dinner. But I'll talk to you for a few moments if you have any questions." People were screaming, bringing up flowers and shit, it was great. It was from that point on that I really got caught up in the theater. One of the high points of my life was when the Old Vic came over after the war with Olivier and Richardson. They did *Oedipus Rex*, and Richardson played Falstaff. I was only fifteen, sixteen. I was on top of the world.

Was your decision to work in the theater in New York related to having a family and settling down in New Jersey?

Somewhat. But another factor was as important as any of the others. Until recently, I was afflicted with a kind of panic disorder—I was a classic agoraphobic. I couldn't travel, which inhibited almost any film work. I couldn't get to certain areas in the city. I couldn't go in elevators. I've had this since I was nineteen. When my wife and I first met, she didn't know about it—I had a macho image to uphold! I couldn't let on that I had any weaknesses, particularly a weakness that seems so childish to other people. When I unburdened myself of the shame, people were very understanding. I then adopted an attitude in my professional life where my agent would outline it beforehand—"Phil can't do such and such, do you still want to see him?" I've met a lot of directors in lobbies.

I don't anymore, thank God. I'm now on medication under a doctor's care, which allows me to do things I couldn't do before. Even if I didn't have this problem, I would have stayed in New York. This made it easier because I couldn't leave if I wanted to.

THOMAS G.
WAITES

Thomas G. Waites

Most people who know him call him Tommy, partly to distinguish him from the pop singer-songwriter Tom Waits and partly because his rumpled street-angel face elicits the kind of affection you might have toward a mixed-up kid brother. He's more savvy and ambitious than he might seem, though. Thirty years old when we met, he had just received a reading of his first play at the Actors Studio and was writing another. A musician and songwriter himself, he was coaching female rock singers who were auditioning for Paul Schrader's movie Light of Day *(Joan Jett got the part). He'd been auditioning for several stage plays and had to choose between a Victorian melodrama, a rock revue, and a small part in* Othello. *He'd just filmed an episode of* Miami Vice, *and he was awaiting the release of* The Clan of the Cave Bear, *in which he starred with Daryl Hannah and Pamela Reed, to see if it would change his life. (It didn't.)*

When did you start acting?

It's actually kind of weird. I wanted to be an athlete all my life, growing up outside of Philadelphia. Then I got hit by a car when I was sixteen and broke both my legs. I had to find something else to do. I was in the hospital for a long time, about nine months. In retrospect it was the greatest thing that ever could have happened to me, because I was a wild kid; I was in a street gang. I was purposely put in this position to sit still for a reason. So I began to read.

I also simultaneously became addicted to Demerol for the pain. In the middle of the night, even though I wasn't in pain, I would put on these incredible scenarios of very high drama in order to get another shot of Demerol. When the doctor finally found out about it and told the nurse, she said to me, "You've been fooling me all this time? You son of a gun. You ought to be an actor." *Bing!* The light went off, and I thought, "Huh. That sounds like an honorable profession."

Most of all, it sounded like what I wanted sports to be, which was a way out of where I was—this ravaged, blue-collar, factory town, very low income, very depressing, very uninspiring, to say the least. I knew I could do better. I became in love with the idea of being an actor; most good actors do in the beginning. You have to withstand the period when you're first realizing you know nothing at all about this. In order to strip yourself to a certain neutral gear so you can play a Jewish transvestite or a street junkie, you have to be willing to be a clean white page. That takes a lot of introspection. Why do you say Phully instead of Philly or Tam instead of Tom? Why, why, why? You keep digging. Why do you jump at certain sounds? Why are you defensive? Why do you see the things you see?

Where did your idea of acting come from?

Romeo. I saw Zefferelli's *Romeo and Juliet* the day after I got out of the hospital. My sister Kathleen took me to see it. I wept like I had never wept in my life. Here I am, this guy in a transition period of my life, and this movie is having this effect on me where I'm crying not just about this movie, but about sixteen years of anxiety, of pain. I want to be able to do that for other people. I used to write songs, and in one of them I describe myself as "a priest ridin' by and spittin' fire in your eyes." It's like a sacrament when I go onstage. That's where theater started, isn't it? The Greeks. The actors were your connection to God, whatever that means.

What do you do before going onstage to prepare for that?

It depends on the part. When I played Petruchio in *Taming of the Shrew*, I'd sit and stare at an ashtray and drink a pint of Guinness stout. Because I saw Petruchio as a hedonist, and this woman purifies him as he purifies her at the same time. For Steve in *Pastorale*, I would take karate class every day and run four or five miles every night before I went onstage, because he was a construction worker, and I wanted to feel what it feels like when you're so tired.

How did you get into studying karate?

When I was very young, I was like a kid in a candy store where everything is free. Getting every job I went up for, under option to Paramount. I needed more discipline, so I sought it out and happened to find one of the greatest men I'll ever know, Sensei Kesh. If you learn to follow someone blind like that, just put your trust in them, you also can do the same with the writer, just trust the language, trust the director and the other actors to be there. You get so much by giving. Not give and take, but give and give. I wasted so much time with self-indulgence that I had to cure myself very quickly. One of my goals is to become a delight to work with. I don't have to worry about being good or not. I can, of course, become better. But I want to be good and fun to work with, dependable and reliable and inspiring and there when the chips fall down.

Did you have formal actor training?

I studied at Juilliard. Most people can't believe that. Most people don't believe I can speak verse either, and I played Prince Hal and Petruchio and *Comedy of Errors* and *Titus Andronicus*. I've done a lot of Shakespeare, and I do well with verse. Part of this business is the element of surprise. When they expect you to be drunk at the bar, show up at the health spa in your gym shorts with a Tiger candy bar in your hand. When they expect you to be Prince Charles . . .

Show up in high heels.

Or whatever. A lot of it is just having the balls to get out there and say, "Yeah, I can be a woman." I mean, people who saw *Forty-Deuce* thought I was a transvestite. One of the other actors brought a friend, and after the show she said, "God, you know, he was such a tacky queen. Why don't they get an actor to play the part instead of dragging in this tacky queen, painting his toenails onstage?" Two days later, he brought her to a karate promotion where I had to fight six people in a row—I got the shit beat out of me—and do one hundred push-ups on my knuckles. He introduced us and said, "By the way, this is the guy who plays Mitchell in *Forty-Deuce*." She was so stunned she dropped her purse. That was very satisfying. I like doing that, making it so real that you don't have any questions. I don't want you to struggle as an audience. I want you to sit back and relax. I'm going to take you somewhere. That's my job, and I like it.

Are there actors who have been inspirations to you?

Al Pacino's been a tremendous inspiration to me. I've known Al since I was a kid, twenty-one or twenty-two. I was sitting in my apartment one day, the phone rang, and this casting director said, "Are your doing anything today? I need you to read for me. Al Pacino is casting this movie called *Born on the Fourth of July*, and we're auditioning for the part of his girlfriend, but he has to go to the dentist. We'll pay you for the day." I said, "Sure." I had thirty of the most beautiful women in the world come in and tear their clothes off and sit on my lap and try to make love to me. I thought, "This is tough, fellas. I get paid for this." Then I met Al the next day to audition for the same film. We've worked together a number of times.

I saw him on Sunday, and we were talking about *And Justice for All*. There was one very beautiful scene between Al and me that they cut out. It was as real as emotion ever gets. He said that if they had kept that scene in, I would have been nominated for an Academy Award that year. A closeup like that can change the entire film.

And your life.

And my life. That's okay. I don't look at any struggle or failure as anything that impedes my progress. You do the job, sometimes you get recognized, sometimes you don't. You go on to the next thing, and it makes you try harder. Someday, I'll get the part that fits me like a glove.

What's your favorite thing about being an actor?

Every time you play a different part, you have to question your motivation for getting into this mess to begin with. Every time you play a part, there's something in that character that's you, whether it's a rapist in *Extremities* or an idealistic young revolutionary in *Awake and Sing*. You have to take yourself apart and you go, "Where in me could I find it to want to do something as horrible as rape somebody?" You go back into your childhood, perhaps, and think of something terribly cruel that was done to you and how angry you are still about that. For example, where I grew up, if you didn't join the football team—and I couldn't—you were a faggot, and you had to fight every day after school, fight your way home, fight your way to the bus. The peer pressure that that involves makes people crazy. It makes them go out and become a serial killer. Going back in time and extracting something from that is my favorite part of acting. I get to find out more about me.

What's the silliest thing about being an actor?

Sometimes you'll work with directors who have the worst taste imaginable, and they'll say, "You know that thing you do, that, like, intense thing? Well, be, like, intense there, okay?" So you have to go *pose* for the camera, and you're thinking, "Is that *intense* enough?"

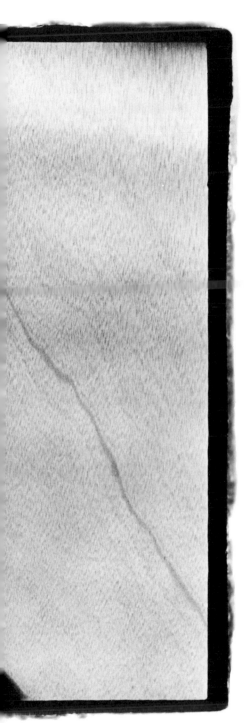

WILL
PATTON

Will Patton

Like many performers originally trained and influenced by actor-director Joseph Chaikin, Will Patton is a spiritually questing and predominantly physical actor —qualities that have carried over to his subsequent work in theater and film. When he replaced Ed Harris in the original New York production of Sam Shepard's Fool for Love, *Will and I worked out at the same gym, and it became a running joke for him to display his battle scars from banging off the walls in that play. He fractured the knuckle of the same little finger twice, and both his hands swelled to almost twice their size. So when we met for this interview, while Will was in rehearsal for another physically strenuous performance in Shepard's* A Lie of the Mind, *we began by catching up on his injuries.*

The arrangement of words on a page cannot adequately convey Will's speech pattern, a cultivated affectation. He talks very hesitantly, in a breathy, slow voice, lingering over any exclamation, only occasionally speaking loudly, clearly, articulately.

How long were you in *Fool for Love*?

I did it for ten months. Physically, I felt all right the whole time, aside from the broken bones and having a split head, black eye, and broken noses. But toward the end, I began to feel emotionally hurt, because I had to change women so many times. It was like falling in and out of love over and over again, having my heart broken over and over and over again when a new actress would take over the part.

How do you like acting in movies?

I don't like the lack of control, being slipped into that nozzle and taken away somewhere where I can't see what's going on. But I do like working in the movies a lot and want to do more. I got to work in front of the camera a lot when I was on *Ryan's Hope* and *Search for Tomorrow*. Soap operas can be good for you, and they can be very harmful. You learn to take the things that matter most, like love and death, throw 'em out like they're candy. You learn to be frivolous and settle for things. Otherwise you kill yourself. Because you have to work fast. You usually get one take. Unless you say "fuck." By accident.

What was working with Martin Scorsese in *After Hours* like?

He was incredible! A lot of directors have a tendency to let the atmosphere be dead and technical and not create an atmosphere of theatricality or intensity or electricity. They'll say, "Here's the camera," and you've got clothes on, and everything's very still and stiff and like a vacuum. And Scorsese made it, like, "This is making movies!" Pow! The room would be made ready for an experience of some sort.

Where did you grow up?

South Carolina, North Carolina. My father was a preacher, and at one time he had a farmhouse for juvenile-deliquent boys. I guess they were all about thirteen when I was about five.

Did your father stop being a preacher?

Yeah, he dropped out. He lost all his morals. Well, no. When I was about thirteen, he ran off, found another woman, and broke from the scene. I was back and forth from my mother to my father. My father was all over the place, never in one place too long.

When did you start acting?

When I was five years old, my mother and my father dressed me up in this hula skirt and put all this makeup on me and danced me in front of all these juvenile-delinquent boys. I remember how much they were excited by me; I was able to dance in this outfit and overwhelm them. That's my first memory of my being able to do something. Later in school I was always kind of crippled and shy, unable to do sports, unable to talk to girls. When I would get up in front of the class to read something I had written or to be in a play, I would feel everyone was my friend all of a sudden. Everyone understood me. It became my way of reaching the world.

Had you been performing before you came to New York?

I went to North Carolina School for the Arts for three-quarters of a year. It's like the Juilliard of the South. I wasn't ready for school. I was totally drunk the whole time. I was out of control and got kicked out, just traveled instead.

Does the work you did with Chaikin help with other work you do?

Yeah, but I think I will never be quite legitimate because of it. I may not ever make a lot of money because of certain feelings I have about acting and certain ways I'm not able to be across a desk. Most of the people you're dealing with from L.A. and in the movies are talking on the phone while you're looking at 'em. They're a really horrible bunch of people. Someone flew me out there one time for a TV thing. I walked into the room, they were talking, and I said, "What's going on in this room? What happened? Did you just have an argument, or what? There's something very strange going on here." They looked at me, like, "What do you mean? This is the way we are, this is the way we behave." I went out in the outer office and said to this guy, "Get me on a plane right away or I'm gonna hit somebody." That was my experience in L.A.

What were they doing that was so horrible?

[He makes a face and emits some inarticulate sounds.] Lying! Or playing this game that doesn't have anything to do with working with you. You'll be here and these people come through the room and they play this game with you. They try to, like, stab you before you even get started.

Stab you?

Take advantage of your vulnerability, strangulate you, and somehow slip your soul into their pocket.

JERRY
ORBACH

Jerry Orbach

Jerry Orbach is a singing actor, a workhorse performer renowned for sticking with a show over the long haul. His first New York job was in Threepenny Opera *Off-Broadway, which he left after three and a half years to play El Gallo in the original production of* The Fantasticks. *He spent three years doing the Bob Fosse musical* Chicago *and four years on Broadway with* 42nd Street *(even longer in the TV commercial for the show). At the time we met, he was on a break.*

What's life in a long run like?

It's easy, really. You have a sense of security and routine, and you have your days free. On the artistic side, there's constant experimentation. I find it fascinating. It's like taking a watch apart and putting it back together, but better because the watch changes every time you open it up. There's always a new audience out there that's never heard the story before. At the end of the run of *Chicago*, we were in San Francisco, and it was the last week. One night after the show I said to Gwen Verdon, "Tonight I did it perfect." It took me three years.

What do you do between long runs?

The daily routine is mostly the gym or playing tennis, working on possibilities for new projects. Right now instead of getting into another show, I'd like to concentrate more on films and television. One needs the national exposure. They now have this insidious computer system called the Q-Rating which, when they punch your name in, gives a rating of how many people in this country know who you are. For instance, Lucille Ball would get 100 on it, and I'll get maybe a 20. Angela Lansbury, prior to doing *Murder, She Wrote*, would have gotten a 20. Now she'll get 95. A couple of months ago, I was up for this television movie. The director wanted me, the producer wanted me, I was perfect for it. The network punched up my name on the computer and said, "No, get somebody else who has a more visible name in television."

Did you always want to be an actor?

From the time I was fourteen or fifteen. A teacher in high school got me an apprentice job in summer stock, so by the time I was a freshman at Northwestern, I already had my Equity card. I was a very serious actor. I wanted to be like Marlon Brando or Montgomery Clift. A strange turning point for me was a college production of Brecht's *The Caucasian Chalk Circle*, which is also a musical. I was deeply immersed in Brecht at the time. When I came to New York in 1956, *Threepenny Opera* had just reopened in the Village, and because of my Brecht background, I went into it as the street singer and understudied Mack the Knife. Suddenly I was doing a musical, so from that I got *The Fantasticks*, and from that my first Broadway show, *Carnival*. During all that time, I studied with Lee Strasberg and Herbert Berghof and Mira Rostova at the Actors Studio, but became pigeonholed as a musical performer. I kept working, though, so I was happy. Friends of mine like Ed Asner and George Segal and Ben Gazzara and Bob Loggia couldn't get arrested, so they were forced to go to California and became movie or television stars.

Was it weird to study at the Actors Studio and do musicals?

One doesn't negate the other. I felt it was interesting to be the type of actor that I was, to do the broad strokes of musicals as a style. It wasn't until *Prince of the City* that people in the business finally said, "My God, he can act naturalistically."

What could you bring to musicals from your serious acting background?

I sang in character as well as acted the character. I came along at a time when the leading people in musicals, like John Raitt and Alfred Drake, sang one way, almost operatically, and pretty much played themselves. But people were getting too sophisticated and starting to laugh at the stiff musical comedy singers who couldn't act. When Barrymore was the great American actor, his broad-stroked, grand style was accepted everywhere. But when Brando came along, he changed the face of American acting. People didn't even think he was an actor the first time he was onstage. It was a revolution in acting, and it permeated everywhere. Finally, it went into the musical, which was very difficult: when you're standing onstage in front of a couple of thousand people without amplification, you have to yell, and that negates any kind of realism.

How do you deal with the fact that onstage you're speaking at three times the volume of what would be realistic?

There's a difference between naturalism and realism. Naturalism is natural behavior—every fluctuation, every moment of natural behavior as this hand hits my knee. But realism is selective naturalism—you select the parts of reality that you want the audience to see. The movie director decides where he's going to cut from me to your reaction. On the stage, you and I have to select when they're going to look at your reaction. If, say, this cup of coffee is poisoned, in film we see you put the poison in, then I come and drink it, and the audience is waiting for me because they know. But on the stage, rather than just drinking the coffee and putting it down, I might do something like this [*he raises an imaginary coffee cup to his mouth very slowly*]. If I slow down the action for that moment, the whole audience's attention focuses in on that cup—"Omigod, what's in the coffee?" It's realistic behavior, but it's unnatural. Speaking three times as loud as life is unnatural. But if you make the character bigger than life, if you make him have more energy than a normal person has walking into a room, then they'll buy it.

Did you think when you started acting that you would do movies?

Yeah. But it didn't work out that way for a while. I tried going to California for a while once, but I had two boys—one's seventeen now, the other will be twenty-four—and when they were in school, I tried not to go away any more than I had to to survive.

Is that why you're attracted to long runs?

It was a matter of financial survival. Why leave something where you're making money to go and take a chance on something else? I envy the people who have what I call a British career, where they go from film to television to stage without much trouble. Here you have to make a commitment to living either in Los Angeles or New York. The travel is not the problem, it's the attitudes. If you're an actor from New York, they still say, "If you're willing to relocate, we feel we can give you more work. You want to become part of this community? Or are you going to stay in New York and be a foreigner?"

What's the silliest thing about being an actor?

The feeling that one is still not a grown-up at fifty. I'm reasonably intelligent, I work hard, and if I'd been thirty-five years in the shoe business, I'd be the president of the corporation or chairman of the board and making my own decisions. As an actor, I'm still waiting for phone calls.

ZELJKO
IVANEK

Zeljko Ivanek

His name, in Slovenian, means "desire." As a child, Zeljko Ivanek (pronounced ZHEL-ko Ee-VAH-nek) went back and forth between his native Yugoslavia and California, where his father did research at Stanford. He speaks five languages—Slovenian and Serbo-Croatian (two Yugoslavian tongues), French, "rusty" German, and unaccented English. Sweet, shy, and rather secretive, Zeljko was twenty-eight when we met. He had just finished performing in David Hare's A Map of the World at the Public Theater and had not yet been cast in Joe Orton's Loot, which opened at Manhattan Theater Club and later moved to Broadway.

What do you do when you're not working?

I see a lot of shows and movies. I spend hundreds and hundreds of dollars a year on other people's work. I don't have the patience to go to class—I went straight from high school to Yale to drama school in England, and I can't take being in a classroom anymore. I learn a lot from watching other people work. I saw a play and two movies yesterday, which is not that unusual for me. I'm insatiable. And I sleep at the strangest times. I go to bed around seven in the morning and sleep 'til two in the afternoon.

What do you stay up all night doing?

That's a good question. It's not like I'm doing anything productive. Until about three in the morning, I really like it. I'll read the *New York Times* or watch something. From three until I fall asleep, that's a waste. When I'm in rehearsal, I lead the healthiest life—getting up at nine in the morning, rehearsing all day, making dinner, looking at my script, going to bed by midnight, one o'clock. It's an incredibly normal life. Then when we start performing, it takes me hours to calm down after a show, so bedtime gets to be three, four in the morning. When I'm not working, it creeps toward five, six, seven. It's just restlessness, mostly. I put my head down and I can't stop thinking. I worry whether I'll read something I feel strongly about. Then if I do, will I get it?

Did you always want to be an actor?

Yeah. It was the only thing that I took any real pleasure from, and it always seemed the most logical thing to pursue. I started out with a juvenile desire for attention, probably. By the time I went to college, I settled into more specific reasons about what it is I get out of it and why I want to continue doing it. Each thing I've done that I was proud to be associated with—*Cloud 9, Master Harold . . . and the Boys, Brighton Beach Memoirs, A Map of the World*—crystallizes why I want to do it but also spoils me for the next time around. It makes it harder to do things I don't feel as passionate about. *Cloud 9*, for instance, ends with two characters, basically the same woman at different ages, embracing each other, a woman embracing her past. One night this woman who was well into her fifties came backstage with her husband and told us, "It took me twenty-seven years of therapy to do what you do on that stage at the end of the play every night." What an incredible feeling! You suddenly want to be part of that all the time.

When you went into acting, did you want to do movies as well?

It was always stage. I didn't grow up with movies. I would go to some American movies, but I never related to movies as something I would actually do, maybe because it was so far removed. I'm not sure I even realized that people in movies were actors.

What did it feel like when you actually did movies?

Very strange. When I showed up, they'd been shooting for a month and a half already—this was *Tex*—and it like landing on foreign ground. It's such a drastic shift from rehearsing a play, where you have a script in your hand, you get up and do it, get a few notes, do it again. You show up on a movie set, and you wait for three hours while they set the lights. Suddenly, you're the least important thing there.

It was also a drastic shift not having an audience, not having someone to tell you what happened. I only had one scene, in a truck, and because we had to shoot it out of order, it was completely disorienting. You finish, and you have no idea of what actually happened. Somebody says, "Good, that was fine," or, "Good, we'll go again," and you don't have a clue that you've actually had an effect on anything. I like it a lot, but I have a lot to learn.

What's the hardest thing for you to do as an actor?

It's hard for me to feel I have the right to sit still and talk slow. If I have three sentences in a row, I have an innate tendency to get through them as fast as possible, on the off-chance that by doing that I'll make less of a fool of myself or have less of a chance of someone in the audience saying, "Have we been listening to him for a minute and a half already?"

JOHN
MALKOVICH

John Malkovich

That John Malkovich became known as a stage actor first, rather than a television or film star, is largely the legacy of his background in Chicago theater, with its strong tradition of continuity and ensemble playing dating back to the Second City company that nurtured the likes of Elaine May, Mike Nichols, Alan Arkin, and Barbara Harris. The rewards of working with a band of like-minded actors in Chicago's Steppenwolf Theater Company encouraged Malkovich to develop his unusual gifts in a tiny Off-Loop theater rather than throw himself into the freelance talent pool in New York or Los Angeles.

With Steppenwolf, Malkovich started out playing a series of brooding sons—Tom in The Glass Menagerie, *Biff in* Death of a Salesman, *the narrator of A Sorrow Beyond Dreams (Peter Handke's memoir of his mother's suicide). All that changed, he says, "when my hair fell out." He started taking roles like Steve in Say Goodnight, Gracie who makes his entrance wearing a gorilla suit and brown derby, or Mr. James in a particularly notorious show called* Big Mother. *"It was a School of Large Props play, all mug-and-run," Malkovich recalls with satisfaction. "I wore a black Afro wig, and I painted on these greasy sideburns, one in the shape of Florida—with a star by Tallahassee—and the other in the shape of a spermatozoa."*

The freedom to experiment with impunity that the Steppenwolf actors allowed each other made him determined not to be pigeonholed. He made his New York debut as Lee in Steppenwolf's production of Sam Shepard's True West. *Practically from the first line he uttered—a balding menace in a grimy, oversize undershirt, he breathed beer in his brother's face and deadpanned, "So, Mom took off for Alaska, huh?"—Malkovich was a sensation. His dangerously infantile performance, later televised in PBS's "American Playhouse" series, started racking up the kind of critical raves, awards, and peer-group adulation that greet an actor's debut maybe once in a generation. But the next time he got onstage, he played Biff Loman, Arthur Miller's All-American good boy, opposite Dustin Hoffman in* Death of a Salesman *on Broadway. His first movie was* The Killing Fields, *in which he played a photographer; next, in* Places in the Heart, *he played the blind Mr. Will, which won him an Oscar nomination. Even while performing on Broadway, Malkovich continued to direct plays, as he frequently had in Chicago with Steppenwolf. He mounted an Off-Broadway revival of Lanford Wilson's* Balm in Gilead *that transformed a lowlife drama into a street opera by pumping it full of rock music, and followed that by directing Kevin Kline, Raul Julia, and Glenne Headley (a Steppenwolf actress and his wife) on Broadway in Shaw's* Arms and the Man.

From the outside, this looks like one of the best-planned careers in show business. When you meet John Malkovich, though, he hardly comes across like a one-man media event. Tall and somewhat stony-faced in repose, he speaks softly in the measured Midwestern drawl of someone who doesn't like to rush into things. When he laughs, he has the lazy grin and goofy rolling eyes of a sheepish kid. His high forehead and curly sidelocks give him an leonine air that, onstage, he can use to scary effect when he wants. Offstage, he's dreamier, a soft-boiled egg. He reminds me of the Cowardly Lion in The Wizard of Oz. *Like many good actors, Malkovich is rarely satisfied with his work: "Most of it has just been a terrible misunderstanding."*

The obstacle in anything you do is that the audience will say, "I've seen that." It was bad enough when all you had to deal with were the performances one person could see onstage in a lifetime. Now, with films, it's more than a lifetime. That's what's scary about films.

Did you find acting for the camera different from acting onstage?

Only in that I am a creature of instinct, and film is anti-instinct and anti-intuition. Everything's got to be planned down to the last minute, which I don't excel at. I keep changing it. The problem is that if you do that, you leave it up to other people's discretion which take they prefer. I'm not exactly a paranoid person, but I don't like my performance to be in anybody else's hands. In theater, it's not. Films are harder for me because I don't have the emotional weight of the night behind me. But I enjoyed doing the movie of *Death of a Salesman*, because by that time we'd gotten the performances we wanted.

I understand that when you first auditioned for *Salesman*, you hit it off with Dustin Hoffman right away.

Well, so many famous people, I mean *stars*, were shaking in their boots waiting to read with Dustin. I wasn't scared. I just went for him and started flinging him around. He loved it. He wanted people who'd challenge him. I'm not the nervous type. Dustin's an excellent actor, but I've worked with some great actors all my life.

Does it feel funny going back and forth from being a director to being an actor?

Although I have enjoyed acting a lot sometimes, I have to say I prefer being a director. Sometimes I wish I could be meaner, because I'd probably get better work done. I could almost never fire someone. I did it once in my life, and I felt so terrible afterward for so long, I don't think I could do it again.

Do you have models as a director?

No. But I had two really good teachers in school. Dr. Gabbard, at Eastern Illinois University, taught me how unforgivable it is to be boring—that it's the worst sin and it's why live theater is always dying. He was very blunt about it. I can remember being in rehearsal and seeing the glow of his cigarette from the back of the theater and his saying, "You're a bullshit actor full of bullshit. You bore the hell out of me. Get off the stage."

Then I had another teacher, Dr. Lane, at Illinois State—which is where most of us at Steppenwolf went to school—who didn't really care what was boring, he only cared about what was true to the human condition. He had an uncanny instinct about what was true and moving, about the aura around an actor that says, "This is true." That's why a lot of the actors at Steppenwolf have a real workers' mentality. They're not devastated by their own gifts. We've been lucky, we've worked together a long time, there was some talent in the group, so we've had glimpses of what theater can be, and that's what we've worked toward.

Did you always make a living as an actor in Chicago?

No, I always had a day job. I worked at Chandler's Office Supply, I was a bus driver for Solomon Schecter Day School, I was head cabbage cutter at Egg Rolls Etc., and I worked in the box office for the Ravinia Festival. I never made more than five thousand dollars a year from Steppenwolf. Usually it was more like two thousand or no thousand.

How did you like going to the Oscars when you were nominated for *Places in the Heart?*

It was fine. Nobody told me about the part before, or I would have gone in the back door. About a minute before we got there, Phyllis [*Carlyle, his manager*] said, "Oh, by the way, there will be a few press people there when we go in." A few—it was more like a few thousand. I wasn't prepared for that. It was a circus. I felt sorry for them. Glenne talked for weeks about Rob Weller from *Entertainment Tonight*, how sad he looked—like a crust of bread. [*He is silent for a moment, replaying the event.*] You know . . . someone offers you a part . . . and you're nominated for this award . . . and you're just a fuckin' *jerk*. I think of myself as a person, not a thing. That stuff celebrates becoming a thing.

BARNARD
HUGHES

Barnard Hughes

Besides being one of the most beloved actors in the business, Barney Hughes is also the head of a distinguished theatrical family. While he was appearing at the Lunt-Fontanne Theater on Broadway with Jason Robards in the acclaimed revival of Eugene O'Neill's The Iceman Cometh, *both his wife, Helen Stenborg, and his daughter Laura were engaged at the Circle Repertory Theater Off-Broadway, and his son Doug, a talented stage director, was working as associate director of the Seattle Repertory Theater.*

It was shortly before Thanksgiving when we met in his dressing room before a matinee, and Barney (who had recently turned seventy) was reassessing the wisdom of his offer to cook Thanksgiving dinner for the whole family. It also turned out to be the last week of The Iceman Cometh, *which opened to sensational reviews but didn't do great business and closed after a surprisingly brief run.*

The time has come for me to go out West and do a mini-series or something like that, and then come back and shoot the roll on another play. I walk into the theater every night under the marquee dangling those banners saying what people think about this production; to think that it's closing after fifty-five, sixty performances is rather disheartening. This has happened to me the last three plays I've done—Arthur Kopit's *End of the World*, a wonderful play, closed in a hurry. The season before that, I was in Lanford Wilson's *Angels Fall*—I'd go anywhere to do it at the drop of a hat. That was a fast close. I must stop doing plays I like, if I intend to make a living in the theater.

Does it seriously disrupt your life when a play closes prematurely?

Well, you just have to sit for a while until you catch the brass ring again. If you're doing films or television, you're in one wheel. If you're doing theater, you're in another wheel. When you try, as I do, to dance back and forth between the two of them, there are disruptions. But at my stage in life, it's kind of nice to have a breather in between.

In sheer number of hours, you've probably been running longer in *Iceman* than any two other plays.

Yes, plays are getting shorter and shorter. I went to Washington to see Ralph Richardson a couple of years ago in *Early Times*. I'd never met him, but Irene Worth heard I was going and had given me a birthday present to deliver to Sir Ralph for his wife. So I went back to see him, and he said, "What brings you to Washington?" I said, "I came down to see your performance." He reared back and started poking me with his cane, dueling with me. I said, "Yes, and I found it well worth my time." He said, "My God, it's only ninety minutes long. Now, let me see—three and a half hours on the train, three and a half hours back. I owe you five hours and thirty minutes—what can I do for you?"

What do you think about onstage in *The Iceman Cometh*?

I must admit that I ran over a couple of shopping lists this week. Generally I've found that you'd better stay with the play; if you drift out of it, you begin to hear the zzzzzs all over the place.

Did you always want to be an actor?

I suppose I did. I always loved the theater. Growing up in New York, I had a great opportunity. My parents went all the time, so I saw everything when I was a kid. I was highly critical of everything. All the actors, especially the young ones—I'd trash them after the show. A friend of mine got annoyed at my being so critical about everything. One day I got a postcard saying that Franklin Short had received my letter and would be very happy to audition me next Tuesday at five o'clock and to bring something I'd prepared, about five minutes long. I didn't know what the hell it was all about, so I showed this mysterious postcard to my friend Art Nesbit. He said he'd read in *The New York Times* about a man forming a Shakespearean repertory company to play schools and colleges and had submitted my name. He said, "You're always shooting off your mouth about how you could do better than so-and-so." I had no idea what the hell an audition was, so I memorized a poem, Pope's "The Dying Christian to His Soul," went down and read it to the old man. He must have been shocked, but he gave me a part.

I made my debut as the haberdasher in *The Taming of the Shrew*. Afterward, I had no conscious memory of having been on. I remember sitting in the dressing room and a big bright spot out there beyond the dark and then suddenly being back in my dressing room. The rest was a total blank. But I stayed with the company about three years, playing all sorts of parts. You were expected to be able to play every part in the play. "You play Hortensio instead of Gremio tonight," and you'd do it. I never felt awed by Shakespeare again.

Did you have any training before that?

Never even been in a play. Always shied away from it. Sometimes I sit looking at myself in the mirror and wonder, if Art Nesbit hadn't given me the goose, would I have ever had the nerve to do it? Of course, it took a long, long time before I knew what the hell I was doing. For six years I worked almost continually in stock companies through the South, and then I went into the army when I was twenty-five, so I had four years to think about what I was going to do. I realized I didn't know anything about acting. All I knew was performing— getting out there and learning your lines and having energy and being as bright as you could. I really didn't know anything about looking at the parts. I was over thirty by the time I began to think seriously about becoming an actor.

I went out to Chicago to work with a young company and stayed for about six years, playing eighteen weeks of stock in Chicago and then in winter going to Palm Springs to play eighteen weeks there. We were always doing nine new plays in each town. My wife joined the company, and we all married each other —the director married the ingenue, and the juvenile got married. It was a fantastic company. Then the time came when Helen and I were driving home thinking, "Jesus, we're leading this wonderful life, making money, playing wonderful parts"—but we felt we didn't deserve it. So we decided to go back to New York.

You went back to New York for penance?

For growth. We went back into a new apartment in London Terrace, and we were just saying good-bye to the telephone installer when the telephone rang. It was Marion Dougherty [*New York casting director*], who didn't even know I'd been out of town, offering me a job. I haven't stopped working since. That was thirty-two years ago or so. After doing some television, I immediately went on the road with *Teahouse of the August Moon* for a year and a half. Doug was born on the road in Palm Springs. I was in Boston playing with Gertrude Berg in *A Majority of One* when Laura was born. So I owe a lot to various friends who've seen my wife to the hospitals and back home again.

Is that what the life of an actor is about, being on the road?
Well, we have a very romantic feeling about the theater, really. We have old traditions and things that we keep up, the pretzels . . . [*He gestures toward his dressing table, and indeed among the various trinkets, toys, letters, and Polaroids scattered across the tabletop and makeup mirror is a curious stockpile of big, doughy pretzels, the kind that vendors sell from pushcarts on New York City street corners.*] Doug was in kindergarten when I had an opening, and he bought a pretzel for me as an opening-night present. So we've always exchanged them since. We fly them out to Seattle when he has openings. Helen got one when she opened at Circle Rep. Everybody gets a pretzel. We used to save them all, but it got ridiculous. The back room was festooned with old stale pretzels. So now we keep them a year or two, then move on and get a fresh batch.

What are the other traditions in your family?
We have aphorisms, very private and personal, that we never go onstage without repeating to ourselves. I don't know what Helen's or Laura's or Doug's is, and they don't know mine. I guess we'll put them in a sealed envelope when the end is near and pass them on.

What did it mean in the '50s to come to New York and work in the theater?
A lot of things to me. It meant I had reached another level of competence. I don't regret all those years I spent out of New York, because, God, I played everything—Ephraim in *Desire Under the Elms*, Chris in *Anna Christie*, all the wonderful Coward leading men, Jack in *The Importance of Being Earnest*, *Charley's Aunt*, everything that was current. But of course, being in the theater, New York was a goal of mine. I became an actor to be a Broadway actor. People didn't go into the theater . . . I suppose they did, to become movie actors, and of course there's television, and radio is something else again. Now you cross all lines and work in radio, television, films, commercials, circuses, or whatever the hell comes along. But in those days, there were stage actors, movie actors, and radio actors. I always wanted to be a stage actor.
Once I was doing a play downtown, and I was walking up Broadway to get the subway to Fiftieth Street and Seventh Avenue. I'd pick up *The New York Times* at the newsstand there going home every night. One night the guy saw me coming, folded the newspaper, and threw it under my arm as I paid him. He just knew that I belonged. I don't know if he even knew I was an actor, but it was a big thrill for me. I still get goose pimples thinking about it.

When you were a young man starting out, did you think you would have this long career in show business?
Fifty-two years! I look at a mirror, and I think, "What the . . . how did you wind up here?" Life has been so random. I don't remember making a choice about anything. Things came, and I did them.
I worked at Macy's one Christmas years ago, I guess over fifty years ago. It was just for six, seven, eight weeks, something like that, but I was a very good salesman, and I had a lot of enthusiasm. I was so good that they asked me to stay on after Christmas. I had this strange feeling—I was so glad when they got rid of me, because I might still be down there behind one of those counters.

When you started doing TV and films, did it feel like a different kind of acting?

No. It was their job to know where to point the camera and where to put the boom and where to turn the knobs, and I just did what I did. Once it's done, I don't like to look at myself, and if it's possible to avoid it, I do. I don't like that gent up there, particularly. I don't connect with him. He makes me uncomfortable when I look at him, me, up there. It's very upsetting to look at yourself—you think, "Oh, fool, why did he do that?" Because you change your mind about it, and you never get a chance to do it again. I think that's the thing actors love about acting in the theater—you always get a chance to atone for your sins the next night. If you continue to do it, you continue to change it.

There are a few things that I kind of think were okay, but they're rare. Jason and I did a television show thirteen or fourteen years ago, a wonderful, gentle thing for Hallmark Hall of Fame or something called *Thanksgiving Treasure*. I played an old farmer who has a relationship with a young girl, Jason's daughter. I have a wonderful, wonderful death scene. I'd never seen it, but Jason has it on videocassette, and just yesterday I had a copy made. When I was at the studio, I saw less than a minute of the thing on the monitor, and there was this wonderful old actor dying—by Jesus, he was good. And it was me.

Appendix
(A selected listing of credits for each actor)

KEVIN BACON (born July 8, 1958)
BROADWAY; Slab Boys
OFF-BROADWAY: Poor Little Lambs, Forty-Deuce, Album, Getting Out, Flux, Glad Tidings, Men Without Dates, Loot
FILM: Enormous Changes at the Last Minute, Diner, Only When I Laugh, Friday the 13th, Hero at Large, Footloose, Forty-Deuce, Quicksilver, Rites of Summer, Animal House, Little Sister
TV: Search for Tomorrow, The Guiding Light, The Gift, The Demon Murder Case

PHILIP BOSCO (born September 26, 1930)
BROADWAY: Whose Life Is It Anyway?, Auntie Mame, Rape of the Belt, Donnybrook, Nightlife, A Man for All Seasons, Stages
CIRCLE IN THE SQUARE: Eminent Domain, The Bacchae, Major Barbara, Man and Superman, Saint Joan, The Caine Mutiny Court-Martial
OFF-BROADWAY: Threepenny Opera, Some Men Need Help, Be Good to Me
ROUNDABOUT THEATER: Misalliance, Hedda Gabler, Ah! Wilderness, Inadmissible Evidence, Don Juan in Hell, A Month in the Country, Master Class
OTHER: Lincoln Center Repertory Company, American Shakespeare Festival (Stratford, Connecticut), Arena Stage (Washington, D.C.)
FILM: Flanagan, Children of a Lesser God, The Money Pit, Heaven Help Us

FRANK CONVERSE (born May 22, 1938)
BROADWAY: Design for Living, Brothers, The Philadelphia Story, First One Asleep Whistle
OFF-BROADWAY: The House of Blue Leaves
OTHER: San Diego Shakespeare Festival, Long Wharf, McCarter Theater
FILM: Hurry Sundown, Hour of the Gun, The Rowdyman, Spring Fever, The Bushido Blade
TV: Coronet Blue, NYPD, Medical Center, Movin' On, The Young Lawyers, The Young Rebels, The FBI, The Mod Squad, The Equalizer, The Widowing of Mrs. Holroyd, Marilyn, Guests of the Nation, The Shadow of a Gunman

WILLEM DAFOE (born July 22, 1955)
WOOSTER GROUP: Nayatt School, Point Judith, Route 1 & 9, North Atlantic, L.S.D., Hula, The Temptation of St. Anthony
FILM: Heaven's Gate, The Loveless, Roadhouse 66, Streets of Fire, To Live and Die in L.A., Platoon
TV: The Hitchhiker

JEFF DANIELS (born February 19, 1955)
BROADWAY: Fifth of July
OFF-BROADWAY: The Golden Age, Lemon Sky, The Farm, The Three Sisters, The Shortchanged Review
CIRCLE REP: Johnny Got His Gun, Minnesota Moon, Brontosaurus, Thymus Vulgaris, Seduction Duet, American Welcome, My Life, 42 Cities in 40 Nights
FILM: Ragtime, Terms of Endearment, The Purple Rose of Cairo, Marie, Heartburn, Something Wild
TV: A Rumor of War, Hawaii Five-O, Asking for It

BRAD DAVIS (born November 6, 1949)
OFF-BROADWAY: Entertaining Mr. Sloane, The Normal Heart, Sissies' Scrapbook, The Elusive Angel
FILM: Midnight Express, A Small Circle of Friends, Chariots of Fire, Querelle
TV: Roots, A Rumor of War, Robert Kennedy and His Times, Mrs. Reinhardt, Class of '65, Song of Myself, Sybil, How to Survive a Marriage, Chiefs

JEFFREY DE MUNN (born April 25, 1947)
BROADWAY: Comedians, Bent, K-2
OFF-BROADWAY: Total Abandon, A Midsummer Night's Dream, Modigliani, A Prayer for My Daughter, The Chekhov Sketchbook, The Country Girl
FILM: Ragtime, I'm Dancing as Fast as I Can, Resurrection, Frances, The Hitcher
TV: All the Sad Young Men, I Married Wyatt Earp, Keeping On, Mourning Becomes Electra, Wild Jackasses: The Forgotten Eagle

MATT DILLON (born February 18, 1964)
BROADWAY: The Boys of Winter
FILM: Over the Edge, Little Darlings, My
Bodyguard, Liar's Moon, Tex, The
Outsiders, Rumblefish, The Flamingo Kid,
Target, No Names, No Pack Drill, Native
Son
TV: The Great American Fourth of July and
Other Disasters

GRIFFIN DUNNE (born June 8, 1955)
OFF-BROADWAY: Just Like the Night, Two
Soliloquies and Several Obscenities, Marie
and Bruce, The Hotel Play, Coming
Attractions, Hooters
FILM: Shiver, Cold Feet, Almost You, Chilly
Scenes of Winter, American Werewolf in
London, The Fan, The Other Side of the
Mountain, Johnny Dangerously, After
Hours
TV: The Wall, The Best of Families, Medical
Center, Amazing Stories

PETER EVANS (born May 27, 1950)
BROADWAY: Night and Day, Children of a
Lesser God
OFF-BROADWAY: Total Eclipse, Endgame,
Streamers, A Life in the Theater,
Company, Geniuses, The Transfiguration of
Benno Blimpie, The American Clock,
Springtime for Henry, Life Class, Don Juan
Comes Back from the War
FILM: Arthur, Impostors
TV: St. Elsewhere, Remington Steele,
George Washington

HARVEY FIERSTEIN (born June 6, 1954)
BROADWAY: Torch Song Trilogy
OFF-BROADWAY: Pork, Flatbush Tosca, The
Pioneer and Pro-Game, The Life of Juanita
Castro, The Silver Bee, How Jacqueline
Kennedy Became Queen of Greece, Persia,
Satyricon, Freaky Pussy, Amerika D.
Cleopatra, Christopher at Sheridan, In
Search of the Cobra Jewels, Xircus
FILM: Annie Hall, Dog Day Afternoon, The
Happy Hooker, Garbo Talks, Apology
TV: Miami Vice

MORGAN FREEMAN (born June 1, 1937)
BROADWAY: Hello, Dolly!, The Mighty Gents
OFF-BROADWAY: The Niggerlovers, Ostrich
Feathers, Exhibition, Black Visions,
Cockfight, White Pelicans, Julius Caesar,
Coriolanus, Mother Courage, The
Connection, Medea and the Doll, The
Gospel at Colonus
FILM: Brubaker, Eyewitness, The
Pawnbroker, Where Were You When the
Lights Went Out?, Adam, Hollow Image,

Marie, That Was Then, This Is Now
TV: The Electric Company, Another World,
Roll of Thunder, Hear My Cry, Charlie
Smith and the Fritter Tree, Attica, The
Marva Collins Story, The Atlanta Child
Murders, Resting Place

JOHN GLOVER (born August 7, 1944)
BROADWAY: Whodunnit, Frankenstein, The
Selling of the President, Design for Living,
The Importance of Being Earnest, The
Visit, Holiday, Don Juan, The Great God
Brown
OFF-BROADWAY: Criminal Minds, The
Government Inspector, Treats, Rebel
Women, Linda Her and The Fairy Garden,
Chemin de Fer, Subject to Fits, The House
of Blue Leaves, A Scent of Flowers, Digby
FILM: White Nights; Julia; Melvin and
Howard; The Incredible Shrinking Woman;
Annie Hall; The Evil That Men Do; A Flash
of Green; Shamus; Willy Nilly; A Little Sex;
Success; The Mountain Men; Somebody
Killed Her Husband; Last Embrace;
Monday, Tuesday, Wednesday; Apology;
52 Pick-up
TV: An Early Frost, Ernie Kovacs—Between
the Laughter, George Washington, Face of
Rage, Rage of Angels, Kennedy, Kojak, You
Are There, Twilight Zone

SPALDING GRAY (born June 5, 1941)
MONOLOGUES: Sex and Death to the Age 14;
Booze, Cars and College Girls; India (And
After); In Search of the Monkey Girl; A
Personal History of the American Theater;
Nobody Ever Wanted to Sit Behind a Desk;
47 Beds; Interviewing the Audience;
Swimming to Cambodia, Travels Through
New England; Terrors of Pleasure
WOOSTER GROUP: Sakonnet Point, Rumstick
Road, Nayatt School, Point Judith, L.S.D.,
North Atlantic
PERFORMANCE GROUP: Dionysus in '69,
Oedipus, Commune, The Tooth of Crime,
Cops, Mother Courage
FILM: The Killing Fields, Hard Choices,
True Stories

ANTHONY HEALD (born August 25, 1944)
BROADWAY: The Wake of Jamey Foster, The
Marriage of Figaro
OFF-BROADWAY: Digby, Principia Scipitoriae,
The Foreigner, Henry V, The
Philanthropist, Quartermaine's Terms, The
Glass Menagerie, The Fox, The Caretaker,
Inadmissible Evidence, Misalliance
FILM: Silkwood, Teachers, Happy New Year
TV: Miami Vice, Spenser for Hire, Tales
from the Dark Side, Deadly Force

294

EDWARD HERRMANN (born July 21, 1943)
BROADWAY: Plenty, Mrs. Warren's Profession, The Philadelphia Story
OFF-BROADWAY: Moonchildren, Twelfth Night, The Caretaker, A Midsummer Night's Dream, The Basic Training of Pavlo Hummel, The Cherry Orchard, Not About Heroes
WILLIAMSTOWN THEATER FESTIVAL: Trelawney of the "Wells," Arms and the Man, The Greeks, Old Times, Candida, Whose Life Is It, Anyway?, The Front Page
FILM: The Purple Rose of Cairo, Compromising Positions, The Paper Chase, The Great Gatsby, Day of the Dolphin, The Great Waldo Pepper, The Betsy, The North Avenue Irregulars, Take Down, Reds, Harry's War, A Little Sex, Annie, The Man with One Red Shoe
TV: Eleanor and Franklin, Eleanor and Franklin: The White House Years, A Love Story: The Eleanor and Lou Gehrig Story, The Sorrows of Gin, Dear Liar, Candida, The Electric Grandmother

GREGORY HINES (born February 14, 1946)
BROADWAY: Sophisticated Ladies, Comin' Uptown, Eubie
FILM: Deal of the Century, Wolfen, The Cotton Club, White Nights, History of the World Part 1, The Muppets Take Manhattan, Running Scared
TV: Amazing Stories, Shirley MacLaine: Illusions

BARNARD HUGHES (born July 16, 1915)
BROADWAY: The Iceman Cometh; End of the World; Angels Fall; Da; All Over Town; The Good Doctor; Much Ado About Nothing; Abelard and Heloise; Sheep on the Runway; The Wrong Way Light Bulb; How Now Dow Jones; I Was Dancing; Hamlet; Nobody Loves an Albatross; The Advocate; Advise and Consent; A Majority of One; Dinosaur Wharf; Teahouse of the August Moon; The Ivy Green; Please, Mrs. Garibaldi; The Cat and the Canary
OFF-BROADWAY: Translations, Pericles, Merry Wives of Windsor, Hamlet, The Three Sisters, The Devil's Disciple, Older People, Uncle Vanya, Line, Hogan's Goat, A Doll's House, The Last Minstrel, The Will and the Way, The Taming of the Shrew
FILM: Tron, First Monday in October, Best Friends, Oh God!, Hospital, Sisters, Rage, Cold Turkey, The Pursuit of Happiness, Where's Poppa?, Midnight Cowboy, The Young Doctors, Play Girl, Treehouse
TV: Under the Biltmore Clock; The Adventures of Huckleberry Finn; Tales from the Dark Side; Little Gloria, Happy at Last; The Caryl Chessman Story; A Memory of Two Mondays; The Judge; Sanctuary of Fear; Lou Grant; Doc; All in the Family; The Guiding Light; Much Ado About Nothing; The Borrowers; The Thanksgiving Treasure; All the Way Home; Look Homeward, Angel; You Are There; A Christmas Carol; Naked City

TOM HULCE (born December 6, 1953)
BROADWAY: Equus
OFF-BROADWAY: Romeo and Juliet, Twelve Dreams, The Rise and Rise of Daniel Rocket
FILM; September 30, 1955; Animal House; Those Lips, Those Eyes; Amadeus; Echo Park
TV: Emily, Emily; The Rise and Rise of Daniel Rocket

WILLIAM HURT (born March 20, 1950)
BROADWAY: Hurlyburly, Man and Superman
CIRCLE REPERTORY COMPANY: Richard II, The Great-Grandson of Jedediah Kohler, Childe Byron, The Diviners, Mary Stuart, Hamlet, The Runner Stumbles, Fifth of July, Lulu, Ulysses in Traction, My Life
OFF-BROADWAY: A Midsummer Night's Dream, Henry V
FILM: Altered States, Eyewitness, Body Heat, The Big Chill, Gorky Park, Kiss of the Spider Woman, Children of a Lesser God
TV: All the Way Home, Verna: USO Girl, The Best of Families

BILL IRWIN (born April 11, 1950)
BROADWAY: Accidental Death of an Anarchist, 5, 6, 7, 8 . . . Dance
OFF-BROADWAY: The Regard of Flight, The Courtroom, Tirai, Not Quite/New York
OTHER: Strike Up the Band (American Musical Theater Festival, Philadelphia), A Man's a Man, The Three Cuckolds (La Jolla Playhouse)
FILM: Popeye
TV: The Regard of Flight

ZELJKO IVANEK (born August 15, 1957)
BROADWAY: The Survivor, Brighton Beach Memoirs, Loot
OFF-BROADWAY: Cloud 9, A Map of the World
OTHER: Master Harold . . . and the Boys (Yale Repertory Theater)
FILM: Tex, The Sender, Mass Appeal
TV: The Edge of Night, Alice in Wonderland, The Sun Also Rises

ROBERT JOY (born August 17, 1951)
BROADWAY: Hay Fever
OFF-BROADWAY: Found a Peanut, Lenny and the Heartbreakers, The Death of von Richthofen as Witnessed from Earth, Lydie Breeze, What I Did Last Summer, Fables for Friends, The Diary of Anne Frank, Life and Limb, Field Day
OTHER: Privates on Parade (Long Wharf), Romeo and Juliet (La Jolla Playhouse), Big River (American Repertory Theater, Boston)
FILM: Atlantic City, Ragtime, Ticket to Heaven, Threshold, Amityville 3-D, Terminal Choice, Joshua Then and Now, Desperately Seeking Susan
TV: The Equalizer, Moonlighting

RAUL JULIA (born March 9, 1940)
BROADWAY: Nine, Threepenny Opera, Where's Charley?, Two Gentlemen of Verona, Betrayal, Dracula, Design for Living, Arms and the Man, The Cuban Thing, Indians
NEW YORK SHAKESPEARE FESTIVAL: Othello, King Lear, The Tempest, Hamlet, The Taming of the Shrew, As You Like It, The Cherry Orchard, Titus Andronicus, The Memorandum
OFF-BROADWAY: Macbeth, Life Is a Dream, Blood Wedding, The Oxcart, No Exit, City Scene, Your Own Thing, The Persians
FILM: Compromising Positions, Kiss of the Spider Woman, Tempest, The Escape Artist, One from the Heart
TV: Mussolini, King Lear

KEVIN KLINE (born October 24, 1947)
BROADWAY: Loose Ends, On the Twentieth Century, The Pirates of Penzance, Arms and the Man
NEW YORK SHAKESPEARE FESTIVAL: Hamlet, Richard III, Henry V
THE ACTING COMPANY: The School for Scandal, The Lower Depths, The Three Sisters, She Stoops to Conquer, The Way of the World, The Knack
FILM: Sophie's Choice, The Pirates of Penzance, The Big Chill, Silverado, Violets Are Blue

JOHN LITHGOW (born June 6, 1945)
BROADWAY: Requiem for a Heavyweight, Beyond Therapy, The Changing Room, My Fat Friend, Anna Christie, Comedians, Bedroom Farce, Division Street, Spokesong, Once in a Lifetime
OFF-BROADWAY: Hamlet, Trelawney of the "Wells," Salt Lake City Skyline, Secret Service, A Memory of Two Mondays, Kaufman at Large
FILM: Obsession, Blow-Out, All That Jazz,

Rich Kids, The Big Fix, The World According to Garp, Twilight Zone—The Movie, Buckaroo Banzai, Dealing, I'm Dancing as Fast as I Can, Footloose, 2010, Terms of Endearment, Santa Claus: The Movie, The Manhattan Project
TV: The Glitter Dome; The Day After; The Oldest Living Graduate; The Big Blonde; Mom, the Wolfman and Me; Resting Place

JOHN LONE (born 1952)
OFF-BROADWAY: F.O.B., The Dance and the Railroad, Sound and Beauty
FILM: Iceman, The Year of the Dragon, The Last Emperor
TV: The Dance and the Railroad

CHARLES LUDLAM (born April 12, 1943)
RIDICULOUS THEATRICAL COMPANY: Conquest of the Universe or When Queens Collide, Big Hotel, Whores of Babylon, The Grand Tarot, Turds in Hell, Bluebeard, Eunuchs of the Forbidden City, Corn, Camille, Hot Ice, Stage Blood, Caprice, The Ventriloquist's Wife, Utopia, Inc., The Enchanted Pig, The Elephant Woman, A Christmas Carol, Reverse Psychology, Love's Tangled Web, Secret Lives of the Sexists, Exquisite Torture, Le Bourgeois Avant-Garde, Galas, The Mystery of Irma Vep, Salammbo
OTHER: Hedda Gabler (American Ibsen Theater, Pittsburgh)
FILM: Impostors
TV: Miami Vice

JOHN MALKOVICH (born December 9, 1954)
BROADWAY: Death of a Salesman, Arms and the Man
OFF-BROADWAY: True West
STEPPENWOLF THEATER: Of Mice and Men; The Glass Menagerie; Philadelphia, Here I Come; Say Goodnight, Gracie; Big Mother; Death of a Salesman; Curse of the Starving Class
CHICAGO: A Streetcar Named Desire, A Sorrow Beyond Dreams
FILM: The Killing Fields, Places in the Heart, Eleni, Death of a Salesman, Making Mister Right
TV: The Chicago Story; Word of Honor; Say Goodnight, Gracie; True West; Rocket to the Moon

KEN MARSHALL (born 1951)
BROADWAY: West Side Story
OFF-BROADWAY: The Playboy of the Western World, Becoming Memories, Caligula, The Mound Builders, Quiet in the Land
FILM: Tilt, La Pelle, Krull
TV: Marco Polo

PAUL McCRANE (born January 19, 1961)
BROADWAY: Runaways, Curse of an Aching
Heart, The Iceman Cometh
OFF-BROADWAY: Fables for Friends, Hooters,
Crossing Niagara, Hunting Scenes from
Lower Bavaria, Dispatches, Landscape of
the Body, Split
FILM: Fame, Rocky II, The Hotel New
Hampshire, Purple Hearts
TV: And Baby Comes Home, We're Fighting
Back

MARK METCALF (born March 11, 1946)
OFF-BROADWAY: Blue Window, Mr. and
Mrs., Romeo and Juliet, Streamers, Creeps,
The Tempest, Hamlet, Salt Lake City
Skyline
OTHER: Henry IV Part I (American National
Theater, Washington), Accent on Youth
(Long Wharf), Long Day's Journey into
Night (Arena Stage), The Tooth of Crime
(McCarter Theater, Princeton)
FILM: Animal House, Final Terror, Almost
You, Oasis, Chilly Scenes of Winter, Where
the Buffalo Roam, The Garden Party
TV: Hotel, For Love and Honor, Barnaby
Jones, Breaking Away, Hill Street Blues

JOE MORTON (born October 18, 1947)
BROADWAY: Hair, Raisin, Jesus Christ
Superstar, Two Gentlemen of Verona
OFF-BROADWAY: Salvation, A Month of
Sundays, I Paid My Dues, Tricks,
Christophe, Charlie Was Here but Now
He's Gone, Souvenirs, Rhinestone, G.R.
Point, Cheapside
BROOKLYN ACADEMY OF MUSIC: Oedipus,
A Winter's Tale, Johnny on the Spot, The
Recruiting Officer, A Midsummer Night's
Dream
FILM: And Justice for All, The Brother from
Another Planet, Trouble in Mind,
Crossroads
TV: Search for Tomorrow, Grady, Another
World, The File on Jill Hatch, Watch Your
Mouth

MICHAEL O'KEEFE (born April 24, 1955)
BROADWAY: Mass Appeal, Fifth of July
OFF-BROADWAY: The Tragedy of Ronnus
Riccus, Christmas on Mars, Short Eyes
OTHER: Streamers (Long Wharf), An
American Tragedy (Arena Stage), The
Count of Monte Cristo (American National
Theater, Washington)
FILM: Grey Lady Down, The Great Santini,
Caddyshack, Split Image, Nate and Hayes,
Finders Keepers, The Slugger's Wife, The
Whoopee Boys
TV: A Rumor of War, Harvest Home,
Friendly Persuasion, The Oath, The
Hitchhiker

JERRY ORBACH (born October 20, 1935)
BROADWAY: Carnival; Guys and Dolls; The
Natural Look; Carousel; Annie Get Your
Gun; Promises, Promises; 6 Rms, Riv Vu;
Chicago; 42nd Street
OFF-BROADWAY: Threepenny Opera, The
Fantasticks, The Cradle Will Rock, Berlin's
Mine, Scuba Duba
FILM: Mad Dog Coll; John Goldfarb, Please
Come Home; A Fan's Notes; The Gang
That Couldn't Shoot Straight; Prince of the
City; Brewster's Millions; The Sentinel; F/X
TV: The Nurses; The Way They Were; An
Invasion of Privacy; The Special Magic of
Herself the Elf; Murder, She Wrote

WILL PATTON (born June 14, 1955)
OFF-BROADWAY: A Lie of the Mind, Fool for
Love, Joan of Lorraine, Goose and Tom-
Tom, Dark Ride, Limbo Tales, The Red
Snake, Tourists and Refugees,
Re-Arrangements
FILM: Desperately Seeking Susan, After
Hours, Chinese Boxes, Silkwood, Belizaire
the Cajun
TV: Kent State, Ryan's Hope, The Equalizer

AIDAN QUINN (born March 8, 1959)
OFF-BROADWAY: A Lie of the Mind, Fool for
Love
CHICAGO: Hamlet, Scheherazade, The Trick,
The Irish Hebrew Lesson, The Man in 605
FILM: Reckless, Desperately Seeking Susan,
The Mission
TV: An Early Frost

DAVID RASCHE (born August 7, 1944)
BROADWAY: The Shadow Box, Loose Ends,
Lunch Hour
OFF-BROADWAY: John, Snow White, Isadora
Duncan Sleeps with the Russian Navy, End
of the War, A Sermon, Geniuses, To Gillian
on Her 37th Birthday, The Custom of the
Country
FILM: Manhattan, An Unmarried Woman,
Just Tell Me What You Want, Honky Tonk
Freeway, Striking Back, Best Defense,
Cobra, Native Son

CHRISTOPHER REEVE (born September
25, 1952)
BROADWAY: A Matter of Gravity, Fifth of
July, The Marriage of Figaro
OFF-BROADWAY: My Life, Berkeley Square,
Summer and Smoke, The Way of the World
LONDON: The Aspern Papers
WILLIAMSTOWN THEATER FESTIVAL: The
Royal Family, Richard Corey, Holiday,
Galileo, Camino Real, The Greeks
FILM: The Bostonians, The Aviator,

Superman, Superman II, Superman III, Deathtrap, Monsignor, Somewhere in Time, Running Man, Streetsmart
TV: Anna Karenina, Enemies, Love of Life, The American Revolution

---

PETER RIEGERT (born April 11, 1947)
BROADWAY: Dance with Me, Censored Scenes from King Kong
OFF-BROADWAY: Call Me Charlie, Sexual Perversity in Chicago, Isn't It Romantic, Sunday Runners in the Rain, A Rosen by Any Other Name
FILM: Animal House, Chilly Scenes of Winter, The City Girl, Local Hero, Le Grand Carnival
TV: Twilight Zone, News at Eleven

HOWARD ROLLINS (born October 17, 1950)
BROADWAY: We Interrupt This Program, The Mighty Gents, G.R. Point
OFF-BROADWAY: Medal of Honor Rag, Streamers, Measure for Measure, The Passing Game, The Taking of Miss Janie, Fathers and Sons, Traps
FILM: House of God, Ragtime, A Soldier's Story
TV: Roots 2; King; For Us, the Living; Moving Right Along; A Member of the Wedding; My Old Man; Thornwell; A Doctor's Story; Wildside; Children of Times Square

---

ROY SCHEIDER (born November 10, 1932)
BROADWAY: The Chinese Prime Minister, The Year Boston Won the Pennant, Betrayal
OFF-BROADWAY: Serjeant Musgrave's Dance, Stephen D, Romeo and Juliet, Henry IV Part I, Richard II, The Nuns
FILM: Curse of the Living Corpse, Stiletto, The French Connection, Klute, The Seven-Ups, Loving, Paper Lion, Star, Puzzle of a Downfall Child, The Outside Man, Sheila Levine Is Dead and Living in New York, L'Attentat, Jaws, Jaws II, Marathon Man, All That Jazz, Blue Thunder, Still of the Night, Last Embrace, Mishima, 2010, Sorcerer, The Men's Club, 52 Pick-Up
TV: Prisoner Without a Name, Cell Without a Number, NYPD, Tiger Town

---

WALLACE SHAWN (born November 12, 1943)
OFF-BROADWAY: The Mandrake, Chinchilla, Carmilla, The Master and Margarita, Marie and Bruce, The Hotel Play, Aunt Dan and Lemon
FILM: Manhattan, Starting Over, Strong

Medicine, A Little Sex, Simon, All That Jazz, Cheaper to Keep Her, Atlantic City, The Hotel New Hampshire, Lovesick, Deal of the Century, Crackers, My Dinner with André, Strange Invaders, The Bostonians, Heaven Help Us, Saigon—The Year of the Cat

---

JOHN SHEA (born April 14, 1949)
BROADWAY: Yentl, End of the World
OFF-BROADWAY: American Days, The Sorrows of Stephen, The Master and Margarita, Safe House, The Dining Room, Romeo and Juliet, Gorky, Battering Ram
FILM: Hussy, Missing, Windy City, It's My Turn, Honeymoon
TV: The Nativity, Eight Is Enough, Barnaby Jones, The Last Convertible, Family Reunion, The Man From Atlantis, Kennedy, Hitler's SS—A Portrait in Evil

---

JOHN TURTURRO (born February 28, 1957)
OFF-BROADWAY: Danny and the Deep Blue Sea, Men Without Dates, Steel on Steel, Chaos and Hard Times
FILM: Desperately Seeking Susan, To Live and Die in L.A., Gung Ho, Hannah and Her Sisters, Offbeat, The Color of Money

---

LENNY VON DOHLEN (born December 22, 1958)
OFF-BROADWAY: Cloud 9, Desire Under the Elms, Asian Shade
FILM: Tender Mercies, Electric Dreams, Billy Galvin
TV: Under the Biltmore Clock, Kent State, Sessions, Mother May I, Don't Touch, How To Be a Perfect Person in Just Three Days

---

THOMAS G. WAITES (born 1955)
BROADWAY: American Buffalo, Richard III, Awake and Sing, Teaneck Tanzi
OFF-BROADWAY: Forty-Deuce, Pastorale, Paradise Lost, The Two Orphans, Extremities
FILM: Pity the Poor Soldier, On the Yard, The Warriors, And Justice for All, O'Malley, The Thing, Clan of the Cave Bear, Light of Day
TV: Miami Vice

CHRISTOPHER WALKEN (born March 31, 1943)
BROADWAY: JB, Baker Street, The Lion in Winter, High Spirits, The Unknown Soldier and His Wife, Iphigenia in Aulis, The Rose Tattoo, Lemon Sky, Enemies, The Plough and the Stars, The Merchant of Venice, Sweet Bird of Youth

OFF-BROADWAY: Best Foot Forward, The Chronicles of Hell, Scenes from American Life, The Judgment, Kid Champion, Macbeth, Measure for Measure, Cymbeline, Troilus and Cressida, Hamlet, The Tempest, The Seagull, Cinders, Hurlyburly, The House of Blue Leaves
FILM: The Boy Who Could See Through Walls; Next Stop, Greenwich Village; The Anderson Tapes; Annie Hall; Roseland; The Sentinel; The Happiness Cage; The Deer Hunter; Last Embrace; Heaven's Gate; The Dogs of War; Pennies from Heaven; Brainstorm; The Dead Zone; A View to a Kill; At Close Range
TV: Naked City, Barefoot in Athens, Histoire du Soldat, Who Am I This Time?

SAM WATERSTON (born November 15, 1940)
BROADWAY: Oh Dad, Poor Dad, Mama's Hung You in the Closet and I'm Feelin' So Sad, Halfway Up the Tree, Indians, Hay Fever, The Trial of the Catonsville Nine, Much Ado About Nothing, Hamlet, A Doll's House, Lunch Hour, Benefactors
OFF-BROADWAY: Thistle in My Bed, The Knack, Fitz, La Turista, Red Cross, Muzeeka, Henry IV, Spitting Image, As You Like It, Cymbeline, Waiting for Godot, The Tempest, Measure for Measure, The Three Sisters, Gardenia
FILM: Fitzwilly, Generation Three, Cover Me, Babe, Who Killed Mary What's'ername?, Savages, A Time for Giving, A Delicate Balance, The Great Gatsby, Rancho Deluxe, Heaven's Gate, Dandy, the All American Girl, Hopscotch, Capricorn One, Interiors, Sweet William, Sweet Revenge, The Eagle's Wing, The Killing Fields, Warning Sign, Flagrant Desir, Hannah and Her Sisters, Just Between Friends
TV: Oppenheimer, Q.E.D., Games Mother Never Taught You, In Defense of Kids, Friendly Fire, Much Ado About Nothing, Dempsey, The Boy Who Loved Trolls, Reflections of Murder, Finnegan Begin Again, Love Lives On

JIMMIE RAY WEEKS (born March 21, 1942)
BROADWAY: My Fat Friend, Enemies, The Merchant of Venice, A Streetcar Named Desire, We Interrupt This Program, Devour the Snow
CIRCLE REPERTORY COMPANY: A Tale Told, The Great Grandson of Jedediah Kohler, Confluence, The Diviners, Feedlot, Glorious Morning, Dysan, Innocent Thoughts, Harmless Intentions, The Runner Stumbles
OFF-BROADWAY: Serenading Louie,

California Dog Fight
FILM: Cruising, Airport 1977, Eyewitness, Heaven Help Us
TV: Kennedy, The Gentleman Bandit, Ryan's Hope, Miami Vice

PETER WELLER (born June 24, 1947)
BROADWAY: Summer Brave, Sticks and Bones, Full Circle
OFF-BROADWAY: Streamers, Daddy Wolf, Rebel Women, The Woolgatherer, The Woods, Serenading Louie
FILM: Butch and Sundance: The Early Years; Just Tell Me What You Want; Shoot the Moon; Of Unknown Origin; The Adventures of Buckaroo Banzai; Vera; First Born; Apology; Monday, Tuesday, Wednesday; Robo Cop
TV: Exit 10, Kentucky Women, Two Kinds of Love

TREAT WILLIAMS (born 1952)
BROADWAY: Grease, Once in a Lifetime, Over Here, The Pirates of Penzance
OFF-BROADWAY: Maybe I'm Doing It Wrong, Some Men Need Help
FILM: The Ritz, The Deadly Game, The Eagle Has Landed, Hair, Prince of the City, 1941, Why Would I Lie?, The Pursuit of D. B. Cooper, Once Upon a Time in America, Flashpoint, Smooth Talk, The Men's Club
TV: Dempsey, A Streetcar Named Desire, The Little Mermaid, Some Men Need Help

JAMES WOODS (born April 18, 1947)
BROADWAY: Borstal Boy, Conduct Unbecoming, The Penny Wars, The Trial of the Catonsville 9, Moonchildren, Finishing Touches
OFF-BROADWAY: South Pacific, Saved, Green Julia, The Siamese Connection, In Fireworks Lie Secret Codes, Vivien, Gardenia,
FILM: The Visitors, The Way We Were, Hickey and Boggs, Alex and the Gypsy, The Choirboys, The Black Marble, Distance, Split Image, The Onion Field, Night Moves, Videodrome, Against All Odds, Once Upon a Time in America, Eyewitness, Joshua Then and Now, Cat's Eye, Salvador
TV: All the Way Home, The Great American Tragedy, And Your Name Is Jonah, The Disappearance of Aimee, Raid on Entebbe, Foster and Laurie, Billion Dollar Bubble, Holocaust, Badge of the Assassin

ANTHONY ZERBE (born May 20)
BROADWAY: The Little Foxes, Solomon's Child, The Moon Besieged
OFF-BROADWAY: Behind the Broken Words, It's All Done with Mirrors, Dear Liar, Terra

Nova, The Merchant of Venice, The Cave
Dwellers
OTHER: Mark Taper Forum (Los Angeles),
Old Globe Theater (San Diego), Stratford
Theater Festival (Canada)
FILM: The Omega Man, The Turning Point,
I Am a Legend, The Life and Times of
Judge Roy Bean, Cool Hand Luke, Will
Penny, The Molly Maguires, The
Liberation of Lord Byron Jones, The
Parallax View, The Balcony, They Call Me
Mr. Tibbs, The Strange Vengeance of
Rosalie, An Investigation of Murder,
Papillon, Rooster Cogburn, Farewell My
Lovely, The Dead Zone, Who'll Stop the
Rain?, The First Deadly Sin
TV: Mission: Impossible, How the West Was
Won, Harry O, The Virginian, Gunsmoke,
Bonanza, Cannon, Kiss Meets the
Phantom, Old Foolishness

Acknowledgments

I would like to thank Annie Walwyn-Jones and Murdoch Morrison, Sophie Craze, Bill Robinson and Leo Chiu, Marc Balet, and Maxi Cohen for allowing me the use of their homes as studio space. I would also like to thank Gael Love and Kate Harrington for permitting me to publish photographs originally made for *Interview*. And I am very grateful to the following people for their help: Sylvia Shapiro, for her legal expertise; Ira Mandelbaum, for his beautiful prints; Elyse Connolly, my rep; Joe Dolce; Robert Starkoff; Bryan Bantry, Lynn Parrish, and Melissa Ekblom; Carol Boissier; and all the hairdressers, especially Pascal Boissier and David Kinigson.

I would like to dedicate this book to my sister Marilyn.

—Susan Shacter

I would like to thank Alice Playten and Josh White, Harry Kondoleon, Billy Toth, and Luis Sanjurjo for their help, friendship, and special treats during the writing of this book; Des McAnuff, for inspiring me to nurture my love for actors; Dr. Marty Seif, who heard about it all; and Stephen Holden, who shared his editorial comments and his love with me on a daily basis.

—Don Shewey

We would both like to thank John Glover, Mark Metcalf, Catherine Olim, Lois Smith, and Betsy Sokolow, who were all of enormous help in rounding up their friends and clients and convincing them to participate in our project. Also thanks to Paul Martino, Peggy Siegal, Roz Corral, Mary Goldberg, Vic Ramos, David Rasche, Robyn Goodman, Bill Treusch, Gerry Siegal, Caitlin Buchman, Robert Warshawsky, Dale Davis, Adrian Bryan-Brown, Annette Shearer, Richard Kornberg, Joan Witkowski, Susan Wright, Gary Lisz, David Powers, Tiki Davies, James Lapine, Lewis Allen, and Cindy Valk. We would like to acknowledge the invaluable assistance of Bobbi John, who consulted on design matters throughout the making of the book, and Sally Morrison, who researched the actors' credits for the appendix. We would like to thank Ross Wetzsteon for suggesting that we work together, our agent Robert Cornfield for his infinite efforts on our behalf, and LuAnn Walther at New American Library, who supervised the final stages of publishing the book. Most of all, we would like to thank Helen Eisenbach, without whose biblical patience, excellent taste, superior editing, and tireless support this book would not have happened.

And, of course, all the actors.

Photography Credits

GROOMING

Pascal Boissier
Lenny Von Dohlen
Griffin Dunne
Brad Davis
Willem Dafoe
Frank Converse
Jeffrey de Munn
John Malkovich

Raymond Camacho
Matt Dillon

Bob Fink
Paul McCrane

Dawn Jacobson
Aidan Quinn

David Kinigson
Kevin Kline
John Lithgow
John Shea
David Rasche
Peter Evans
Anthony Zerbe
Mark Metcalf
Michael O'Keefe
Thomas G. Waites
Jerry Orbach

Michael Knight
Anthony Heald

Mitsuru Kono
Jeff Daniels

James Lebon
Bill Irwin

Rodney Martin
William Hurt
Sam Waterston

Thom Priano
Kevin Bacon

Gabriel Saba
Raul Julia

Shunji
Edward Herrmann
John Lone
Robert Joy

Danny Velasco
Spalding Gray
John Glover
Will Patton

Deborah Wardwell
Roy Scheider
Peter Weller

MAKEUP

Letha Rodman
Peter Weller

STYLING

Leslie Holzman
Griffin Dunne
John Glover

About the Authors

SUSAN SHACTER is a New York-based photographer. Her portraits and fashion photographs have been published in many magazines, both in the United States and abroad, including *Interview*, German and British *Vogue*, *Tatler*, *GQ*, *Linea Italiana*, German and Spanish *Harper's Bazaar*, *Harper's & Queen* and *L'Uomo Vogue*. Her commercial clients have included Giorgio Armani and Calvin Klein.

DON SHEWEY is a journalist and theater critic in New York. His articles have appeared in *The New York Times*, *The Village Voice*, *Esquire*, *Rolling Stone*, and many other publications. He is the author of the biography *Sam Shepard*.